THE
SARSEN WITCH

EILEEN KERNAGHAN

ACE BOOKS, NEW YORK

THE SARSEN WITCH

An Ace Book / published by arrangement with
the author

PRINTING HISTORY
Ace edition / April 1989

This one is for Sue.

PROLOGUE

The land belonged first to the hunters. After them came the planters of seed and the miners of flint—the Mother's people.

Then horsemen rode out of their wide, flat lands at the foot of the ice, sweeping north and west through the rich river valleys, until they came in the course of centuries to the Narrow Sea.

Their god was the great lord of the sky, the thunder-bringer, whose chariot was drawn by the golden horses of the Sun. Though the horsemen knew no sorcery and little science, they were born to the art of kingship and the craft of war.

In that time of heroes the lands of the west, the chalk lands, stood at the center of the world. The Sun-god ruled, and the Mother's people served him.

But in the wild lands, in the hills and forests and secret places of the earth, the hunters lived as they had always lived. And among them dwelt the last of the witchfolk, who in their own time, in the Lost Lands, had themselves been kings.

1

Naeri

She had had a name once, and a place in the world—preordained, unquestioned. Naeri, they had called her, the brown lily. A flower-name, because she had been a pretty child, smooth-skinned and delicately made. In time, when she grew into full womanhood and wisdom, she should have had another, secret name: a name of power.

Remembering those years, she saw circles within circles, like ramparts of banked earth, with herself—warm, loved, secure—inhabiting the center. Tribe, clan, hearth-family—the strong high walls of kinship had sheltered and surrounded her. With time, the faces had grown remote and shadowy, like figures out of Legend. But at night, sometimes still, she woke with a hand clutching her heart.

She pushed back the ragged ends of her hair as she knelt beside her supper fire. No flower-name would suit me now, she thought with irony. She saw herself in her mind's eye—chapped lips, windburned face, lean, hard-muscled body. A creature spare and strong and hardy as the gorse. In one terrible hour the horsemen had stripped her of everything—tribe, name, mother, hearth-place—leaving her only her sharp wits and a certain quiescent, unschooled power. And yet they had left her better armed than they knew.

She set a pot of barleymeal and water over the hot coals, and stirred in a duck egg from the morning's forage. While the porridge thickened, she cracked and ate a handful of hazelnuts.

The round, shallow eyes of the Mother-figure watched her—benignly, or so it seemed. Some long-departed miner had carved that little squat, swollen-bellied chalk woman, hoping no doubt that her fecundity would by example call forth a greater yield of flint. In this dark chamber the Mother-figure's presence was a comfort. She seemed to say, "Here beneath the earth, in the womb of the hill, is my hearth-place. I will share it with you, who have no name and no place of your own."

The mine entrance, three-quarters jammed with rubble and chalk blocks, was further concealed by a tangle of furze and juniper scrub. It was more like a cave than a mine shaft, running for a few feet into the slope of the chalk cliff, then angling sharply downward. As a rule these worked-out shafts were filled with chalk rubble, as though to repair the damage done to the earth. This one, for whatever reason, had been left open.

Perhaps a dozen handspans below the entrance passage, a lateral gallery opened off the main shaft. It had an air hole to the outside and was large enough to sleep and cook and move about in. Once it must have served as an underground workroom; the floor was littered with flint chips and odd bits of tools.

It was a good place, sheltered from wind and rain, well hidden from men's eyes, hidden too from the wolves that howled at night in these upland pastures. And she knew that she could not be trapped here, as too often earth-dwelling creatures were trapped in their burrows. Below her living gallery was a network of passages leading off from the main shaft at many levels and in many directions, connecting it with dozens of other exits to the surface.

She had been frightened at first to sleep above those black subterranean tunnels. Some nights, thinking she heard ghosts wandering there, she would build a fire between her bed and the shaft mouth, and huddle trembling against the farthest wall. In time she realized that the sounds she heard were the patterings and rustlings of small animals, or the noise of the wind finding its way along a passage.

As she grew braver, she climbed down the shaft and explored the maze of tunnels, so that now she carried their twistings and turnings like a map in her head. Sometimes she came across a skull, or scattered bones, but she was no longer frightened. Though men had worked and more than likely died here, they did not seem to have left their spirits behind.

For the first months she had lived by foraging for birds' eggs, snaring rabbits, fishing for trout and salmon in the streams. Like a squirrel, she laid by what she could for winter—nuts, roots, rose hips, seeds.

When the cold came, she grew bolder. She traveled by night, swiftly and silently as the red deer, down into the valley towns, up to the gates of the cattle farms on the hills. She shared no kinship with these people. If they caught her they would kill her, or make her a hearth-slave, according to their whim. But they had corn plots, vegetable patches, midden heaps. She lived like the fera, those little wild folk half out of Legend, stealing what she could in the night and hiding her booty in the hollow hill.

Thus she had come to possess a fine store of chipped crockery; two leather water jugs; an incense cup with no incense; and a badly dinted copper bowl. All these were arranged on a chalk ledge over her bed of bracken and skins. In a lower gallery, where it was cool and dry, she kept her winter stores, eked out by emmer and barley from unguarded fields.

Whatever she found on her forays that might one day prove useful, she kept—bits of rope, scraps of woven cloth, a wicker basket, discarded tools. Among these things were treasures—a belt-fastener and one button of glossy jet, an amber bead. These last were wrapped carefully in a piece of doeskin and stuffed for safekeeping under her bed.

Accustomed from childhood to warmth, safety, a measure of comfort, she had set out to make her dwelling place secure and pleasant: covering the floor with bracken, and lining the chalk walls with the skins of small animals, pegged into place with sharpened sticks.

The daughters of the witchfolk learned early those skills they needed to survive. More than once, as a child, she had gone with her sisters to hunt the fallow deer. Now, thanks to the flint miners, she was well supplied with spear heads. What she yearned to find, or steal, was a good straight unbroken shaft. With luck and a hunter's weapon, she could supply for herself those things like lamp fat, needles, sinew, that were hardest to steal and most difficult to do without.

She finished her meal and heaped chalk rubble on the embers of her fire. By now, she judged, it must be full dark. She put her dagger into her belt, laced up her sandals. Then, quick as a cat, she scaled the notched tree trunk that led to the outside world.

The high chalk pastures rolled away into distance, dipping and swelling like black water before the wind. On a high point to the west, two black stones leaned against the horizon, marking the ridge track. To the southeast, at the escarpment's edge, bare wind-wracked thorns held up their branches. It was almost midnight, a clear moonless night, the air cold enough to sting her cheeks. Stars, glittering and sharp as ice, were beginning to appear among tag ends of clouds. She could feel the crunch of frost on the short turf underfoot. She liked this weather, welcomed the rush of nervous energy it brought after the long melancholy weeks of rain. All the same, a wet night would have served her purpose better; sound carried too well in this sharp dry air.

She came to the edge of the chalk, where steep woods plunged down to the bottomlands. A long way below, between the trees, she could see the gleam of black water with light reflected in it. Sheltered by beech and ancient yews, she started down the hill path.

2

Gwi

Gwi held the copper bracelet up to the lamp for a final inspection. Satisfied, he polished it with a scrap of doeskin to bring up the shine. It was a simple piece, but elegantly wrought, and could have come from no hand but his own. Assuming she had the sense to know fine work from shoddy, the chief's wife should be pleased with it.

He set the bracelet aside, along with the belt-rings. They had no work for him here that challenged his skills or his imagination, but still, he had paid for his supper and lodging. He picked up the flat-tanged ceremonial dagger, testing its grip. Not that it mattered—it was copper, not bronze, meant only for show. The village was a small one, off the main track. Here, flint knives were still in ordinary use; copper reserved for ritual; bronze and gold beyond even the headman's reach. All the same, this chief had his copper worked to order, as the great horse-chiefs did. That in itself showed a large measure of pride—or ambition—when most village folk were content to buy cheap foreign-made goods from wandering merchants.

Remembering the great workrooms of the horse-chiefs, Gwi was restless to move on. He thought of gold inlay, jet studs, faience, amber; axes of good bronze and golden ceremonial breastplates. His hands itched for his tools.

Then he started and looked up, hearing a faint noise, like the snap of a twig, behind the hut where he had set up his makeshift forge.

Soft-shod, he moved in darkness along the side of the hut, with his hand on his dagger pommel.

The intruder was crouched over the smithy fire. His back was turned, and he appeared to be poking with a stick through the dead coals. Gwi caught him by surprise. He set his foot in the small of the man's back and sent him sprawling, face first, into the still-warm ashes. Then, while the thief was coughing and rubbing soot out of his mouth, Gwi seized both his wrists and dragged them sharply behind his back.

Gwi was surprised at the strength in those narrow shoulders—it was all that he could do to hold on. Finally, at dagger point, he turned the fellow round—and found, to his mild astonishment, that his captive was a woman.

She was a tall girl, with a spare angular grace about her. Her dark brown hair was cropped to shoulder length, pulled back from her brow and tied with a thong. She had a rather long, somber face—straight-nosed, stern-jawed, with high prominent cheekbones burnished by the cold. Her body was as taut as a strung bow, her gray eyes wide and startled.

"Well," said Gwi, examining her with interest. "You may thank the Mother it was me who found you. The villagers would have killed you on the spot."

Her gaze was cool, defiant. Not a thief's boldness, he thought, but the look of a warrior, almost.

"And you?" she asked. "What will you do with me, instead?"

Gwi shook his head. "Girl, you misjudge me. That was not in my mind either. But like any other man, I value my possessions. If I catch a prowler behind my house, I have a right to ask what she is after."

She spread her hands out before him. "Nothing. As you see, I have taken nothing."

He glanced at the pouch hanging from her belt. She shrugged, opened it, spilled the contents at his feet. He saw pieces of flint, tinder scraps, something—probably food— wrapped up in linen. A broken amber bead. A painted potsherd. Nothing of his. Nothing, except for the flint and the food, of the slightest value.

"I take what is thrown out. Or sometimes what is spared easily—a handful of grain. I saw your forge place, and I thought I might find a bit of sky-stone, or maybe fools gold, for my tinder pouch."

"So, not a thief, then. Only a harmless scavenger."

She shrugged again, but he saw that his words had brought a darker flush to her cheeks. He could sense the fierce pride in her, and was suddenly ashamed of his mockery.

"I do what I must to live. I take only what I need."

And then, looking down at the broken bead and the potsherd, she surprised him with a rueful look, the ghost of a grin. "And those—well, those are pretty," she said.

He laughed. "Are you hungry? I have stew on the fire."

She nodded, somewhat dubiously. He sat her down at his table before she could change her mind, and ladled stew into a bowl.

He was a man of lively curiosity. He wanted to keep this strange wild bird in his hand a little longer.

"Where do you live?" he asked, while she ate.

She gestured vaguely. "Up there," she said. "On the chalk." Her look was evasive.

"Alone?"

She nodded.

"An odd choice for a young woman."

"Not so odd," she replied. "You live alone, do you not?"

"Aye. But wandering the roads as I do, I never lack for society. You, I think, are not often in the company of other folk."

Once again, that noncommittal lift of the shoulders. She made no reply, only went on with her meal.

Finally she looked up and said dryly, "I did not expect to be in your company, either. After all, it is the middle of the night."

"I was working," Gwi said. "Sometimes I lose sense of the time."

He saw that she had a streak of soot across her temple. He picked up a polishing cloth and went to wipe it away. She looked warily at him, but stood quiet under his hand.

He could hear the faint pop and crackle of the fire, dying down to embers. Somewhere nearby a baby was crying. Before long dogs would bark and cattle would begin shuffling and lowing in the byres. Soon, too, the village women would crawl out of their warm beds to light the hearth-fires.

"Well," he said to the girl, "I will not keep you longer. Go while it is safe still."

A thought struck him. Where was that buckle he had set aside? He hesitated, thinking, this is not a woman to be given baubles. A good bronze knife is what she needs, if I had one not spoken for.

Still, he thought, sometimes you should obey your first impulse, if it is a harmless one.

She was half out the door when he said, "Wait. This is for you. Put it away in your pouch."

Her eyes widened. "It is of no value," Gwi said. "See, there is a flaw here, where I was careless with the hammer. It will serve you well enough to fasten your belt, but I can't sell it." He smiled at her, "That is what you look for, is it not—things that other folk would throw away?"

She held it in her hand for a moment, turning and examining it. She looked at him with faint puzzlement. Then she opened her pouch and dropped the buckle inside. In the blink of an eye she was gone.

∼ 3 ∼

Ricca

The Lord Ricca stamped his feet hard and blew on his hands. Though the morning was half-gone, the roofs glistened with frost; the mud of the courtyard was frozen in ridges, stone-stiff. Ricca had put on his great sheepskin surcoat over his jerkin, and his woolen cloak over that. Still the cold bit at him. Never, he thought, watching his breath smoke, could he remember such a queer winter as this. For weeks it had been warm and wet as springtime. Now, all at once, as new life was beginning to stir in the ground, this hard, bitter weather gripped them.

All the same, he felt uncommonly cheerful. The promise of a winter sun glimmered behind thin clouds. His head, thick and sore from last night's feasting, was starting to clear in the sharp bright air. He thought that he might ride out to hunt, later.

"My Lord Ricca. Your pardon, my lord." A young stammering voice, just at his elbow.

From his great height Ricca glowered down at the slave. The boy was plainly terrified—obliged to deliver his message, but convinced nonetheless that he would be thrashed for daring to speak.

"What do they call you?"

"Harn, lord."

Ricca scratched his beard and spat. He remembered this slave—a thin stick of a lad, at eighteen beardless as a girl, good

10

for nothing but kitchen work. Still, the boy had been born in the camp, and had cost him nothing.

He waited, watching the boy cringe under his cold eye. Each day, as for the first time, Ricca savored the sweetness of power. It was his, now, until his dying-time.

Harn had found his tongue. "Lord Ricca, they have sent me to say that the smith has come."

Abruptly, thoughts of the hunt vanished. "Have those fools of women fed him yet? Has the furnace been lit?"

"He has eaten, lord. He says he would rather see to the fire himself."

Ricca grunted. It was Gwi himself then, not the whey-faced easterner who had come last spring.

"Go," he said, in so mild a voice that the boy looked up, astonished. "Tell the smith I am coming."

Gwi had his broad back turned to the door. He was stoking the great stone charcoal pit, the sorcerer's fire that blasted the skin like the sun's heat. He turned and straightened at Ricca's approach, his face glistening with sweat.

"My Lord Ricca," said Gwi—but he did not bow his head, or bend his knees. It was true that Ricca was Great Chief; but a master-smith, like an archmage, was any man's equal.

"You have risen in the world since I was last here," Gwi said. "You do your father honor."

Graciously, as befitted his new station, Lord Ricca inclined his chin. Gwi's greeting pleased him. In truth, it was a great thing that he had done. He had feared, in secret, that the vote might favor his cousin Cian, who was subtle and clever, as Ricca was not. But it was the War-Council, in the end, that carried the vote—men who had the good sense to prize strength and valor and great deeds above all else.

"There is plenty of work for you," Ricca told the smith. "The funeral games near emptied my treasury, and soon now there is the Planting Feast."

"Good," said Gwi. "I am weary of traveling these winter roads."

"You will stay until spring, then?"

"Aye—longer, if you can keep me busy. I will see that the Spring Feast does you honor."

Ricca watched Gwi curiously as he laid out his tools, wondering what there was about this mild-tempered quiet man that so commanded his respect. Gwi was, by repute, the finest artisan in all the west country, or come to that, as far as the Narrow Sea. Yet he did not speak of his skill, as a warrior might; his fame came only from the mouths of other folk. He was paid well for his work, yet he dressed like a farmer, in rough-woven tunic and mended cloak. He said that it was for fear of robbers on the road; but he came as plainly garbed to Ricca's feast-table, his only ornament a single narrow bracelet of coiled bronze, when he might have worn all the gold of the west in perfect safety.

For the rest, he was of ordinary height, neither fair nor dark; thickset in build, with no spare flesh on his bones; like all smiths well-muscled in the arms and shoulders, but without the great thews and massive neck that marked a warrior.

He was gentle-mannered, soft-spoken; talking no more than he needed to, but smiling often. No man would mistake him for a warrior; he might have been a priest, or a bard. In Ricca's eyes he was as great a sorcerer as old Magha the priest. In Gwi's magic fire the green dull rock was transformed into bright metal, red-gold and shining as the evening sun. Under his clever hands, rough lumps of gold or bronze swelled flowerlike into thin, lovely shapes.

"Come with me," Ricca said. "You will be pleased when I show you what is in my storeroom." He was impatient to reveal his treasures—ingots of copper and gold, tin for bronze-making, black, glossy jet, huge warm lumps of amber . . .

"Time enough for that later," said Gwi. "First bring me your broken weapons, whatever you want recast. This oven is as nervous as a colt—I must first give it something easy to chew on, to gentle it down."

Ricca opened his mouth to protest, but remembered that would get him nowhere at all with the smith. Like a child, he swallowed his disappointment.

"Well," he conceded, "there is plenty of cracked bronze, after last week's raid."

"Ah," said Gwi. "I heard about that. Brega's tribe, was it not? And did you win the day?"

"Aye," said Ricca, surprised. How could it have been otherwise? Brega was an old man, who had put off too long his dying. His war-band fought among itself, with too little thought for other foes.

"Two hundred head of cattle we took that day," said Ricca, "and forty horses."

"In truth," said Gwi, "your time was not wasted." He smiled as he said it. Gwi appeared to see jests, sometimes, that were not plain to other men.

"I will send the armsmaster to you," Ricca said. "But tomorrow you must promise to look at the gold, for I have in mind such a shield as no other chief in this country possesses. And," said Ricca, "since we spoke of feasts . . . tonight you shall sit in the war-circle, on my left hand, and tell me the news from the east."

Neither the two great hearth-fires nor all the bearskins on the walls could keep the cold out of Ricca's feast-hall that night. The wind's icy fingers reached round the door hangings, crept beneath the hides at the windows and through every chink in the timbers. Men came into the feast-circles with furs and cloaks over their fine clothes, while hearth-slaves scurried among them with beakers of hot barley-beer and mead.

"Eat," Ricca told Gwi. He tossed a gnawed joint to his hounds, his arm clanking with its weight of gold and copper bracelets. He could see out of the corner of his eye that the smith, in his drab cloak, ate sparingly, with eastern manners.

"Fill your belly while you can," Ricca said. "If this weather takes hold, we may all starve by spring."

Ricca's brother Finga looked at the great platter of venison and beef that a slave had just set in front of him, and he guffawed.

"That is a good joke, Ricca," he said. "The cribs are half-full still, and the cattle shelters are jammed with cattle. Your woods are full of pigs and deer. If spring does not come at all this year, none of us will go hungry."

"You are a fool, little brother," Ricca said. "Look around you, see how many mouths I must feed. The grass does not grow when the ground is frozen. The corncribs do not fill up by themselves."

For answer, Finga belched. "Well then," he said amiably, "if we have not enough, we will steal from our neighbors."

All around the war-circle, men bellowed with laughter and thumped their beakers on the tables.

After a time, a lazy contentment stole over Ricca. The air was warmer now, shimmering with woodsmoke and pungent with the smell of sizzling pork. The hot mead and the beer had thawed his bones; his belly was full of good red meat.

The women, too, had been into the beer vats. Some of them danced, rather lewdly, showing generous glimpses of breast and buttock, while the men grinned and beat time with their beakers.

Two of Ricca's wives were among the dancers. Watching them, he felt the mead-warmth gathering in his loins. Idly he wondered which one he would summon to his bed tonight. Both, maybe.

Then abruptly the room fell silent, for the minstrel had come in with his string-box. He took his place in the center of the war-circle, and for a moment bent his dark head over his instrument. In a hush broken only by the crackle of the fires and the low moaning of the wind, the first notes rose on the smoky air.

> "Terrible to see in battle
> is the face of the Lord Ricca.
> Terrible and mighty is his ax
> as the thunder-ax of the heavens,
> gold-glittering and round his shield
> as the face of the Sky-Lord.
> The tall spears of his war-band
> are as numerous as the barley.
> All the bright gold of the Westland
> he has gathered into his storehouse.
> Chief among chiefs, Lord Ricca,
> we conceal not your praises.
> Tall are you among chiefs
> as the great oak that looks down
> on all the trees of the forest."

This bard had appeared one day out of nowhere, footsore and ragged, begging a chunk of barley-bread for a song. His own folk had been slaughtered, he said—the chief and all the warriors dead, the camp burned, the people killed or carried off as slaves. Too proud to sing the praises of the conqueror, the bard had fled into the countryside with only the clothes on his back and his string-box.

Ricca glanced up. There was some kind of commotion outside. Heads turned, and hands went to daggers. Presently the cattle-master burst in, followed by two slaves dragging between them a thin youth, who in spite of his bound hands and feet was struggling furiously.

The cattlemaster had to shout to make himself heard over the din.

"Lord, we were riding out after a stray steer, and we found this thief in your oakwoods stealing a pig."

"Bring him here," Ricca bellowed. By now, like most of the war-circle, he was quite drunk.

They hauled the pig thief across the room, still twisting and writhing and trying to reach his captors' hands with his teeth. His ragged cloak had been pulled off, and his tunic was ripped. Ricca took a closer look and blinked in surprise. This pig thief was not a lad at all, but a skinny, crop-haired girl. This indeed was a fine joke, Ricca thought. Had it been a boy, he would have ordered his throat cut on the spot. But now he saw the chance of a livelier entertainment.

"Bind up her mouth so she will not bite," Ricca said to the women. Giggling, one of them brought a strip of linen. Meanwhile, Ricca pulled the torn tunic down to the girl's waist. Though skinny, she was well made, he noticed.

"Fetch the knucklebones," he said. "We will cast lots to see who goes first."

Hearing that, the women screeched with excitement and crowded close for fear of missing something.

Afterward, Ricca thought, I may still cut her throat, if there is any point in it. He objected to having his pigs stolen.

"Wait," said a quiet voice in his ear. "A moment, Ricca."

Ricca grinned at Gwi and elbowed him in the ribs. "What, smith, do you fancy her for yourself, then?"

"I might at that," Gwi said. "Listen, I will make you that gold shield for nothing, if you let me have her."

Ricca roared with laughter, while the warriors grumbled among themselves like dogs robbed of a bone.

"Smith, she is yours, and by the Sky-Lord, I wish you pleasure of her."

All the while the minstrel, who had set down his string-box, was watching intently. When Ricca took the girl by her bare, bruised shoulders and pushed her into Gwi's arms, the minstrel's puzzled eyes followed her.

"Well, girl," said Gwi, when he had her safely back to the smithy, with the door barred. "We did well to bring you alive out of that."

She hunched herself against the wall of his bed-place, her knees drawn up tight against her chest. Her eyes were wide and blank with shock; she was shuddering, as though chilled to the bone.

Gwi felt in his pack for a pin, and drawing up the torn flaps of her tunic, he fastened them on her shoulder. Her cloak was still on the floor of the feast-hall; in his haste he had forgotten to pick it up. He took off his own and wrapped it around her.

Mildly he said, "You are growing overbold, my lass. It seems they were not through with that pig just yet."

She chose to take his small joke seriously. Through chattering teeth she replied, "I was hungry for meat. Who was to know whose pigs they were?"

"Never mind," he said. "You're safe enough here. Lie down now. Sleep. I've had a long day on the road—and it's growing longer by the minute." A thought struck him. "Are you hungry? I have some hardcake in my pack."

She shook her head.

"Well, drink this, at least," he said, holding out his waterskin. "Though mulled ale would do you more good."

She tipped back her head and drank thirstily. Then, still shivering, she lay down on her back on the far side of the bed, log-stiff and with her eyes wide open, waiting.

"Pull those skins over you," Gwi said gently.

She turned her great gray eyes on him.

"Lass," he said, "go to sleep. For that is all I mean to do myself."

Now, hot-faced, she was looking up into the rafters. "I thought . . ."

"Yes, well," said Gwi. "And so did Ricca think so—for which you may praise the Mother. One must talk to the Great Chief in words which make sense to him. Suppose I had told him I spoke for you only out friendship?"

She gave him a puzzled look.

"Well, did you not eat of my bread, lass? And are you not wearing my hearth-gift? In my country we treat our hearth-guests with courtesy. I will not take from you anything you do not wish to give."

He lay down in his clothes and pulled the sheepskins over both of them. He put one arm round her shoulders, and when he drew her closer to him she did not resist. After a while he heard her teeth stop chattering and her breath grow quiet and even.

Weary as he was, it was a long time before sleep came for Gwi. In the deep night he woke again, and feeling her close and warm beside him, his loins stirred. He turned over, leaving a little space between them, and did not wake again till dawn.

∼ 4 ∼

The Apprentice

As soon as Gwi opened his eyes he realized that she was gone; and thinking at first that by craft or sorcery she had fled the camp, he felt an irrational pang of disappointment.

Then he heard someone moving quietly about in the smithy. He thrust his head through the bed-hangings. She had left his cloak on the bed, and in tunic and leg-wrappings, in the bitter air, she was using a broken spear shaft to stir the coals.

"It's cold," she explained, glancing up.

"Let me tend to that," Gwi said. "That is not a bake-oven you see there; the fire must be made right if I am to do any work today. I can see your breath on the air, girl—come back to bed for a while."

He got up, and she took his place under the covers. Soon after, though, she emerged again with a sheepskin over her shoulders and watched him stoke the furnace. Her wariness had all but vanished with the night; she seemed, now, quite at ease in his presence. Altogether, Gwi thought, for one who had so recently escaped death, she was remarkably self-possessed.

"Have you any of that bread left?" she wanted to know.

"Never mind that—in the Lord Ricca's house, no smith goes hungry." Gwi leaned through the smithy door into the courtyard and hailed a passing slave. Presently a kitchen girl knocked at the door bearing a great platter of food.

The meal did Ricca's kitchens proud. There was barley-bread

17

warm from the hearth, with a pot of honey; pig sausage, soft
cheese, wheaten porridge with cream, and a basket of apples.

Gwi watched the girl finish off the last of the porridge and lick
the corners of her mouth as delicately as a cat. For so slender a
creature, her appetite was impressive.

Munching on an apple, she began to wander about the workroom, looking curiously at his anvil, his hammers and files and
punches, but careful not to touch them. The day before, Gwi had
sorted Ricca's bronze and copper into two great piles—in one the
battered and dented shields, the bent knives and blunted axheads
that could be heated and hammered new again; in the other, the
scrap destined for the furnace. Coming across these, she began to
pick things up one by one, touching and stroking and examining
them. Her face was intent, absorbed.

Gwi finished his own meal and called out for a slave to take
away the dishes and another to bring washwater. Then he said to
the girl, "I am recasting that bronze today. You may watch, if you
wish."

In truth, now that she was here, he had no clear idea what to do
with her. He could hardly turn her loose, after robbing Ricca's
war-band of its amusement on a whim. Still, he noticed as she
lifted the weapons how strong and dexterous her hands were. An
extra pair of hands in the smithy would not come amiss, especially
when it came to the mold-pouring. He had always to send for
slaves to help carry the crucibles. Few of Ricca's slaves were as
intelligent as this woman appeared to be.

"Do you have a name?" he asked her.

A small shadow crossed her face. "I had a name once," she
said. "A birth-name. My mother called me Naeri. It must do still,
I suppose, since I have been given no other."

"Well, Naeri," he said, "let us find out if you have the patience
for smithy work."

As he spoke, he loaded a clay crucible with pieces of scrap
bronze and nested it in the coals.

"What am I to do?"

He handed Naeri the goatskin bellows. "Since we are cooking
bronze here, not barley-bread, the fire must be very hot. It takes
a steady flow of air to bring the temperature up." He showed her
where to rest the bellows nozzle on the flat stones at the edge of
the pit.

Obediently, she knelt by the fire pit and began to work the

bellows, pausing now and again to wipe her face against her sleeve.

"Enough," he said after a time, for he could see that she was tiring. "I will take a turn at it." Finally he said, "that should serve."

"Look," said the girl, with satisfaction. The metal in the crucible had turned into a smooth, glowing mass like crimson honey.

"Now," said Gwi, "comes the hardest part. Fetch me those two green branches there by the wall."

He slipped the branches under the lips of the crucible, one on either side, making a carry-cradle.

"Lift when I say the word," he told Naeri. "A splash or spill, and one of us will be howling fit to be heard on the eastern coast."

Her brow was set in fierce lines of concentration as they lifted the molten bronze. Working as with a single mind, they sidled to the waiting ax mold and poured the stream of glowing metal through the gate.

Finally Gwi looked up at the girl and smiled. "My trust was not misplaced," he said. "I have the scars on my foot yet where a helper slipped and splashed me with hot copper."

In the days that followed, Gwi showed Naeri the simpler skills of his craft, and taught her to heat copper in the fire so that she could twist and coil and hammer it into pins, rings, buckles, earrings. He was pleased by her facility with tools, her quickness to learn and the care with which she handled the metal; pleasantly surprised, too, by her inventiveness. He no longer thought of her as another smithy-slave; she had become in the fullest sense his apprentice.

At the end of the first week, thinking that they were comfortable with one another and the time was right, Gwi reached out in the darkness to embrace her. But she shrank away as though his touch burned her.

"What is it, lass?" he whispered.

"You swore you would not ask of me what I did not wish to give."

"Aye, so I did." Reluctantly he drew his hand away. "I would not take any woman against her will." Though the Mother knew, he thought to himself, the women he met on the road were willing enough.

Another thought struck him. Because she lived free and alone, like a creature of the fields, it had not occurred to him before.

"Naeri, have you never lain with a man?"

She did not answer; her silence was reply enough.

He thought that she must be dedicated to some goddess or other, like temple maidens in southern lands. Such vows were not meant to be broken. He did not press her further, but the next day ordered a bed made up for her in another part of the smithy, with a horsehide curtain for privacy. He knew that the servants would gossip, and that more than likely the talk would come to Ricca's ears. But it was no great matter. What the smith did, or chose not to do, was no man's business but his own.

And so, through those last days of winter, they settled into an odd, chaste domesticity. Within the safety of the smithy walls, in Gwi's company, the girl seemed content enough. And yet he saw that she had an ear always on the door, and would grow suddenly tense, alert, at even such ordinary sounds as footsteps approaching through the outer court. It was, he thought, for all the world like asking some wild forest bird to nest peacefully at one's hearth.

Sometimes, as the weather grew milder, they would take bread and ale and set out for a morning's wanderings on the chalk hills above the camp. Here, in the open, climbing the long ridges under the wide pale curve of the sky, Naeri seemed to find a deep contentment. The lines that so often creased her brow were for a while erased; all the movements of her young body grew broader, more expansive.

One day they came upon an old half-ruined circle of standing stones. As a rule Gwi, like the horsemen, gave such places a wide berth; but Naeri walked boldly into the middle of the circle. There was, in her manner, a curious mix of awe and familiarity—so, thought Gwi, did some southern folk approach the statues of their antique gods.

"There is nothing to fear," she said—and for once it was her voice, not his own, that was calm and reassuring. "See, the circle is broken, the power of the stones is diffused."

It was true, in the shadowless noon the stones seemed ordinary enough, a part of the landscape like the wind-bent thorns and the faint crisscrossing of ancient tracks.

She sat down in the lee of a toppled stone and motioned for Gwi to join her. Handing him barley-bread, she said, "In your country, are there no circles?"

"Some," he replied. "Not so large as this. As children we were taught to stay clear of them. They were built by the Lost Ones, the sorcerer-folk."

"I know," she said. And then, surprising him, she began to sing in a clear fluting voice,

"Gray and cold are the mists of the Western Sea,
White are the bones of the folk who sleep beneath the wave.
Drowned, drowned are the towers of ancient time . . ."

"Where did you learn that?" he asked.

"From my mother. I was born of hill-folk. They say we bear the blood of sorcerers and warriors both."

"And what witchery do you do, my lass? If you read thoughts, or shape-shift . . ."

She laughed. "Never fear, I have not the gift for those things. I will not turn into a wolf in the night and devour you. Or read all your heart's secrets, either."

"What, then?"

"I cannot say. I was not yet a woman when I left the witchfolk. I had not discovered my true gift." And then she added in a small, wistful voice, a child's voice, "There is no one, now, to help me find it."

She shook her head, as though to clear it of memories. "Put your hand on this stone," she said. "I will show you something."

He did as she directed. The stone was rough to his palm, faintly warm in the thin sunlight.

"Let your mind be free," she said, "and empty as the wind. Think of nothing. Let your heart be in your hand."

She waited. "Can you feel it?" Her face was solemn, expectant.

Gwi shook his head. "What should I feel, Naeri?"

She put her own two hands flat against the stone and closed her eyes. Presently she said, "In my fingers and my wrists and arms, warmth, that flows into the blood like mead-warmth. A tingling, like the crackle of the air on a frosty morning." She glanced up. "If you touch the stones for too long, you are apt to grow faint and dizzy."

"Girl," said Gwi softly, "what is it that you feel there?"

"It is the old power," she said, "that comes from the world's roots. The earth-magic." And Gwi wondered that she had not already guessed where her true birthgift lay.

~~ 5 ~~

Daui

The end of that long winter came at last. The spring rains fell, and there were small new leaves on the rowan branches. Once again the chalk roads were well traveled. Many visitors came to Ricca's hall—merchants, amber-workers, chiefs and warriors of tribes with whom Ricca's people lived in ax-truce. Each night there were new faces in the feast-hall.

On a warm wet spring evening, with the smell of blossoms hanging in the air, Gwi said to Naeri, "There is a feast tonight in honor of the amber-worker Fahan, who has come from Brethna across the Narrow Sea."

She looked up from the bronze breastplate she had been embossing with quick delicate hammer blows.

"I am bidden by Ricca to attend. Anyway, I want to be there. Fahan is an old acquaintance of mine."

She waited, her face without expression.

"Naeri, will you come to the feast with me tonight? You have bided long enough within these four walls."

Her mouth grew suddenly stubborn, and she shook her head. "By your leave, I will stay here and finish this," she said.

"Come with me, lass. It will be safe enough for you now. No man would dare to lay a hand on the bronze-smith's woman."

"It is not that," she said. "I know they will not touch me. It is the memories I fear, the dreams that come back when I see the horsemen."

"I know they have ill-used you . . ."

Her mouth twisted. She said, with bitter irony, "Ill-used me, yes. Someday, smith, I will put words to my memories, and then you will understand why I do not wish to feast with them."

"Listen to me," Gwi said. "There is a great deal of art in those hands of yours. I think you may turn out to be the best apprentice I have had; and when I leave here I mean to take you with me, if you agree to it."

He looked down at her. She was still holding the breastplate and was examining it with great intentness, so that she did not have to meet his eyes.

"What I am saying to you, girl, is this. I think in time I can make a smith of you. And when your apprenticeship is done, what then? A master-smith must work for men who value her skills and are prepared to pay for them. If she is to do any work worth doing. Do you understand what I am saying, Naeri?"

She lifted her chin, and her gray eyes looked straight into his. They were full of a somber resolution, like a warrior's on the eve of battle. "That I must learn to live among the horsemen." She shrugged. "So be it, then. Must I put on woman's garb to attend this feast?"

He smiled. "Not if you don't want to. Since my apprentice is what you are, in truth, that is how Ricca must accept you."

And so she went to the feast-table in a boy's tunic and leggings, clean and fairly new but as plain-made and as drab-colored as Gwi's own. And Gwi insisted that as a craftswoman she must have a place between him and Fahan the amber-worker in the guest-circle, where as a rule only the wives of the Great Chiefs were privileged to sit.

Mild though the night was, fires leaped in the round hearths. The hall was loud with the roar of flames, the hiss and crackle of roasting fat, the clatter of metal and a great hubbub of voices, already boisterous with mead.

In spite of Gwi's quiet, steadying presence Naeri's nerves were drawn taut as harpstrings. When a tankard of the strong, sweet honey-liquor was set before her, she gulped it faster than was wise.

The mead-warmth gave her courage. Her natural curiosity returned, and she began to look around her. From one corner of her eye she watched the Great Chief, Ricca, resplendent in his feast-night finery. Flushed with mead and with the fire's heat, he had thrown back his cloak. Beneath it he wore a woolen tunic, fastened with gold buttons and fringed at hem and shoulder with polished bone. A dagger with a gold-inlaid hilt hung from a chased gold plaque on his belt. His breastplate also was made of gold, and his heavy neck-ring, and the half-dozen narrower rings on either arm. Down the sides of his broad, high-cheekboned face hung the warrior's plaits, as thick and pale as barley sheaves. His eyes were very blue, and as clear and cold as spring water.

Soon those eyes, which missed nothing, fell on Naeri.

"By our Father's beard," remarked the Great Chief, in a voice which carried the length of the hall, "he has brought the witch-girl to the feast."

"Well, smith," he said, grinning at Gwi, "has she tried to bite off your ear, as she did Nudd's?" There was a sudden silence in the hall as everyone turned to listen. "Show us your shoulders, man," Ricca urged with drunken hilarity. "Has she given you clawmarks there?"

Naeri had learned enough of their speech to understand his words. She felt ashamed, unclean.

Gwi reached out and put his hand over hers. There was nothing sensual in his touch. It was a father's gesture, or a brother's. She was grateful for the sudden courage it gave her. "This lady," said Gwi, coldly and distinctly, "is a princess among her own folk. On her behalf, Ricca, I beg your courtesy."

Ricca's eyes narrowed, and his face took on a deeper flush. But then, through the fumes in his head, he seemed to remember that it was the smith who spoke; and he accepted the rebuke without resentment, or maybe chose to ignore it, letting the joke drop as carelessly as he had taken it up.

"Thank you," said Naeri into Gwi's shoulder. He turned his head and smiled at her. "Lass, it is no more than your due," he said. "Not even Ricca has the right to mock you before company."

How good he is, she thought. She knew she had it in her power to repay that goodness. Ignorant though she might be of men's ways, she was wise enough to read the wistful passion in Gwi's eyes. What he wished of her was small payment indeed. She knew that with Gwi the act would be a shared, unselfish thing; yet still the thought of it brought the dreams back, the red visions of flames and blood. And so tonight she would go to her narrow bed and leave him to lie in his; letting him believe it was her priestess's vows that kept her chaste, not her own blind, unreasoning terror.

But now the minstrel had come into the hall—that tall, magelike, mysterious figure in his hooded cloak. His face was in shadow; Naeri could not see his eyes. Yet somehow, curiously, she felt that he was watching her.

Music flowed through the long room, drifted up to the high smoke-blackened beams. The minstrel sang of ancient wars and ancient kings: the plucked strings sounding the wild rhythm of hooves, like drums. He sang the praises of the Great Chief Ricca and the favorites of the war-circle; and he strummed a southern lay in honor of the First Wife, the Lady Suais.

And at the very last, when the hearth-fires had sunk to embers and the warriors lay snoring with their heads in puddles of spilled mead, the minstrel threw back his hood, and his gray eyes looked straight into Naeri's own. The music changed, grew faint and strange as a far-off bell pealing. His voice was wistful, melancholy:

"Gray and cold are the mists of the Western Sea,
White are the bones of the folk who sleep beneath the wave.
Drowned, drowned, are the towers of ancient time . . ."

Naeri's hand reached out for Gwi's and gripped it hard. There was a sudden aching tightness in her throat, and the room blurred.

In the minstrel's face she saw reflected those other well-loved faces, the shadowy images of her childhood. It was her own face, too—older, harder, sadder, deep-etched by knowledge and despair; yet with that same hawk-look about the eyes, the same strong sculptured bones.

"Daui," she whispered. "Cousin." She went to him, picking her way among the drunken warriors, the overturned benches and sleeping hounds. And she embraced him, weeping openly now for the place in the world they both had known and had so suddenly, cruelly lost.

"Girl," said the minstrel. "Little cousin. Do you know how long I have searched for you? How I wept for you, thinking you were dead, or a slave, or worse? I saw you when they dragged you into the hall as a pig thief; something tugged at my memory then, but I did not know you."

"How could you?" said Naeri. "I was a child when last you saw me . . ."

"Well, you have changed, there is no denying that—as I have also. But tonight it came to me, and I saw in the smith's apprentice the one that I had been seeking."

It was very late. Through the small high window of the smithy they could see the sky paling to gray as the dawn approached.

The minstrel Daui said softly to Gwi, "She was the daughter of the chief. The youngest child. She had a skin like petals and a smile to charm the birds out of the trees. And the deadliest aim I ever saw in a girl of twelve."

"Not so deadly as now," said Naeri. "I did not have to depend on it for my dinner in those days."

"But then the horsemen came," Daui said. "At first I thought I was the only one left of our clan. But I heard stories told of the witch-girl who lived alone on the high chalk, no one knew where. And a man who had caught a glimpse of her once, said she was like enough to me to be my sister. My Naeri, what became of you that night?"

Naeri caught her breath. Some of the fierce joy she had felt in this meeting was lost now in the memories that came rushing back. Remembering that night, she felt her heart hammering against her ribs.

"I hid," she said. "When my mother heard the hooves and the shouting outside, she told me to hide in the wicker chest where she kept her summer garments. It was nearly empty then, and I was not very big. The horsemen did not think to look inside, so I stayed safe through all that long night. They burned the other houses of the village, but ours was set apart a little, being the chief's house, and somehow it did not catch alight. For a long time I could hear the roar of the flames and the screams of those who were caught alive in them; and I was terrified that the smoke would make me cough and give me away, so I pulled the sleeve of my mother's best linen gown over my face. But I heard everything," she said. "I tried to stop my ears with my fingers, but still I could hear the screams.

"Sometime the next day, when it was quiet and I thought the horsemen had gone, I crept out. I saw my mother, and my sisters . . ."

She met the minstrel's steady gray gaze, and the tears she had not shed for her kinfolk these five years slid out from under her lids. With them came the words she had not spoken to Gwi, or to anyone.

"They were lying in a great pool of blood—several pools, I suppose, that had run together into one great red lake. My mother and my three sisters. My sisters looked all white and waxy, like dolls, and their clothes were ripped to shreds, though I could see no knife wounds on them, only great bruises on their arms and breasts. But when I looked lower down . . ." Her voice faltered. "Well, I did not look long. My mother had been carrying a four-month's child. When last I saw her she was carrying it no longer. It would have been a boy . . ." Her voice trailed off, and she gazed down at her clenched hands. "There was so much blood," she whispered. "That was all I dreamed about, for years, the blood."

She put her head into the hollow of Gwi's shoulder, and his arms tightened around her. Over her head she heard Gwi say to the minstrel, "And you?"

"I? I was taken as a slave." Daui hesitated. "Do you want to hear this, smith? It is not the kind of tale one makes songs about . . ."

Naeri could feel Gwi's quiet breath in her ear; could feel the rough weave of his tunic against her cheek and the warm solid flesh beneath. In spite of everything she felt safe, protected.

She lifted her head. "Tell me," she said. "Let everything be said now, then we will not have to speak of it again."

"The horsemen took us by surprise," Daui said. "We supposed we were safe, up there in the hills. It was summer, and a great many of the men, and the women too, had gone to the hunting grounds. When I heard the horsemen ride through the gates I ran out with my spear, but I was no warrior, even then. When I drew back my spear to throw it at one horseman, another rode up from behind and snatched it out of my hand. Then he dragged me off into the trees and used me as a woman, for a joke. Because the women of my tribe carried spears, he said.

"I thought he would kill me, after, but for some reason or other he decided to keep me as a slave. Later on, in their camp, they found that I could sing and play the string-box, and the chief wanted to make a minstrel of me. But I had a little honor left—I would not be his praise-singer, and so I ran away, and took to the roads as a wandering musician."

"And so became a minstrel after all," Gwi said.

"I can still sing Ricca's praises," Daui said. "He has killed many folk, it's true, but none of them were my blood-kin."

He was silent for a moment, and then he said, "All that is in the past. And it is not a bad thing, to be minstrel to the Great Chief. It brings a measure of privilege with it, and what is more important, freedom . . ."

As he spoke, his mind seemed to be half in another place. Then, as though suddenly gathering his thoughts, he said to Naeri, "When the horsemen came, you had not discovered your gift. But I had found mine."

"I remember," she said. "You were a scholar. You were learning the meanings of numbers, the patterns of the earth, the movements of the sun and moon and stars."

"Those things," he said, "and more. And listen, Naeri. When I thought you were dead, I grieved for you because you were my blood-cousin, and my friend. But when I sought you on the chalkhills I had another reason besides."

Puzzled, she looked up at him.

"I know—I think I know—the nature of your birthgift. It is a gift that once I longed desperately to possess. It seems the Mother has denied it to me, and I have accepted that. But Naeri, without you, without your particular powers, the Great Circle is forever broken, the Pattern is incomplete."

"Then Daui, you must first tell me what those powers are."

"Cousin, if I am right, I will do better to show you. But look, it is nearly sunrise. Today we will sleep. Tomorrow you must wake early, for I will be here knocking at your door at dawn."

⚒ 6 ⚒

Nhiall

Daui arrived, as he had promised, at sunup. Naeri, who had been awake and restless for an hour, was sopping up the last of her barley-gruel. She glanced impatiently at Gwi.

"Yes, yes," muttered the smith. Yawning, he laced up his boots. As always, early rising had made him drowsy and ill-humored.

Daui leaned gracefully against the doorsill. In leggings and tunic, with his black bard's cloak thrown over his arm, he looked younger and less somber.

"Have you brought food?" he asked. "We've a long day's walk ahead of us."

For answer Naeri lifted her pack, showing him its weight: it bulged with bread, apples, sausages.

"Where are we going?" she wanted to know, as she poured barley-beer into a goatskin.

"South, along the ridge track," Daui told her.

"Our destination, I meant. And what it is we will do when we get there."

"Girl, girl," said Daui, in a voice that brought back sudden memories of childhood. "You have not changed in all these years. You always asked more questions than anyone had time to answer. Must every journey have a purpose, then?"

"Clearly," said Naeri, "this one does. I remember, you never did anything without a reason."

He laughed. "Well, then. Let us say, I am taking you to meet someone whose business it is to answer questions."

She looked at him with guarded interest. "A priest?"

"So you might call him. Priest, teacher, sorcerer—he is many things. Smith, are you ready?"

Hoisting the beerskin, Gwi nodded without much enthusiasm.

The morning was chill and overcast, the combes and hollows of the downs half-filled with thin white mist. They followed the ridge road down the flanks of the hills until it lost itself in a wooded valley bottom. Just then the sun broke through, its pale rays glistening on the wet foliage. Looking up, they could see to the south the scarps and buttresses of the Great Down, and above them a huge sky with high slow-moving banks of clouds.

They climbed again, up the juniper-covered slopes and over the long turf ridges. The road they followed now was worn by centuries of use; white chalk gleamed through the sparse, well-trodden grass. On this side of the valley the contours of the land grew broader, calmer, swelling and falling away like a great green ocean—and like the ocean, evoking a sense of limitless, unbroken distance.

Midday came. They rested briefly, shared their food, and traveled on through the afternoon. The sun was warm and yellow now. Light and shadow moved mysteriously over the folds and hollows of the chalk.

Late in the day they passed a solitary barrow. Sentrylike, it crowned its high lonely prominence, the name of its warrior-king forgotten, but its crouching shape a familiar landmark for travelers on the downs. Soon after, they came to a deserted hill fort, and beyond, a southward flowing river. The fort belonged to the folk of ancient days, Gwi said—a place of power, where many roads converged.

They followed the river valley through wide green water meadows, with the chalk hills rising up on either side. Primroses grew in bright patches along the river banks; the willows glistened with new-risen sap.

At sunset, at the confluence of three rivers, they came to a temple fallen into ruins; and close by, a village of wattle huts. It was a pleasant place, set among green fields and poplars, quiet and peaceful in the fading light. One hut stood a little apart from the others, in the shadow of the chalk slope. It was toward this dwelling that Daui led them.

It was no more than a farmer's hut—a small round house on

stone foundations sunk partway into the ground, with a skin roof and walls of mud-chinked branches. Within, a peat fire burned, and there was a savory fragrance of meat and herbs.

A tall, white-haired man rose from his place by the fire and approached with hands outstretched in greeting.

"Master," Daui said, and in the old formal way of priests he grasped the man's two hands in his own and touched them to his forehead.

The white-haired man turned to smile at Naeri. His face was at once strange to her, and achingly familiar. Clearly, the blood she shared with Daui flowed in his veins also.

As though reading that thought, he took her hands and said quietly, "Welcome, cousin."

Forgetting courtesy in her surprise, she gazed intently at him. He returned her look with clear and penetrating sea-gray eyes. Although she guessed he must be older by forty years than Daui, he seemed, in some curious fashion, younger. Lined as his face was, there was an ageless quality about it. His mouth had none of the bitterness, the sad stern quality of Daui's. In the depths of his eyes there was a great quietness—the look of a soul that has made peace with itself.

"What do they call you?" he asked.

"I am Naeri," she replied.

"And I am Nhiall. We are blood-kin, you and I—though I daresay by now the records of such things are forgotten . . . Come, sit. And you, Daui. And you, sir." This to Gwi, who, not wishing to intrude, was hovering awkwardly on the threshold.

"Will you sup with me?" asked Nhiall. And without waiting for a reply, he set out bowls and beakers, and lifted a pot of stew from the hearth.

It was pork, stewed with dried fruit and some unfamiliar herb—odd-tasting, but delicious. Naeri, who, as usual, was ravenous, scraped her bowl and gratefully accepted more.

Then, sipping a mulled beer, she looked sleepily around the room. It contained a box-bed with a mattress of skins and heather, a low bench and some stools, a collection of red-glazed cooking pots. On a wooden dresser, strangely out of place among those commonplace furnishings, stood a little horse exquisitely carved in ivory; a chased gold beaker of foreign design; and a black polished vase that appeared, though it was made of stone, to be as light and delicate as a bubble.

There was a woven rug on the floor and another on the wall,

glowing with deep jewel-colors. Nhiall saw her stroking the soft bright wool, and he smiled. "That came from a long way off," he said. "From a brown, dusty southern land."

"How did it come here?" asked Naeri, forever curious.

"How? By caravan, and ship, and on my back for the last part of the way. Heavy it was, too, I can assure you."

Naeri's eyes widened. "You have traveled in those lands? Were you a trader then, before you were a priest?"

"Aye, lass. Horse-trader, sailor, dock laborer, mule-tender—I have turned my hand to a great many things. All that was a long time ago, but these few things I have with me still."

Naeri went to the dresser and very carefully, with one forefinger, she stroked the little white horse's ivory mane. "It's beautiful," she murmured.

"Living in the south," Nhiall said, "one acquires a taste for beautiful things. Here, the earth itself is beautiful enough. What need is there for artifice, when you can look out over the downs on a spring morning? But in those dry desert lands men must create beauty with their hands. See, Gwi is nodding, he understands what I mean."

Wandering back to the hearthside, Naeri curled up like a cat on the beautiful southern rug. Filled with lazy contentment, she basked in the fire's warmth.

"Look at the child," she heard Nhiall say presently. "Put her on my bed, Gwi."

Naeri muttered a sleepy protest. "I must not take the priest's bed, put me on the floor, Gwi . . ." and then she drifted into oblivion.

She woke to a smell of smoke and the sizzle of meat cooking in a pan. Pale sunshine slanted across her bed. She sat up, rubbing sleep out of her eyes. Gwi, who was eating barley-porridge, smiled at her.

"Where is Daui? And the priest?"

"Nhiall has gone to walk the stiffness out of his bones," he said. "And Daui has gone with him."

She stretched and yawned, luxuriating. She liked this place. Somehow it filled her with a sense of ease, of safety. After awhile she got out of bed, stretched again, rough-combed her hair with her fingers, and went to wash in the stream that ran beside the hut. When she returned Gwi had set out her breakfast—goat's milk, porridge, fried strips of pork.

As she scraped up the last of the porridge with a piece of flatbread, she heard Daui and Nhiall returning.

"Well, lass," said the priest. "You have slept half the morning away. But no matter."

She smiled her apology, feeling suddenly shy and uncertain in his presence. To cover her awkwardness, she began to gather up the bowls and beakers.

"Leave those," he said, waving her to a bench. "You are here to learn, girl. That is why Daui brought you to me, whether he has explained it to you or not. Now, let us make a beginning."

He went to a wicker chest standing in a corner and raised the lid, moving not so much stiffly as with economy of effort. Now he was holding up a bauble suspended on a thread. It was a small, perfect sphere, the off-white of old bone, and delicately carved. Ivory, Nhiall told her, like the little horse, hanging from a nearly invisible thread of silk.

"From an eastern land," he said. "I bought it in the market from a girl with skin like amber, and slanted eyes." With a look of wistful recollection he went on, "I could imagine no possible use for it. But she was like a carved ornament herself, and I wanted a reason for lingering at her booth, and so I bargained for it." His mouth quirked. "I remember I gave her a whole handful of copper—three times what the thing was worth. Still, I have found it useful since. In another country, I met a man who showed me that even such a simple toy as this could be put to the use of science.

"Take it," he said to Naeri. "Hold it so, between your thumb and your first finger. Let it swing free. You observe," he said after a moment, "what happens."

She watched the ivory ball. It was gyrating slowly, circling as the moon-priest's marker moves round the moon-circle.

"Now," Nhiall said, "without moving your wrist, or your fingers, make it reverse its motion— make it swing in the opposite direction."

She glanced up at him. "How can I do that?"

"Easily enough. Use your thought, your will. Tell the ball to obey you."

She wrinkled her forehead, pursed her lips, concentrating. The ball slowed, hung motionless. "I cannot."

"Here. The thread is too short for you. Play it out a little more. Now try."

This time, to her wonderment, the ivory bauble swung in a

moonwise circle, reversed, swayed to and fro, stopped, started as she directed it.

Gwi said, "You are moving it with your wrist."

Her concentration broken, Naeri gave him a look of annoyance. "I am not," she said, affronted.

"Not consciously, perhaps," said Gwi. "Let me try." He took the ball, and it swung obediently to his unspoken command.

"You see? And I would swear that I was moving neither my wrist nor my fingers."

"It is a trick almost anyone can do," Nhiall said. "Though the eye may detect no movement, the impulse of the mind is interpreted through nerve and muscle and bone." As he spoke, he took the ivory ball from Gwi's hand and returned it to Naeri's grasp.

"Now, cousin," he said, "we must find how the pendulum speaks to you—what language it uses. Let it swing free again, so. Ask yourself a question—something to which the reply is known, that can be answered simply yes or no."

She thought for a moment, then said aloud, "Am I called Naeri?"

The ball began slowly to gyrate moonwise.

She looked sidelong at Gwi, mischievously. "My friend, is he called Gehri?" she asked—naming the dull-witted lad who emptied slops in Ricca's camp.

"No," replied the pendulum, clearly enough, as it slowed and reversed its swing.

"Gwi, then?" The pendulum agreed.

She chuckled, delighted as a child in possession of a new toy.

"Did I travel northward to reach this place?"

"No," said the ball.

"South?—Does it do that of its own accord," she wanted to know, as the pendulum again reversed its swing, "or am I causing it to answer so?"

"Almost certainly, you are causing it, because the answer is there, in your mind. But now you will know how it speaks to you, how it shapes its answers. And that will not vary. Now I will show you something else."

He took two pieces of copper and set them on the table, a little way apart.

"Let the pendulum hang between the two, and just above."

Immediately the pendulum set up an even rhythm, swinging between the two coins.

Nhiall reached out and took away one of the copper coins, replacing it with a scrap of silver. The pendulum hesitated, then began to gyrate. He took away the silver, put back the copper. They watched the ball resume its former motion.

"There, you see," said Naeri, on a note of satisfaction. "The thing has a mind of its own, after all—this time I did not tell it anything."

Nhiall smiled at her. "And I see you are waiting for an explanation. Magic? Coincidence? A stray draft down the chimney? Or maybe the nerves and the flesh know things the mind does not."

"I have seen this done in the southern countries," Gwi said. "The pendulums are made of copper and are used to seek out copper ore. I had a mind to try it myself, but I am not a great believer in magic, or in anything I cannot test with my own five senses. In any case, I could not get the trick of it."

"In the dry lands they use wands or osier rods to find hidden water," Nhiall told him. "Among the desert people, such diviners are honored like princes. Still, as you say, it is an art, a gift, like so much else. It will not work for everyone. Well, Naeri," he said, getting up from his bench. "Are you ready? Or did you believe your work was finished for the day?"

It was a soft cool morning, with a pale sun just breaking through the mist. There were clumps of white violets in bloom under the hazel trees, and cowslips in the long grass beside the stream. Beyond the village, in the wide fields, sheep grazed peacefully.

This, thought Naeri wistfully, as she breathed the fragrance of damp earth and woodsmoke, this is a place I could bide, and be well content.

Nhiall led her out to the meadow's edge. "Take the pendulum," he said. "Hold your arm extended—so. Let the ball swing freely, and behave as it will."

"Now walk forward," he told her. "The ball will lead you."

She followed the direction of the pendulum's swing, out into the middle of the meadow, where the sheep raised their heads to gaze incuriously at her. As she walked, a tag end of memory surfaced—she saw herself as a small child with Elin, her red-haired cousin. They had played a game like this with bone-fasteners and flax thread borrowed from her mother's sewing bag.

At first she was half-curious and half-amused, seeing the pendulum as some obscure priest's ritual, another of those complex and mysterious temple ceremonies in which, as a child,

she had been expected to take part. But now suddenly she felt a
rising excitement, as though something long hidden, uncompre-
hended, were about to be revealed.

Nhiall was walking just behind her, his eyes on the motion of
the ball. As she advanced, the bauble paused in its even rhythm,
as though hesitating, pondering its next move; and then began to
swing in a ragged ellipse.

"Stop now," Nhiall said,

All at once the ivory ball was moving strongly, steadily, in
ever-widening circles—a thing with a life, a volition of its own.
She felt the strong tension of it against the thread, and what had
been a child's game was suddenly frightening, as though she had
plunged without warning into deep cold water.

She shivered, and the movement of her arms and shoulders
broke the rhythm. As she stepped back—as though from the edge
of an abyss—the pendulum slowed and returned to rest.

"Girl, you have turned as white as chalk," said Nhiall. He put
his hand on her shoulder, steadying her. "There is no need to be
afraid. What you have found is a forceline that runs straight
through this place. See, I will show you how to mark the course
of it."

He set a peg into the ground, and then sent Naeri off at random
through the long wet grass until she was a good fifty paces distant.
"Stop there," he said. "Now turn to the west and walk forward.
Stop when the pendulum begins to gyrate."

Again, that insistent pull against her fingers, the strong,
regular, unequivocal motion. Nhiall caught up with her, and
marked the place. "Again."

By noon they had marked the ground with a long straight line
of pegs stretching out onto the open downland. Under the calm
guidance of the priest, Naeri's nervousness had vanished. What
took its place was an enormous, exhilarating sense of purpose.
She felt half-drunk, euphoric. Each time she approached the
forceline, a tingling ran through her flesh, as though she had
touched metal in cold dry air. And yet, all the same, as the
morning wore on and the line of pegs grew longer, she began to
feel drained, chilled, lightheaded with weariness.

"Enough," Nhiall said, seeing her wan, exhausted look. "We
should have stopped before. Rest now. Tomorrow we will follow
the line a little farther."

~⎯⎯ 7 ⎯⎯

Standing Stones

Next morning at dawn Nhiall roused them. Hot tea and porridge were waiting on the hearth. "Dress warmly," Nhiall advised them, as he went out to fetch more fuel. Sitting up among her rumpled bedskins, Naeri saw white tendrils of mist curling through the doorway.

The sky was a pale unbroken grayish-white, the color of cold gruel; the trees and stream and village huts were half-lost in vapor. As they set out on the road over the high chalk, a raw wind blew down from the north, biting through their heavy winter cloaks.

They were traveling, Nhiall said, to the temple of blue stones, the Broken Circle. For the three men, who had spent half their lifetimes traveling the southern chalk country, its mystery had long been eroded by familiarity. But to Naeri, that ancient haunted place was a thing of legend, of half-remembered fireside tales and childhood dreams. In her mind's eye she saw the stones as luminous, translucent—crystalline shapes like the dark blue jewel her mother had once shown her, that had fallen centuries before from a Great One's dagger.

When at last they came upon the temple, Naeri's first thought was one of disappointment, that the stones were not as marvelous as she had wished them; and her second, that they were, in some other unforeseen way, incalculably stranger.

Wraithlike in the blowing mist, they stood within an earthen bank in a high empty place—a double half-circle of standing stones, some leaning now, or toppled to earth—the whole half-finished structure fallen into ruin. On this sunless morning the stones were not blue, as she had imagined, but a dark gray which, as she came closer, assumed a faintly greenish tinge.

Heads into the wind, the four of them plodded over the greensward, finding some slight shelter at last among the stones. Here the air seemed charged, vibrant, as though a storm threatened. Half-expecting thunder and a sudden onslaught of rain, Naeri huddled deeper into her cloak.

She said to Nhiall, "Were they sorcerers, then, the men who brought the stones?" She spoke in a whisper, as though imagining those ancient folk might wake, and overhear.

"So I was taught. Sorcerers, scientists—geomancers. Men of great skill and learning, who knew how to impose order on the world through the patterning of stones."

"And yet," she said in a small puzzled voice, "they did not finish what they began."

Nhiall looked down at her, and something unspoken passed between them—a sense of overwhelming loss, shared and irrevocable; a grief that welled up out of some deep memory of the blood.

"If I wished," he said, "I could tell you that story, sometime when we are sitting warm and comfortable by the hearth. But then it would be just that, a fireside tale—words only, with no true knowledge."

She waited. "And the true knowledge?" she asked softly, guessing somehow what was to come.

"Is written in the stones, for those who have the skill—and the courage—to read it. For as time leaves its imprint on human memory, so too it leaves its mark on wood, and metal, and stone. You have the geomancer's gift, my Naeri. You have found out for yourself how the earth speaks to you. Now you must listen for the voices in the stone."

She put out her hand to take the pendulum, but Nhiall shook his head. "The ball is no more than a tool, a kind of marker," he said. "The power is here." And he picked up her two hands and set them against the cold damp surface of the stone.

After a time she felt a tingling in her hands, her arms; and a great dizziness. The world was slipping away from her. It was as though she were moving in darkness down a long narrow corridor. At intervals along that passageway were rooms that opened into wider vistas, some shadowy and dim, some luminous with other-worldly light.

There was death in the first room, a vast, howling cataclysmic force leaping out at her, as though the memory of terror had soaked like blood into the stones. It was not her own death she saw there, but a world shattered, inundated. And then she had broken through that wall of thundering destruction, had fled beyond the drowned towers and broken columns; to find herself in a great waiting quiet.

Then she was in a high lonely place where a woman stood alone and cried out defiance to the gods of chaos. And after that she came to a higher, wilder country, where winds blew ceaselessly among the rocks, and the cold bit to the bone.

She went on; and now, glimpsed just at the limit of perception, there were forests of white columns, temples and palaces, pale and glimmering as the courtyards of the moon. The people of those cities moved like shadows at the edge of dreams. Their faces were like petals of exotic flowers; their garments were of gold cloth, woven of sunlight, or silver lace as delicate as spiderweb.

Through halls of light rode warriors armed with the weapons of ancient songs. Beneath their golden cloaks gleamed torques, breastplates, daggers, buckles of river-gold and bronze. As splendid were they and as glittering as Ricca's horse-chiefs. Yet their eyes were grave and gentle; there was nothing of the horsemen's savagery in those fine-boned narrow faces.

The warriors were gone, vanishing suddenly as a dream fades, and their place was taken by a small dark-haired people, in a dim savage world of blood and stone.

After, there was only the green gloom of ancient forests; and no voices but the cries of beasts.

At the last, there was a sense of something hard, gray, inert, a dragging weight, unbearable pressure. Abruptly she felt a crack-ing, a breaking through, like a plunge through thin lake ice. What lay below was naked flame, the intense, unimaginable heat of a million furnaces. She screamed, and her hands flew off the stone's face as though her flesh were seared. Her head was filled with the crimson glare, the dreadful noise of the inferno.

She held her hands against her breast, her knees drawn up, crouching, so that no part of her flesh should touch the stone. She was sobbing, openly and without shame.

Nhiall knelt beside her, rubbing the taut muscles of her neck and shoulders till she felt calm flowing into her like cool water.

"So hot," she whispered. She held up her hands, expecting to see them blistered, charred; but the flesh was unmarked.

"Child, forgive me," Nhiall said. "I could not warn you, or you would have held back. You have been all the way down, to the beginning, to the region of chaos. To the country of the faceless gods."

"Do not ask me to go back," she whispered.

"No," he said. "There are few of us with the power to reach that country, and none who would wish to return to it."

He took her hands. Frightened, she tried to snatch them away, but he gripped her fingers gently and set them against the stone.

"Even if you tried, you could not go so far, so deep, again . . . any more than a burned child will reach twice into the flame."

Nhiall put an arm around Naeri's shoulders and helped her to her feet. She leaned against him as he led her out of the circle, away from the charged presence of the stones and into the meager shelter of some hawthorn bushes.

Silently he gathered twigs and broken branches, and coaxed into life a small, capricious fire. Crouched over the flames, with her cloak pulled close around her, Naeri began to shiver. Her teeth chattered, and there was a fierce pounding in her temples.

"Eat these," said Nhiall, reaching into his pack and passing her a handful of travel cakes. "My poor child, we have demanded too much of you today."

He watched her with concern as she devoured the cakes. "More?"

She nodded, her mouth full.

Daui whistled softly between his teeth as he warmed his hands over the fire. Naeri glanced up and caught his eye, and unexpectedly he grinned. For an instant his bleak features softened and became almost boyish. There rose vividly before her the memory of a younger Daui—the scholar whose thin face, bent over his star-charts, had glowed with an intense and private joy.

"Cousin," Daui said, "truly, the Mother has chosen you. The gift burns in you like a clear flame."

When Nhiall spoke, Naeri thought she heard a slight hesitation, an edge of uncertainty in his voice. "A flame," he said, "that must be carefully nurtured, that must be shielded from draughts, if it is to go on burning."

She knew that there was something between these two that had not been spoken; something that concerned her, had power to change her; that she could no more resist than a storm-bent thorn resists the wind.

"Naeri," Daui said—and as he spoke he was looking, not at her, but into the heart of the fire— "will you bide with Nhiall these summer months? Be his willing pupil, study diligently all that he has to teach you?"

Though it was framed as a question, and gently spoken, still it had the force of a command. She nodded. Had a choice truly been offered, she might not have answered any differently.

~ 8 ~

The Initiate

The blossoms fell from the whitethorn; dog roses bloomed, and in the long warm grass there were clouds of harebells, blue as the summer sky on their threadlike stalks.

Daylong Naeri wandered over the broad backs of the hills, down wooded slopes, through water meadows shaded by gnarled ancient willows. Through the long hours of sunlight she tested and explored her birthgift. The pendulum on its silken string became as much a part of her as her hands, her eyes—a natural extension of spirit and flesh.

Insistently, unerringly, it drew her to the hidden currents of power within and above the earth. She came to recognize at once those fields and garden plots where all the earth forces were in harmony, where living things were bound to flourish. And she learned, as well, where the black streams ran—those deep underground water courses which destroyed the earth's balance, making it unsafe to build or plant above them.

Sometimes she found in the grass a flint arrowhead, a chipped stone tool, a bit of broken pottery. Holding one of these objects clutched in her hand, she would invite into her mind the small faint voices of the past. Behind her closed eyes the visions flickered. At times there might be a child's face or a woman's, the moon seen through oak branches, a leaping stag. But more often than not, there was only blood and fire and the memory of ancient pain.

She had long since lost her fear of earth-magic. Still, after a day on the chalk, she was apt to feel weak and feverish, light-headed; and she knew that Nhiall kept a close watch on her, fearing that those powerful forces of earth and stone with which she seemed now irrevocably linked might sap too much of her own spirit.

The holly bloomed, and the fields were pale gold with the ripening barley. One blazing hot morning Nhiall gathered up an armload of tablets and scrolls, and beckoning Naeri to follow, he strode down to the poplar grove beside the brook. It was shady and cool there, with no sound to disturb them; only the whisper of leaves, the peewit's call, the soft chuckle of the stream on its pebbled bed.

The air was heavy with the fragrance of the summer fields: wild thyme, marjoram, agrimony, self-heal and clover in sun-warmed grass. Lulled by the heat and the hum of bees and the slow quiet cadence of Nhiall's voice, Naeri listened, and drowsed, and listened again.

"Once," Nhiall said, "a gray-eyed lady sat beside me in a garden on an island that seemed to me, then, at the world's end. I remember, it was the southern springtime, and very hot, as it is today; but the garden was shady. There was a fountain, and a smell of herbs and flowers.

"I was not much older than you are now, as eager to learn, as innocent of where that learning might take me. The lady told me that she was sending me on a long journey, on a hard narrow path. The place where I must travel was on no map of this world—each one of us who goes there must chart it for himself or herself. If we are to find our way, we must speak the language of the country, must recognize the landmarks—the barrows, cairns, hill notches—along the way. For in the landscape of the mind, as in the Westland, there is both wild pathless country and the straight track that leads us to our destination."

And so he began, through the days that followed, to teach her the mind's language, as once it had been taught to him. She learned to read the runes that southern people carved in stone and clay; and the secret alphabet of the witchfolk, hidden since ancient times in song.

As a sorcerer works with spells, she worked with lines, angles, circles, measures, formulae; she made patterns with numbers till they danced in her dreams like bright beads on a string. As well, she learned to map the real countryside that lay around them, charting on vellum, with charcoal ink, the courses of streams and rivers, the shapes of hills and valleys, the patterns of the major forcelines.

At night, they lay in the long sweet-smelling meadow grass and studied the patterns of the stars. Nhiall told her how the tides and currents of power that flow beneath the earth correspond to the patterns of the heavens, making a great web that imposes order on primeval chaos. "For all things must be in harmony," he said. "The sun's rising and the sun's setting, the moon's phases, the slow journeys of the stars, the shape of the land and the patterns of the standing stones."

"Look there," he said, pointing. "There are the north stars, in the constellation of the Dragon. And there is the Bear, who has been moving with infinite patience, over many millennia, into the Dragon's place. For thousands of years wise men have observed their progress across the sky. The people of the northern forests have a legend—they say that when the Bear, who is their hero, triumphs at last over the Dragon of the Underworld, order will reign forever over chaos."

He turned to look at her in the starlight, and there was a wistful sadness in his voice. "Perhaps one day it will be so. But I think not in our time, my Naeri. In the meantime, we must go on fighting our small battles in the name of order. To understand order and balance, to preserve and restore the Pattern, that is the geomancer's art. In him—or in her— knowledge and instinct, science and sorcery, come together and make a whole."

It was late. The ground was growing damp and cold. Naeri folded her cloak carefully and put it under her.

"And you, Nhiall," she asked sleepily, "are you a geomancer?"

He shook his head. "I learned, when I was about as old as you, that my art is an inward-seeking one. There is no power in me to affect the pattern of things. All that I can hope to change, for all my striving, is the shape of my own soul." He smiled at her. "It took me a long time to accept that—as long as it took Daui to accept that he had no earth-magic."

He touched her cheek with his cool dexterous magician's hand. "But you, Naeri—you are the crystal that captures the sun's fire and draws it down to earth. You are the copper blade through which the lightning passes. The power of earth and the power of stone flows through you and does not change you. It may be you have the power to change the world."

As though their two minds were suddenly linked, she saw his vision of her. All at once the stars were too near, and terrifying in their brilliance. She rubbed the heels of her palms into her eyes to shut them out.

She could hear the night wind murmuring in the beeches, frogs croaking, crickets in the grass. These, too, were a part of the Pattern. She put her hands over her ears.

She said, very softly, hearing the words only in her mind, "Priest, you ask too much of me."

Nhiall's hands captured her own as though they were wild birds, enfolding them. She met his eyes. In the starlight they were silver-colored, transparent-seeming.

"It is true," she said, "that the stones and the earth speak to me. I knew that, before ever I came here. The first time I touched a standing stone and felt its power in my flesh, I knew what gift had been given me. If gift it is, and not a curse upon me. But such powers we are born with, they are not ours to choose. Now you ask me to choose . . . what? Not to practice the small gift I was born with. Something so much greater that I cannot even begin to grasp what you are saying to me. To stand at the center of the world, with the sun and moon and stars wheeling round me, the power of the stones beneath my hands and the tides of the earth flowing through me—to understand all this, to hold all these things in rhythm and balance . . ." She stared at him. "Surely this is the work of gods, not mortal folk."

Then, breathless and flushed, she looked down at her hands. It was the longest speech she could ever remember making.

"Gods," Nhiall said, "and geomancers. You, my Naeri."

There was a long silence. She threw herself down on the grass, listening to the small voices of the night, contemplating the fiery patterns of the stars.

"By the Mother," she said softly, "I think you have your work cut out for you."

She heard him laugh.

"Yes," he said. "But I never had a better pupil."

"Now," said Naeri, "I am going to ask you a question."

"Ask what you will."

He waited. She spoke slowly, measuring her words—a swimmer testing unknown waters.

"I was happy with Gwi. He was kind to me. More than that, I would have been his apprentice, maybe someday a master-smith. I would have had a place in the world. Maybe what he taught me was not what you, or Daui, or the world would call sorcery, but it seemed to me there was a kind of magic in it.

"And then Daui found me, and took me away from a place where I was well content. He did not tell me why I must leave, or what I was to gain in exchange for what I had given up. I did not ask, then. But I am asking now."

Nhiall did not reply at once. He seemed to be weighing his words as carefully as she had weighed hers. Finally he said, "I will give you first of all the answer Daui would have given. He would have said, because you are born of the witchfolk, and there is placed upon you—upon all of us—an ancient obligation. Like the Bear of the North, our race dies and is forever reborn. Each of us must discover what our birthgift is, and lay claim to it. We must use what weapons we are given, to defeat the Dragon of Chaos."

"And you, Nhiall? What would you say to me?" She waited, watching his grave, gentle face, blanched by starlight.

"I would say . . . because your name and your birthright were taken from you, and I wish to give them back to you. I might talk to you of duty . . . not duty to—" he hesitated, "to the memory of some past greatness. But simply duty to yourself. And," he finished softly, "because it has been lonely on the high track, and I delight in the prospect of your company."

The summer ripened into harvest-time. Naeri rose at dawn, while the mist still curled over the fields, to finish her lessons in the cool of morning. In the long yellow afternoons she gathered mint and rose hips at the pasture's edge; or, when it was too hot to walk abroad, she and Nhiall would take their trout lines down to the banks of the Greenwillow. There she would sit propped for hours against a willow trunk, watching the patterns of light and shadow on the river; listening in rapt silence while Nhiall talked of his journeyings in far lands.

The summer had changed her. Though she was slender and hard-muscled still, she no longer had the shape of a half-grown, half-starved boy. Where once hip and collarbone had jutted beneath the skin, now flesh curved smoothly. She had let her cropped hair grow down to her shoulders, and given its way, it had abandoned itself to curl. Her face, under the dark mass of waves, had lost its gaunt look, had softened into something close to beauty.

These nights, the moon hung ripe and huge and saffron-colored over the village. Often she could not sleep, but wandering out of doors lay under the trees in the warm dark; filled with something that was neither loneliness nor melancholy, but a shapeless, inexplicable longing.

One night her restlessness drove her across the moon-washed fields to a low marshy place where a stream widened into a shallow pool. Her skin seemed moist and sticky under her linen shift; impatiently she pulled the shift over her head and tossed it aside.

The pond, fed by a chalk stream, was stinging cold. She waded out to the center. There was a hollow there, and she stood in molten silver to her thighs. She crouched, scooped up handfuls of water and, wincing with the sudden shock of the cold, let it fall in silver rivulets on her breasts and belly.

After a while she straightened and began to run her hands down her ribs, into the hollows of her waist and over her hips' curve. Her skin was chill to the touch, faintly puckered by gooseflesh. She wondered at her possession of this stranger's body—this smooth, alien woman's flesh, roused by the moon to strange hungers, formless yearnings.

~~ 9 ~~

In-Gathering

The summer drew to an end at last. There were bright splashes of copper in the beechwoods; in the mornings the pastures and the shorn fields were wrapped in an opalescent haze. Every day, while the fine weather held, Naeri went out into the woods and meadows with the women of the village, to gather the autumn's harvest of wild fruits and hazelnuts.

Every evening she and Nhiall ate huge mounds of blackberries, and those that were left she mixed with dried meat and fat for travel cakes, or boiled up with honey for sweet preserves. Nhiall laughed when he looked into his larder and saw the neat rows of jelly pots and heaped baskets of nuts and apples; pointing out that as a single man and a priest—with knowledge of healing and small sorceries—he was amply provisioned by the village wives. But he knew, as Naeri did, that this in-gathering had nothing to do with need or logic; like a creature of the fields she was driven by pure instinct, a compulsion old as the changing of the seasons.

Soon enough the gray rains of autumn came. On those chill wet mornings, with the mist hanging heavy over the fields, Naeri was well content to sprawl beside the hearth, puzzling by firelight over runes carved southern-fashion in tablets of clay, or scraps of vellum covered with geomantic patterns.

One morning a traveling herbalist knocked at their door. He was full of self-importance, for he had left Lord Ricca's camp a day or two earlier, and brought with him a message from Lord Ricca's minstrel. "The maid Naeri is bid return to Ricca's court for the New Year's Games. The minstrel will come for her in the moon's next quarter."

The message was no surprise to her; Daui had promised to send word before the leaves fell. All the same a sudden excitement seized her, a curious rush of anticipation. She, who had sworn when she left Ricca's camp that she wished never to return.

The herbalist must have observed the look in Naeri's eyes. Since it was women, mostly, who bought from him, he made it his business to understand what went on in their heads.

"Ah, the young maids, how they love a feasting . . ." he said with a wink and a grin. As he spoke, he edged over the sill and began, uninvited, to unpack his wares. Fascinated, Naeri watched him spread out his display of vials, sachets and powder packets on Nhiall's worktable. The merchant named them for her, one by one—love potions (these with a sly look and another wink), blood powders, sleeping tisanes, stomach nostrums—the whole complex pharmacopia of field and wood and pasture.

Naeri pondered for a while, picking things up and setting them down again; finally, for reasons she could not have explained to anyone, least of all herself, she settled on a honey and marigold lotion to smooth her skin; and rosemary-and-nettle oil to make her hair grow long and glossy.

Nhiall watched with amusement as she paid the merchant with two loaves of fresh-baked seedcake. She met her teacher's eyes, blushed furiously; and hid her purchases away with her other treasures, behind her bed.

Daui arrived with the hunter's moon, and raised his eyebrows a little at the sight of her, in teasing admiration. He spoke little of Ricca's court, but was full of questions for Naeri. What had she learned, these months?

She showed him her charts of the sun's and the moon's risings; mapped for him the crossing of forcelines that brought harmony and prosperity to this village; recited for him the alphabet of the trees.

Proudly she displayed her knowledge, as a warrior displays his shields or a chief's wife her golden ornaments. He did not praise her, as Nhiall would have done; he merely nodded, accepting each new proof of her learning with grave satisfaction, but no surprise.

It was blustery and cold on the day that Daui and Naeri set out for Ricca's camp, with rain threatening all through the forenoon.

The gray weather had drained the chalk hills of color. The wind roared like the surf, bending the pale grasses, tearing the last leaves from the thorns. By the time they came down into the wooded valley that divided the south downs from the north, the sky had entirely clouded over and a thin cold rain was falling. The path through the valley bottom was slick with beechmast and brown sodden leaves.

Well before they came in sight of the earthworks and the tall ramparts of earth and stone, they knew they had reached Lord Ricca's lands. Huge flocks of sheep and goats grazed on the green turf; the oakwoods were filled with swine. On the flanks of the hills were wide fields of wheat and barley stubble; the chief's share had long since gone to fill Lord Ricca's corncribs.

As they climbed the slope of the chalk toward the camp, a hundred unsettling memories rushed back. How many times had she come here as a thief, under cover of darkness, to raid the rich midden heap outside the bank? She tried not to think of that last disastrous foray, when they had dragged her, bound and hobbled and out of her mind with terror, through Ricca's gates.

All that belonged to another lifetime. Her name was hers again, restored to her by her blood-kin. She had memories now, wisdom and shared knowledge. She had a place in the world that could not easily be taken from her. And so she walked proudly beside Daui, through the banked-earth circle and across the ditch, up to the great gates of Ricca's camp.

She looked up, seeing the palace compound for the first time as a hearth-guest might. Two full stories high rose the timbered house-places on their firm foundations of hill stone, with tall roofs of wickerwork and skins. Below were workrooms, corncribs, cattle byres, sleeping places for the hearth-slaves; in the dry upper chambers the horse-lords and their women slept.

Encircling those warm secure rooms was a rampart walk which looked out over the green chalk pastures, the barley fields and oakwoods. From there one could watch the approach of chiefs, warriors, craftsmen, merchants, minstrels—kinsmen and strangers alike, traveling the high white roads from all the world's corners to pay Lord Ricca homage.

By the time they reached the gates the wind was blowing harder and lashing cold rain into their faces. Naeri was grateful for the shelter of the inner courtyard, still more for the muggy warmth of the feast-hall. Two huge fires were blazing on the hearths. There were vast loaves baking on the hot flagstones, legs of mutton simmering in the cooking troughs. Now that the autumn slaughter had begun, the hearths would never be allowed to grow cold. The courtyard had been pungent with smoke and the smell of fresh blood, with carcasses of pigs and cattle dangling everywhere.

It was the time of in-gathering, when the herdsmen returned with their flocks from the summer pastures, when—once more before the roads were closed by winter rains—the clans came together from the scattered chiefdoms.

This was the time of year when empty spaces were left in the feast-circles for any wandering strangers who might knock upon the gates to ask shelter from the storm. And—it was said in whispers—at this festival of winter's beginning the shivering hungry spirits of the dead rose from their barrows on the hills, seeking the warmth of familiar hearthsides.

There was no one in the place at this hour but hearth-servants; still, Naeri could find no ease in Ricca's feast-hall. She bolted her supper as quickly as she could, and got up from the fire.

"Bide a while," said Daui. "Dry your feet, girl. You can leave when the war-band comes."

Shaking her head, she stood up and threw her cloak over her shoulders. The sodden hem clung to the backs of her legs. Squelching in her wet boots, she made her way out of the feast-hall, across the courtyard to the smithy.

She looked inside, saw that the forge was cold, the dark room deserted. She called out to a slave-girl who was crouched over a basket sorting winter pippins in a nearby shed.

"The smith—do you know where he has gone?"

"Aye, lady." It was a shock to hear herself called that—had she changed so much, then, in these few months? "He went west with the last full moon to buy white-metal for Lord Ricca."

"And did he say when he would be back?"

"Nay, lady. When he has bought enough white-metal, I expect."

Naeri turned back into the dank chill of the smithy. She made up a small fire in the charcoal-oven, set her boots and leggings beside it, and huddled over the flames, listening to the rain dripping from the eaves. When the fire had burned down to coals she got up, feeling stiff and weary and more dispirited than ever. She drew aside the horsehide curtain that Gwi had put up for her—and found her bed made up exactly as she had left it. The sight of it for some reason was more than she could bear, and she curled up on the fur coverlet, sobbing.

After that she felt better; she sat up and wiped her face on her sleeve. "Fool," she told herself. She pulled back the bed-rugs, expecting to find her pallet damp and musty-smelling; but it was quite dry, and it occurred to her that Gwi must have told the slaves to air it, and bring in fresh bracken; or maybe he had hung out the rugs and blankets himself. At that thought the ache in her throat returned, and fresh tears sprang forth. In the end she cried herself to sleep.

Next morning she found, as she should have known well enough, that her moontime had started. She dressed and went out into the courtyard to walk the stiffness out of her joints. The weather had cleared overnight, and the air was brisk and wintry; the wet ground smoked in thin sunlight.

Smells of griddle-bread and roast pig were drifting out of the hearth-hall. Suddenly ravenous, she followed them.

At this hour the war-band would still be sleeping off last night's barley-beer. Later, their women would come down to the hall to supervise the midday meal; in the meantime, Naeri and the hearth-slaves had the place to themselves. Or so she had imagined.

"Well," said a voice like a bear's growl in her ear, "what do I see here? It is the smith's wench."

She started, spilling her mead, and her heart seemed to shrivel inside her like a winter apple. Lord Ricca, dressed for the hunt and holding a dripping pork rib, was glowering down at her.

She swallowed hard. He cannot harm me, she told herself. Though Gwi is not here, still I am under Daui's protection. Meanwhile her heart was thudding against her ribs.

"Or is it?" mused Ricca, enjoying his game of hound and hare. "The face is the same, though more like a maid's now, less like a starved bird's. But as for the rest . . ." He left the thought unfinished. His face was brown from the wind and sun, with a high color under the tan, the stiff yellow plaits of his beard glistening where he had dripped pork fat on them. His eyes were as cold as ever, appraising her as he might have appraised a brood mare.

Suddenly he bellowed with laughter. "Don't look so scared, woman, I won't touch you. But tell the smith when he comes back, he's a fool to leave such a ripe fruit unplucked."

He collected a spear from the hearthside and went out in great good humor, whistling for his dogs. Abandoning her meal, Naeri crept back to the smithy. Within these hostile walls it was the only refuge she knew.

She was still there hours later, crouched over the cold fire pit, when Daui found her. In her hands she cradled a half-finished copper bowl.

"I have been looking for you," Daui said. He sounded annoyed. "No one thought to tell me you were here."

"No one knew," she said. Absently, she stroked the gleaming surfaces of the copper.

"What are you doing here, girl, sitting by yourself in the dark? If it's the smith you're waiting for, he'll not be back tonight."

"I know. He has gone west to buy more tin. I expect that Ricca has wasted it all on feast-goods."

Daui smiled. "I am thinking that was the smith's voice I heard just then."

"Well, it's true," she said, feeling somehow defensive. "Gwi told me that at the funeral games Ricca gave away half the weapons in the armory to impress the clan-chiefs; and after, he had no copper left for new ones."

"And Gwi would be the first to tell you that Ricca is no fool. The place of the Great Chief is neither bought nor held cheaply. Among the horse-clans, an open hand means strength and virtue."

He folded his long elegant form so that his eyes were on a level with hers, and reached out to touch the copper bowl. "What have you there? Is that your work?"

She shook her head. "I can't do anything like that. Raising metal—that is work for a master-smith, like Gwi."

"But you were learning?"

"Not that. Only easier things. One day, though, when I was ready, Gwi would have taught me to do bowls and cups."

"You have a hunger to learn," Daui observed. "Nhiall tells me you are an apt and willing student."

She looked down at the floor, pleased and embarrassed by his praise.

Daui was silent for a moment; his thoughts seemed to be elsewhere. Then, catching her by surprise, he said, "What *were* you doing with the bowl?"

Flustered, she said, "Nothing. Only practising a thing the priest taught me . . ."

His piercing gray eyes demanded an answer. She collected her thoughts and explained, "Gwi spent a long time working on this bowl, and took pride in his work. I wanted to see if somehow I could reach him, through the part of his spirit that is in the metal."

"And did you?"

Something in the way the question was asked, the sudden quickening of his interest, made her uncomfortable.

"Maybe . . . I don't know." It was not quite the truth. But she had no wish to share with Daui, or anyone, that fleeting vision of cliffs and sea coves, and gulls wheeling in the bright air— images so sharp and immediate that, for the instant they endured, her breath caught in her throat.

Daui shrugged and stood up, brushing dust from his cloak. "In any event, the smithy is no place for you to spend the night."

"My bed is here," she pointed out.

"Let us have none of your obstinacy, cousin." He spoke lightly, but underneath, the command was clear enough. "You are my kinswoman, and under my protection. If you want respect from the horsemen, you must behave accordingly."

She sighed, and stood up. "Show me where, then."

Her room was on the second story, facing inward over the courtyard; she had to climb a ladder to reach it. She had never slept in a place as fine as this. There were furs and woven hangings on the walls to keep out the winter chill, more rugs and furs scattered underfoot. The bed-place was heaped with white rabbitskins; on a chest in a corner stood beakers, an incense cup, an assortment of meat knives and ladles in wood and bone. On either side of her, through the flimsy wattle partitions, she could hear the warriors and their women, talking, laughing, arguing.

A single small window on the near wall looked down into the courtyard. She watched the hearth-slaves rushing between the pantries and the feast-hall with loaves of bread and mead jugs for the evening meal. She felt as remote from that ordinary world, and as lonely, as if she had slipped through a gateway into the Bright Land.

A serving girl came in, carrying garments over her arm. Shyly, she held them up for Naeri's approval. They were clothes that a warrior's woman might wear—long-sleeved tunic, ankle-length linen skirt, an overjerkin of soft deerhide fringed with bone and jet.

"The minstrel bade me bring these to you," said the girl. "To wear in the hearth-hall tonight. Oh, and these, too." She held up a string of blue faience beads. It was on the tip of Naeri's tongue to say, "Take these things away. I will wear my boots and leggings, as I have always done," but then she remembered that she was Daui's hearth-guest, and his kinswoman. She must not shame him before Ricca. That simple courtesy, at least, she owed him.

She sent the girl for water, and when she had washed as much of herself as she could easily manage, she began to rummage through her travel pack, looking for the two small vials she had bought from the herbalist. Awkwardly she smoothed her hair with rosemary oil, and rubbed marigold lotion on her cheeks and chin. Then she put on the fine feast-garments, and waited resignedly for Daui to fetch her.

The feast dragged on interminably. Nervous and miserable in her woman's finery, Naeri sat crumbling a piece of barley-cake between her fingers. The noise and the smell of the place, and the anxious knotting of her belly, had robbed her of appetite.

On this wet night, with the window flaps drawn against the autumn chill, the air in the hall was thick and oppressive. Steam billowed from the cauldrons and the hot stones of the roasting troughs, to mix with the smells of smoke, damp leather, pork grease and unwashed flesh.

Daui had left her in the women's circle. Here the smoke and stench was overlaid with a mingling of flower fragrances, so strong they made her stomach queasy. She recalled that the herbalist had lately visited the camp.

The babble of voices died down a little while they watched a tumbler and a pair of jugglers; and a man with a shabby old bear that shambled about and jerked its chain in a grotesque dance. Each year the New Year's Games drew wandering folk who danced and played the fool to fill their bellies.

But now the minstrel was tuning his string-box, and a sudden silence descended. He strummed a few melodies without words, time-worn airs tossed off as lightly as a jest. Then, as always, came the praise-songs—to Ricca, to the war-circle, and then to the First Wife, Suais.

She was a woman of the south, from across the Narrow Sea—a black-haired, brown-eyed, deep-bosomed beauty, heavy of hip and thigh, who stalked through Ricca's palace with a slow-moving, indolent grace. Her temper was legendary: provoked, she could display a casual cruelty that raised eyebrows even among the horsemen. Daui said he had once seen her break a slave-girl's arm—snapping it across a table edge, as one might break a piece of kindling for the fire.

Tonight she was dressed in a long loose robe of honey-colored wool, with a gorget of gold and amber at her throat, and beads of amber plaited into her glossy hair. Her eyes were painted in the southern fashion with kohl and green malachite. Flanked by her bower-women, she smiled and ate sweetmeats and tossed her head so that her plaits swung in time to the music; basking in favor like a great sleek cat before the fire.

It was a new song that Daui played for the First Wife that night: southern music, full of sun and shadow—hot dry days and flower-scented midnights. Langorous, sensual music, like Suais herself.

The song ended; Daui smiled, inclined his head, and his hand hovered for a moment over the strings. Then a new music rose, tentative at first, as though the notes were inventing themselves beneath his agile fingers—at first faint, wild music like the wind over the chalk lands, and then a soft rush of notes falling like spring rain.

> She is the green rowan tree
> that puts forth tender leaves.
> She is the white hawthorn flower
> that blooms upon the chalk.
> The swallow is she upon the bright air
> and the roe deer upon the mountain.
> She is the wild lily that grows alone
> in the untrodden meadow.

He ended in a shower of grace notes. A silence followed. Someone, a warrior, gave a shout of laughter; then a more sober companion must have nudged him, for the laugh died suddenly, choked back.

Naeri cringed, hunching her shoulders, feeling scores of eyes upon her like ropes stinging her flesh.

The women stirred first, making a soft clatter of earrings and baubles and bracelets as they turned to whisper among themselves. Now and again one would glance sidelong at Naeri, with her hand over her mouth to cover her smile.

They remembered her well in the feast-hall—pig thief, witch-girl, the smith's wench who dressed like a boy and was rumored to sleep by herself. Now the minstrel sang songs in her praise, like some new favorite of Suais's bower. All the same, what Ricca's

minstrel had singled out for praise, no man—or woman either—
dared publicly to mock.

Daui struck up a new song, a hymn of battle, and the slaves
brought more platters of roast meat and hot bread. In the
war-circle they bellowed out the familiar refrain and banged their
dagger handles on the table.

A hearth-slave tripped over someone's outstretched leg, and
dropped a basketful of empty beakers. Startled out of sleep by the
noise, Ricca's hounds began barking. The growing din of the
feast-hall was, for Naeri, as welcome as fog rising on the hills—a
sheltering and concealing cloak. Someone slid a beaker of mead in
front of her. As she drank, she felt the knot in her stomach loosen;
after a time she felt warm and almost content.

When the music began again, she closed her eyes, seeing the
notes hanging in darkness like small perfect pearls, like beads of
amber.

> "Loud is the voice of the gull over the
> high crags of Nynnia.
> Mournful is the sea's song as it breaks
> upon the gray shingle . . ."

The music washed over her like the surf's roar, the west wind's
keening. It was an old sad air from the Western Isles that Daui
played, a lament for sailors.

Listening, she found herself in another place, a landscape of
gray rock and gorse. She was walking on a high cliff top over the
sea, with the salt wind in her face, and Gwi was beside
her . . . Then suddenly the cliff fell away beneath her, the rocks
shattering and crumbling, and she plummeted headlong into the
sea.

Her whole body jerked and her eyes flew open. She woke, not
to Gwi's reassuring presence, but to the sight of Ricca standing
over her.

Startled and disoriented, she flinched away from him. Ricca
reached out a leisurely hand and grasped her by the chin, tipping
her head back so that she was forced to meet his eyes. She sat
perfectly still, like a rabbit in the grip of the stoat, mesmerized by
fright.

Ricca straightened then, and flung his heavy yellow braids
behind his shoulders. "Magha," he shouted. His voice was huge,
echoing. It filled the room like thunder.

The sorcerer looked up from his special place beside the fire. He was older than any man in the feast-hall, frail and stiff from the agues of many winters. His beard trailed like gray tree moss down the front of his stained red robe.

"Old man, tell me how the rowan-flames spoke to you at last winter's soothsaying."

Cracked and thin as Magha's voice was, it carried like an ox-horn in the sudden quiet. "Thus they spoke: that with the next New Year, a stranger, a dark woman of the hills, would bring fortune to the House of Ricca, and many victories to his war-band."

"So, old one, you have bidden me choose, and I have done so. She is young, and you will grant, not unpleasing to the eye. If my minstrel speaks truth, she is virgin." With less roughness than she might have expected, Ricca seized Naeri by her elbows and lifted her to her feet.

"Witchgirl, smith's woman, whatever you be. Dark woman, stranger. I name you Winter Queen."

And so she stood, heartsick and afraid, in the midst of a throng that must now shout her praises, as a few moons ago they had shouted derision. She knew that a pattern was being made—a pattern in which she could read no meaning. Daui had a hand in it, and Nhiall, too, it seemed. She wondered what Gwi would have said, had he known. But Gwi was not here—and that too was part of the pattern.

~ 10 ~

Winter Queen

All day long the wooden wagons rolled up the chalk roads. Next morning Naeri looked out from the rampart walk and saw the autumn sun shining on circles of horsehide tents, sprung up on the bare slopes like toadstool rings. At night, fires blossomed on the dark hills where the clansmen feasted and quarreled and slept among the barrows of dead chieftains.

The women's rooms were in a fever of excitement. Daylong they stitched and decorated new feast-day garments, directed the bread-baking and the stuffing of endless sausage links, counted honeycombs and cheeses. Two days before the New Year's Games all the women of the camp gathered in the feast-hall carrying armloads of clothing—the faded and cast-off finery of past festivals. Amid much laughter and mead-drinking, they tore the cloth into strips, which they boiled and stirred in dye vats, and hung to dry in the windy courtyard. At sunup next morning they trooped out onto the slopes of the hills to tie all these bright rags to trees and bushes, so that the leafless branches blossomed again in exotic splendor.

At night by lamplight the old women told tales that made the young girls shriek and throw their skirts over their heads and wives shift nervously on their benches, glancing into corners and gripping one another's arms for comfort.

They told of the Host of the Dead, that fleshless army whose feet never touch the earth, who drift forever at the wind's bidding.

They spoke of the strange shadowless dusk that falls over the land on the eve of the New Year, of beckoning ghost-maidens and of warriors who rode out of their barrows in that unearthly twilight, armed with the weapons of ancient time. They told of the woman who stands at the ford, washing the limbs and heads of dead warriors, who is death to any man who encounters her; of folk who, wandering abroad on New Year's Night, were found dead and cold at dawn inside the stone circles, with black marks of fingers on their flesh.

An old grandmother spoke of a long-ago feast-night when, with a head full of barley-fumes, she had lost her way back to the tents of her clan. "I came down to the edge of a lake," she said, and her voice trembled with the memory of ancient terror. "There I saw a great stallion, with hide the color of new grass, browsing among the reeds. It raised its head and looked at me with its sad, gentle eyes, and I, being a wild girl, with my thoughts all awry from feasting and lovemaking, thought it would be a fine thing to capture this horse and ride it back to the camp. As though it read my very thoughts it came closer, and so I caught hold of its mane, that was long and green and dank as waterweed, and it sank down upon its knees so that I could mount. And then it galloped twice, thrice around the lakeshore, swift as the wind out of the east; and I clinging to its mane and gripping its sides with all the strength of my body, and praying to the Sky-Father for my life.

"At the very last, as it veered in its headlong course, I knew it meant to carry me into the waters of the lake and drown me; and I gave a great scream, and let go its mane, and threw myself to the ground. There they found me at dawn, with half the life knocked out of me, and my hair and cloak wringing wet as a drowned corpse's. And they told me when I came to myself that I had ridden the Water-Horse, that dwells beneath the lake and lures folk into riding him, so that he can drown them and devour their flesh."

Crouched over the dying fire in that half-lit room, Naeri felt the skin crawl on her nape. She hugged herself for comfort, and poked the fire with a stick to stir it into life.

Feast-morning came. Naeri looked out and saw clear autumn skies, the mist on the fields shimmering in early sunlight. A good omen. Ricca would be pleased, for on this day, as at Spring Feast, the fortunes of the year turned.

On the slopes beyond the walls smoke rose from hundreds of

campfires. Already the traveling peddlers, purveyors of buttons and beads and ribbons, cheap copper knives and painted pottery, were setting out their wares. From high on their tent poles, bright streamers blew in the wind.

The herdsmen were leading the two-year-old colts into the banked-earth corral for branding. Later in the day the traders would come to barter for the small, swift chalk-bred ponies.

Naeri pulled on her old mended tunic and her leggings, and half-slid down the ladder to the inner court. Unnoticed, she slipped through the gates and across the earthworks into the marketplace. She had no goods with which to barter, but was content to wander among the merchant tents and the cowhides spread out on the wet grass, examining copper mirrors and burnished mead cups, daggers with bone and amber pommels, honeyed sweetmeats and incense pots filled with burning aromatic leaves—a secret herb, the peddler told her, more potent than the strongest mead.

As the sun climbed higher, jugglers and acrobats performed among the tents; musicians played on drums of clay and leather, shepherd's pipes and swan-bone flutes. The marketplace became crowded with free farmers and herdsmen from the chalk farms, camp women, clansmen of Ricca's own tribe and those who rode as his allies; even a few hunters from the wild hills, who went their way as silently as shadows.

And still the merchants continued to arrive with their pack-mules and ox-carts along the white ridge roads. With them came itinerant coppersmiths and leatherworkers with their bags of tools; and a few quiet-spoken men who had come to bargain privately, exchanging amber, faience and exotic eastern metalwork for western gold and copper.

On a level field beyond the market the New Year's Games were in progress: wrestling, foot-racing, stone-throwing; mock battles with spears that sometimes, half by accident, grew serious, leaving dark patches of blood on the pale turf.

Naeri stood for a while watching two warriors locked in close combat. Their greased bodies gleamed in the sunlight as they grappled and clutched at one another, and rolled wildly about in the wet grass. Then some of the women of the camp came out to fetch her, and berated her for slipping away; today, by custom, she must bide alone in her bower, preparing for the rituals of the turning year.

At day's end the women came to bathe her with perfumed

water. They brushed her hair and rubbed it with sage and rosemary oil till it lay smooth and gleaming on her shoulders. When it was nearly time they dressed her in white linen, the color of snow and moonlight, woven with gold threads for the promise of the sun's returning, and green threads for the new shoots that would stir again in springtime.

At her throat and on her brow, instead of jet and amber, they hung the winter-blooming mistletoe. And so she went forth as Winter's Queen, the moon-virgin, bride of the Old Lord, the dying Sun.

They led her into the feast-hall, where all the clan-chiefs and tribal lords were gathered, and the young warriors who, having triumphed in the Games, had come to receive their honors.

Old Magha the sorcerer met her, bowed before her; and led her to the place of honor in the war-circle, at the Great Chief's left hand.

She moved like a sleepwalker through the ritual, the drinking of ivy-ale from amber cups, the extinguishing of torches. Afterward, all she remembered was the silence; the long shadows that flickered behind the hearth-fire; and oddly enough, the coarse golden hairs on the backs of Ricca's hands.

Thus sang Magha, in his old man's wavering voice:

> Moonborn, winterborn,
> Lady of Snows,
> White maiden.
> Skyborn, nightborn,
> Bride of the Sun,
> Seed-bearer.
> Here is the Sun's child.
> the young warrior.

And he put into her arms the last ear of wheat from the harvest, token of the strong new Sun that at midwinter would spring from her loins.

In the old days, before the horse-tribes crossed the Narrow Sea, they would have killed her, in the dark of the moon that came before the solstice. In these quieter times the ritual was enough.

It was finished, for now. Ricca held up his great stone-headed scepter. She was Queen of the Games, and with Ricca must honor the winners and welcome the clan-chiefs.

She saw for the first time the huge glittering mound of feast-goods: battle-axes with narrow drooping blades, daggers whose hilts were inlaid with gold or studded with thousands of tiny golden pins; gold plaques, buckles, a fine bronze helmet, torques and gorgets, halberds and rapiers in the fashion of the Western Isle. Some of these things would be presented, with much ceremony, to the young men; the rest would go to the clan-chiefs, and to the chiefs of friendly tribes in pledge of ax-truce.

Two slaves came in with armloads of rowan branches, which they laid on the hearth-flags at Magha's feet. Magha stood in his scarlet robe with his head thrown back, his arms wide-flung, crying out to the rowan-spirits in the syllables of some arcane sorcerer's tongue.

When he had done with his invocations, he gathered up the leafless branches and began to feed them into the fire. They were tinder-dry and made the flames leap roofward with a sudden roar.

Magha paced slowly around the fire pit, shielding his eyes with his two hands as he stared into the flames. Sometimes he bent his head to one side, listening to the hiss and crackle of the burning branches. Now and then he paused to throw more fuel upon the fire. When the last bough had flared up and burned to ashes, he turned to Ricca.

"Great Chief." He spoke softly. At the far end of the feast-hall men held their breath and strained to hear. "I have looked into the leaping flames. I have heard the voices of the rowan-spirits."

Ricca gazed at him without expression; but glancing down, Naeri saw that the Great Chief's hand had tightened around his mead cup, and the knuckles were showing white. This, she thought, was a thing more frightening than any ghost tale. What courage must a man possess, to hear his destiny and maybe even his own death forespoken?

"Speak, soothsayer." Ricca's voice was as low and as steady as Magha's own. This was between the two of them and the spirit voices. They might have been alone in an empty hall.

"This have I seen in the shape of the flames and heard in the fire's roaring: that in Ricca's time, he will be king over the chalk lands, and the chiefs of all tribes will bow down to him. Loud will be the hooves of his war-band as the thunder of the Sky-Lord's chariot. He will be as the storm upon the hills that bends tall trees before it as easily as summer grasses."

Ricca swirled his mead thoughtfully in its golden cup, and he nodded. "This is a good prophecy," he said. "But so spake the flames last New Year, and also the year before. Old man, have the rowan-spirits no new thing to tell me?"

"This also," said Magha, "have I seen in the flames. These words would the rowan-spirits have me say to Ricca." He paused, while the tribe of Ricca hung upon his silence. "That neither by land nor by water will Death seek you out; neither by day nor by night will he discover you. Neither by stone nor bronze nor by any substance of this world will he destroy you."

There was a stirring and rustling in the feast-hall, like the sound of the wind blowing through the forest. One name was whispered again and again, like a conjure word, and that name was Ricca's.

"Thus," said Magha, "have the voices spoken." He sat down, drained a beaker of mead and began to chew ravenously on a piece of barley-bread. For two days and two nights the old man had fasted to clear his head for visions.

Ricca stood up in the Great Chief's place. He was tall and splendid in his marten-trimmed cloak, his yellow-dyed tunic with the great ceremonial plate upon his breast. The look in his eyes—amazed, exultant—belied the hard set of his jaw, his dour unsmiling mouth.

"Men of the High Chalk," he shouted, his great voice echoing among the rafters. So does the Lord of the War-Host cry out the battle-challenge. "I am Ricca, Chief among Chiefs, with whom Death himself has this day sworn ax-truce."

He held out his cup once, twice, thrice; each time, when it had been filled to the brim, he threw back his head and drained it.

"Clan-chiefs of the tribe of Ricca, I call upon you. And upon the Great Chiefs of the hills and the south down, who sit as hearth-guests in the house of Ricca." His voice was rough-edged, too loud, but steady. "Who will ride with Ricca? Who will sit in his War-Council? For those who will not ride with me must flee before me and fall beneath my hooves.

"I have thought long," said Ricca, "and I have decided, from today forward, it must be like this: the men of the tribe of Garech sitting in feast-hall with Rath's warriors; the sons of Rath's tribes training for battle with the sons of Ricca; the maidens of Aithra's camp given in marriage to the young men of the tribe of Garech. Thus will we make bonds among us that are not lightly broken. The Lords of the High Chalk will sit together in war-council. Of ourselves, we are strong; together, there will be none can stand before us.

"In token of this," he said, "I have emptied my treasure-house, knowing that before this year is out my storerooms will again be full. I bid you share in the riches of the house of Ricca."

One by one the Lords of the Chalk came forward to make their blood-vows; and to each one was given rich gifts to seal the bargain.

First came Ricca's underlords, the clan-chiefs of his own tribe: Derga One-Eye, Black Uigh, Rudra of the River, Tighern Longbeard. After them came the Great Chiefs of the out-tribes sworn to ax-truce: Garech the Red, brother of Ricca's Third Wife, Clia; Rath Wolfslayer, Lord of the North—gaunt, dark-visaged, with the fierce eyes of a gyr-falcon—a man one would not wish to have for an enemy. And Aithra of the Long Spear, a stout man who, though he smiled often and was mild and jovial-looking, was known as the most ruthless and bloodthirsty of warriors.

Finally the young champions of the Games were called up to claim their prizes. And when the wealth of Ricca's treasure-house had dwindled away to nothing, Ricca spoke again.

"Such a war-host as ours must have a mustering place," he said. "A place that will strike fear and awe into all those who come upon it. A gathering place for the tribes and a temple to our father the Sky-Lord. Of stone should it be built, that endures forever; with many doorways opening to the Sun."

At this moment Daui's fingers began to dance upon his harp strings, making a music that was small at first, but slowly gathered power. Notes built upon notes, harmony upon harmony. Almost one could hear in that music the temple of Ricca's imagining, the tall house of many doorways rising upon the chalk.

"This will we build to the glory of the Sun-Lord," Ricca said. "Soon now I will choose the place. When the Sun returns and the seeds stir, then will the work begin. Go now," he told them. "Let the gates of the camp be thrown open. Let the fires of the New Year be kindled on the hills. Now we will dance for the Old Lord's death, and the New Lord's birth-time."

On the heights of the chalk the New Year's fires were burning—one last glorious blaze of light before the drawing in of winter. Just outside Ricca's camp, in a level place tucked into a fold of the downs, yet another great fire had been kindled, and here a drunken, boisterous crowd was gathering. More barley-beer, in skins and earthenware jugs, passed from hand to hand, and presently the dancing started.

Long lines of men and women—both down farmers and people of the horse-clans—moved through the ancient figures of the fire dance: advancing, retreating, stamping, leaping, circling. Some, in the old way, wore the heads and skins of animals. Beyond the firelight's edge the spirits of the dead danced also, to their own faint eldritch music.

It was the Winter Queen who, by custom, led the women of Ricca's camp. Naeri had danced like this as a child in the hills, under the white stars and the hunting moon. The pulse of the drums was in her blood; her body swayed, her feet moved in remembered rhythms. The reed pipes made a high, sweet music, clear and silvery: moon-music. In her head the mead sang like the pipes; her blood pounded in time to the drum's insistent throbbing. There were two great circles now, spinning in opposite directions. Faces were blurred ovals flashing past her as she whirled and stamped. Winter-bride, moon-dancer, she leaped like the flames on the hill, swayed like a young rowan in the wind.

After a time the circles began to break up. Laughing and gasping, the dancers fell out two by two and wandered away into the fields.

For a moment it seemed they had left her to dance alone in the dying firelight. But no, here was her partner, the chosen one who must end the dance with her. Nearer and nearer he circled, matching his steps and the rhythm of his body to her own.

He was the Lord of the Black Sun, the Dark Dancer. It was he who led the warrior's line, as the winter-maiden led the women's. He danced in the black hide of a bull, with a horned bull-mask hiding his face; yet she knew him by his long barley-colored plaits, bound with rings of darker river-gold. His eyes, behind the mask, were not cold and water-pale as they had always seemed to her before, but blue as the burning edge of flame

The music ended suddenly. The black bull, the winter-god, reached out to claim her.

She swayed, dizzy with barley-beer, breathless with dancing; and the world began to fall away from her.

Someone caught her from behind and held her firmly. "Remember she is mine, Ricca," a voice said. And she saw the bull-man stand back, his arms dropping to his sides, his eyes full of baffled rage.

Limp as a barley-doll, she hung in Gwi's arms. She tried to speak, but her lips and tongue felt swollen, and she could not properly form the words. Her limbs were clumsy as sticks of wood.

"Smith," said Ricca. His voice behind the mask was dangerously quiet, knife-edged with fury. "You ask too much of friendship. The Winter Queen is the chief's by custom. Twice now you have snatched this woman away from me; and yet it seems you have no use for her yourself."

"That was then," Gwi said softly. "A man can change his mind. Anyway, you can see what a state the girl is in. You will get no amusement from her this night."

She felt Gwi lifting her, settling her into his arms, carrying her into the refuge of the dark. In her mead stupor she felt heavy-limbed, muzzy-headed—and irrationally happy. The warmth of Gwi's body stirred something in her—an answering warmth, a vague unfocused yearning. She murmured something she could not afterward remember, turned her head, and put her lips against his throat. And then, as his arms tightened around her, her head fell back on his shoulder and she slid away into sleep.

She woke in her old bed in the smithy, with rugs piled over her; the drums were still beating in her head.

"Gwi," she called out in a small, forlorn voice. The smith put his head around the horsehide curtain. "I feel like death itself— what is the matter with me?"

"Nothing," said Gwi with amusement, "that a day or two will not put right."

He ducked out and came back in a moment with a beaker of hot tea. "Girl," he said as he watched her sip it, "you were drunker last night than I have seen any woman who was still on her feet."

Gingerly she shifted her limbs. Her stomach was queasy, but all the pain had settled in her head. She seemed sound enough elsewhere. Gwi smiled at her, and reached out a hand to tuck back the tangled locks of hair that were falling into her eyes. She remembered the warmth in her loins last night when he carried her, and felt a curious sadness. Something she had wanted had been held out to her last night, and she had let it slip away.

Quick footsteps crossed the courtyard, approached the door of the smithy. For one terrified moment Naeri thought that it was Ricca.

"Is the girl there?" Daui's voice. She relaxed, and the breath she had been holding rushed out all at once. But that brief alarm had set her heart pounding, and fresh pain stabbed through her skull.

She could hear Daui talking to Gwi in an angry whisper. His words carried across the room, though clearly they were not meant to. She sat up, straining to hear.

"Have you taken leave of your wits, man? Ricca is in a fury."

"With me? Or with Naeri?"

"Does it matter? Both, I suppose. No . . . with you in particular."

"Because I did not wish to see that poor child come to harm? What would you have done, in my place?"

"She's not a child, as you very well know. As to harm—it was no more than happened to every woman in camp last night . . . and none of them are the worse for it. The New Year's Queen is Ricca's by custom."

"So Ricca reminded me," Gwi said. "And how did she come to be New Year's Queen? As I recall, no one asked me—and after all she is supposed to be my bondswoman."

"It seems she has caught Ricca's eye," Daui told him. "Of his own accord, he singled her out."

She heard Gwi swear, and then he stamped into her bedchamber. Daui followed, stooping to miss the lintel.

"You knew," Naeri said to Daui accusingly, before he had a chance to speak. "You sang that praise-song for me, in feast-hall, and you knew he would choose me. Also, you knew what was meant to come after."

"Cousin," said Daui, "you credit me with too much foresight. You know I lack that gift."

There was no humor in his voice, only a faint edge of sarcasm. He seemed ill at ease in her presence. He is afraid to meet my eyes, Naeri thought suddenly; and the realization startled her.

Daui shrugged, finally, and said, "In any case, that was a fool's trick, Gwi, bringing her back to the smithy—like rubbing salt in the wound."

"Where else would she have been safe?" Gwi asked. "Ricca may bellow for a while, but he'll get over it. He knows well enough I was within my rights. Look, I'll show you something. You too, Naeri—it's time you were up."

She slid out of bed in her crumpled feast-gown, trailing a rug from her shoulders.

Gwi led them across the smithy to a storeroom and pulled back a curtain to reveal a huge ceremonial shield: sheet gold over a frame of wood and leather, round and dazzling as the sun's face, and masterfully incised with a pattern of radiating lines. He pulled it out into the smithy and propped it against a wall, where it seemed to gather up all the light of the forge fire and fling it back into their eyes.

"I have been a long time making it," Gwi said, "for there was much else to do. But now it is finished, and Ricca will carry it at the Planting Feast."

Naeri said, with utter sincerity, "It is the most wonderful thing that I have ever seen." She added, with a hint of malice, "It's a pity Ricca must have it—I hope you made him pay a good price for it."

Gwi's mouth quirked. "Aye, a very good price," he said. "Ricca thought he had bested me at the time, but in truth, I never made a better bargain."

And when she waited, clearly not understanding, he laughed. "Ah, girl, have you so soon forgotten? That shield was the price I paid to free a certain pig thief."

She felt the blood rising in her face.

"Well, lady, that surprises you, does it?" said Gwi. He was once again in good humor, relishing the joke. "But you can spare your blushes," he added kindly. "I would have made the shield in any case. Still, you can see why Ricca's anger is no great matter to me. I have the shield, and at the moment he does not."

"Your point is well made," observed Daui. "It seems that a fair bargain was struck. Ricca may fume for a while, but he can hardly dispute your claim to what is yours by purchase-right."

Hearing those words, so casually spoken, all the fear and bewilderment of the last few weeks swelled up like a great lump in Naeri's chest. She thought that if she did not speak now, she would choke on her anger.

"What right?" she burst out. "You talk of purchase-rights and bargains, as though I were a pile of scrap metal, or a brood mare. I was a free woman when I came here. I went my own way and did as I saw fit. Now no one asks what I want or what pleases me. Or cares, come to that. "No, Gwi," she added hastily, seeing his guilt-stricken look. "You bought my life and freely returned it to me. You have laid no claims on me but those of friend, and craft-master. But you, Daui." She took a deep breath. "You claim the rights of kinship. That may be well and proper, and I suppose I should be grateful to you. But I have lived without kinfolk for a long time and am accustomed to it. What I am not accustomed to is being pulled this way and that, treated as a child with no wits of its own, ordered about to do your bidding without question."

"Cousin," Daui said softly. "I have given you back your birthgift. Does that count for nothing?"

"It frightens me," she said. "When I use that gift, I feel it draining the life from me, sucking the very marrow from my bones. Daui, this power uses me. It makes of me its slave, its instrument." She hesitated, twisting her hands in front of her. "As you will, Daui, if I let you."

She saw his eyes widen slightly, heard the quick sharp intake of his breath, and she knew that she had shocked him.

After a long, uncomfortable moment he reached out and took her hands. "You must trust me, cousin. You must believe me when I say that I mean you nothing but good. You must believe me, too, when I tell you it will not always be so—that the power one day will come more easily to you."

Truly, he has mastered the bard's craft, thought Naeri, as his soft voice flowed on, gentle as harp music, persuasive as strong mead.

He said, "Remember when you learned to draw a yew bow? How your arms ached at first? Little cousin, this is not so very different. In time the will, like the bowman's arm, grows stronger, and control comes."

His eyes, gray as storm clouds, met and held her own. There was no evasion now. Behind that steady gaze she saw the powerful, seeking mind, the passionate intensity of purpose. It frightened her, and held her spellbound.

"Naeri, there is so much that I must share with you. So much knowledge to be poured into that eager mind of yours—like mead into a flagon that can never be filled up." He leaned back suddenly and laughed, as though mocking his own seriousness. "Listen. It would not be a bad thing to take you away for awhile—until Ricca forgets his anger, and some new woman catches his eye."

"To Nhiall's village?" She hoped that was what he meant. She would be safe and comfortable there, through the dreary winter months. But Daui was shaking his head. "Later, perhaps. I had another place in mind."

He saw the look in her eyes and added hastily, "No, don't be angry. Hear me out." Putting his two hands on her shoulders, he drew her down beside him on a bench by the fire.

"In all these months, there is one question you have never asked me."

She raised an eyebrow, waiting.

"You have never asked me, 'where are the others?' "

She stared at him as a faint impossible hope took shape and grew.

"Do you mean, the witchfolk?"

He nodded.

"Why should I ask that? I knew the answer. I saw my family die. I knew that was neither the beginning of the bloodshed nor the ending." Feeling her throat tighten, she bit hard on her lip. "Why should the horsemen let others live, and not my sisters?"

"But you and I have survived," he said. "As others have. Through quick wits or sorcery—or simple cunning. They live in hiding now, among the Hunters—gone to ground like foxes in the hills."

Wide-eyed, she hung on his words, still not daring to believe.

"Not a morning's journey from here, there is a temple," he said. "An ancient place where the Mother is honored still, and the old ceremonies are preserved. Will you go there with me, cousin?"

She knew this was all a part of the net that he was weaving— that intricately, patiently knotted web of magic and power and kinship. Yet when she thought there might be others like herself— for an instant there rose before her an image of her mother and her sisters: the strong-boned, beautiful faces, the grey eyes touched by laughter. A terrible homesickness welled up in her.

"Yes, of course I will go with you, cousin," she said.

～ 11 ～

Cathra

They made an early start on a brisk dry morning, traveling the river road to the west. In tunic and soft boots, wrapped in a winter cloak, Naeri strode chest-deep through trailing scarves of mist. She had grown taller this past summer. She and Daui were nearly of a height now, and her long legs ate up distance as rapidly as his.

She carried a yew bow, and tucked into her belt was a fine bronze knife with an amber pommel, which Gwi had given her as a journey-gift. She was, by her reckoning, seventeen years old—and for today at least she was her own woman. She whistled for the sheer joy of the occasion.

After a while the river path dwindled away into marsh and reed beds, and they turned up the wooded slope to higher ground. Here, on the forest track, brambles clawed at them, and wet bracken crowded against their legs; the ground was littered with acorns and beechmast. As she walked Naeri gathered a few hazelnuts the squirrels had missed, and a handful of late black-berries.

It was cold and dank among the trees, the paths still clotted with night shadow; but already shafts of sunlight were spilling through the high branches. Briars, bushes, ferns all shimmered with gossamer; before long it would be hoar-frost weather.

Presently the trees thinned, and they came out into open country, following a high track over the chalk.

Cresting a ridge, Naeri saw beneath her a vast saucer-shaped depression strewn with a multitude of gray sarsen boulders. Half-embedded in turf, they looked from this height like a great flock of grazing sheep. Suddenly uneasy, Naeri put her hands to the sides of her head. She was aware of a pressure, a tension within her skull; she felt rather than heard a faint hum like the sound of distant bees. Broken and scattered, without form or pattern to concentrate their power, still the terrible raw energy of the stones shimmered upon the air.

She called down the hill to Daui, "What place is this?"

In a moment he came up beside her, his thin dark face flushed a little from the climb.

"The downsfolk call it the Valley of the Rocks."

"The stones—how did they come to be here?"

"They have always been here," he said. "They are the First Ones—older than humankind, maybe as old as the earth itself." He stood beside her, catching his breath, as they looked down into the valley. It was a wild, desolate place—a wilderness of bramble and juniper scrub and long, tawny grass.

"The Lost Ones, the Gray-Eyed People, knew this valley," Daui said, "as they knew the Mountain of Blue Stones, farther to the west. They came with their geomancers and master-builders and harvested these tall stones as we might gather pebbles on a beach. And then they carried them to the temple-sites—the places of power where the forcelines meet."

"To bind the powers of earth and sky in circles of stone, to impose order and harmony on the world," said Naeri, quoting. Daui gave her a quick pleased look and threw his arm across her shoulders. He seemed not to hear the irony that lurked beneath her words.

She shivered, and turned her back on the Valley of the Rocks. Under racing clouds, in the fitful autumn sunlight, they made their way across the hills.

Soon they crossed the great ridge road that ran down from the northeast along a shoulder of the downs—a broad green highway, deep-rutted from centuries of use. The land fell away below them. Southward was the Sedge River, a thin line glimpsed among the trees; and beyond, to the southwest, rose an enormous thrusting hill of chalk and turf, too regular in shape to have been formed by nature.

From the rim of the chalk they came down again into open woodland—hawthorns, hazels, blackthorns, growing along the deeper forest's edge. From somewhere nearby there came a high birdlike trilling, and Daui, with his two fingers to his lips, answered it.

A tall woman stepped out of the trees, carrying a wicker shield and a flint-headed ashwood spear. In her strong features and wide-set gray eyes, in her long light bones, she bore the clear marks of witchblood. Save that her hair was crow-black and Naeri's was brown, the two were like enough to be sisters.

Behind the huntress came a long-legged, red-haired girl of perhaps thirteen. The child seemed shy and hung back a little, watching them out of wide green eyes under a tangle of curls.

"Cathra," Daui said. "Greetings, cousin." He took the tall woman's hands in his own, touching his forehead to them.

"They sent us to meet you," the woman said. She spoke in the lilting dialect of the hills—Naeri's mother tongue.

Daui raised an eyebrow. She grinned and reached under her jerkin, pulling out a willow twig to which an elder and a hawthorn leaf had been fastened with linen thread.

"A witch-maiden, traveling in the company of a poet," she read. And added slyly, "Not traveling very fast. As you see, news of your coming preceded you."

"I counted on the dark of the moon to bring you down from the hills," Daui said.

Cathra nodded. "Tomorrow night is the ceremony . . ." She broke off abruptly, and glanced at Naeri with a question in her eyes.

"This is a kinswoman of yours," Daui told her.

"So I can see," the huntress said. She put a hand on Naeri's shoulder and from her slight advantage of height looked curiously down at her. "Girl, your face is strange to me. I have never seen you in the temple. To what clan do you belong?"

Naeri said, "I am of the House of the Lady Arhan, of the Alder clan." It seemed a lifetime since she had spoken those names aloud; they were strange and bittersweet on her tongue.

The red-haired girl's eyes widened until they seemed to fill most of her small face. "But," she said in a clear childish voice, "They are all dead, the women of that house."

"So we had thought," Cathra said. "There is a song about it."

"I made that song," Daui reminded her. "The Lament for Arhan's Daughters. And never guessed that the youngest of the daughters had escaped by her own quick wits. She was younger than you, little Fearnn," he said to the girl. "One day I will make another song, of the four long winters she lived alone in the chalk hills, for I like that story better than the first."

Cathra's sinewy arms reached out to Naeri, and their cheeks touched in a quick hard embrace. Then Cathra stepped back and, kneeling, silently laid her spear at Naeri's feet. At that warrior's tribute, Naeri swallowed hard and blinked back tears.

"We must take you to the Old One," Cathra said.

She led them by a circuitous route along the bronze and russet pathways of an oakwood and through a tangle of bramble thickets into a narrow clearing. The tent camp itself was surrounded by a palisade of sharpened stakes, and, behind that, a ditch overlaid with branches.

"Wait here," Cathra said, as she ducked under a tent flap and vanished. The girl Fearnn stood gravely observing them from a few paces off. She put Naeri in mind of a wood sprite, who at a loud voice or sudden footfall might vanish like smoke into the trees.

Waiting in the deep shade inside the wall, Naeri shivered and stamped her feet. At this time of year scant light or warmth penetrated the forest gloom; she could see her breath faintly curling on the air.

In a moment Cathra reappeared and beckoned them inside. The air in the tent was warm and humid, smelling of meadow herbs and smoke. A small banked fire cast a reddish glow against the walls, and on the face of the woman who sat warming her hands over the coals.

She was the oldest woman Naeri had ever seen—older even than the frail great-grandmother who had died when Naeri was three. Her face had the spare stark beauty of weathered wood or stone, the skin taut-stretched like fine parchment, with deep hollows under the jutting cheekbones. Her priestess's robe of white linen, her cloak of pale ermine-edged wool, hung loosely on her shrunken frame. There was a great white sea-pearl at her throat, and on her wrists were bands of the pale moon-gold from the Western Isle.

When she raised her head, her slate gray eyes, in their shadowed sockets, were clear and intelligent as a girl's. Her gaze met Naeri's, and she smiled.

"Come to me, child," she said. There was nothing imperious in her tone—she spoke fondly, gently, as a grandmother might.

Then she turned to Daui and Cathra and said quietly, "Go. Leave me a while with this kinswoman of mine."

"Well, girl," said the moon-priestess, when the two of them were alone. Her voice, like her eyes, was strong and youthful. "I knew your mother. A woman of courage and keen wits— the cleverest of the Alder clan, I always thought."

She leaned forward and took Naeri's two hands in her own. She held them lightly, loosely; there was no longer any strength in those gnarled, misshapen fingers.

"It seems you are your mother's daughter," she said. "You have that same somber questioning look she had. 'Little Owl,' I used to say, when I wished to tease her. And it appears you have her cleverness, too. Cathra has told me how you have survived these four years past."

Her eyes searched Naeri's face, and for a strange instant it was as though their thoughts touched.

"There is a great gift in you," the Old One said. "Child, have they told you that?"

While Naeri was wondering how to answer, the priestess nodded and said, "Yes, yes, I see they have. And made you afraid, where there should be cause only for rejoicing." There was pity in her voice, faintly touched with anger.

"I was a healer once," the Old One said. "Not a great gift, like yours—a smaller magic. But it takes skill, for the hands must work in perfect harmony with the heart and mind. Out there on the downs, among the witch-rocks, I had my garden of herbs and healing mosses. The power was strong in me then, and I was happy, for I had found my true place in the world. But you see—" and she held up her time-ravaged, twisted hands— "when it came to it, I could cure all sicknesses but my own. The power is gone now, drained out of me like river water. I am a dry spring at summer's end." Then, "Never mind that," she said. "I have my place in the world still. I tend the bone gardens, underneath the hills." She gave her chin a small jerk, and Naeri knew that she meant the barrows of the dead.

"I cannot heal the dead any more than I can cure the living. But when you are as old as I, the wall between life and death grows thin. Down there in the earth's womb I talk to the skulls, and now and again they answer me."

Her eyes, brilliant and penetrating as an ancient hawk's, turned suddenly on Naeri. "Do you believe me, girl?"

"Yes," said Naeri. "I believe you, Old One."

"And you, little daughter—do the dead speak to you?"

"Yes," Naeri whispered. "When I touch the tall stones I see the dead; I hear their voices."

The old woman laughed suddenly, a high shrill unexpected sound. "Well, little one, it is not a matter for weeping, that."

Naeri swiped at her eyes with the back of her hand and thought, I cry too easily these days. There had been no tears, all that time on the high chalk. Now it seemed that her nerves had grown too close beneath the skin, so that every thought that touched her—of loneliness, fear, self-pity—set them thrumming like plucked strings.

"Fear not the gifts the Mother has given you," the Old One said with a curious gentleness. "They are yours to use, and to rejoice in." And then, as she crouched over the coals, her voice rose in a high, crooning chant:

> Warriorborn,
> fear not the sharp point of your spear
> nor the cutting edge of your knife.
> Witchborn,
> fear not the earth's nor the mind's darkness.
> These are the gifts of the Great Goddess.
> These are your weapons against your enemies . . .

She broke off abruptly and said in a matter-of-fact voice, "Daughter, will you walk behind me in the New Moon's Procession?"

"With much pride," said Naeri, for she knew the honor was an extraordinary one.

The Old One nodded, and made a small gesture of dismissal. "Tell them to give you food," she said. "I remember, the young are always hungry." And then her eyes grew shuttered and remote. It was as though she had fled the airless confines of the tent, and had gone away into some distant place.

The others had almost finished their midday meal. As soon as she saw Naeri, Fearnn rushed forward with a steaming bowl of game stew and a beaker. In her excitement she had filled the cup to overflowing; some of the yellow liquor splashed into Naeri's lap. It was scented lime-honey mead, Naeri found when she tasted it—a guest-drink, not meant to be wasted. She had caught Fearnn's sidelong glance in Cathra's direction, half sheepish and half-gleeful. But Cathra was fletching an arrow, and paid no heed.

Her task finished, Cathra rose lazily, fed a log to the fire, and came to sit on her heels beside Naeri. "Tomorrow," she said, "if you wish, I will show you the temple. But today is for talk. Do you know, even in the hills the stories reached us about the witchwoman who lived under the chalk? We thought she must be a slave who had run away from a horse-camp. No one imagined the truth."

So through that afternoon, until the long twilight of the forest deepened into black night, Naeri spoke of those years in hiding. It surprised her that there was so much to tell, when each day had seemed at the time identical to the rest. But Cathra was hungry for details—how did Naeri hunt, what weapons did she use, how did she escape capture through all those months of foraging within a stone's throw of the horse-camps?

Across the fire, Naeri could see Daui's dark head bent over his string-box, his fingers plucking strings apparently at random. From time to time he hummed brief tentative snatches of melody. She knew that under his lithe, clever fingers a new song—her own song—was taking shape.

It was growing late. Someone passed around a goatskin of beer; someone else started a batch of cakes on the hot stones of the cooking fire. In the midst of telling how she had come to meet Gwi the smith—and how he had kicked her head first into the smithy fire, by mistake—Naeri found herself dozing off. Cathra laughed.

"Go to bed," she said. "There is room for you in my tent."

Cathra, as hunt-captain, had a small tent to herself, which she shared with Fearnn. Most of the space inside was taken up with hunting gear, but there was a crumpled pile of furs and skins in one corner that served as a bed-place.

Cathra had the next watch. Before she went out she refilled the oil lamp, rumpled Fearnn's red curls, and bade them a good night.

Fearnn yawned and rubbed her eyes. Her shyness and her long-limbed, fawnlike look made her seem younger than she was. When she stripped off her jerkin for bed it was clear that she had already entered her first womanhood. A rug pulled up to her chin, she lay watching Naeri with her long, leaf-colored eyes. She seemed more at ease now, and in a mood to talk.

"Will you stay for the moon-rites?" she wanted to know.

"So Daui tells me."

"I am to lead the procession," Fearnn said. "I have been chosen New Moon Maiden."

"That is a great honor," Naeri said. She remembered how, as a child, she had prayed one day to be chosen, and had waited impatiently for the signs of her own womanhood.

"So Cathra says," replied Fearnn complacently. And with the abruptness of a small child, she turned over and fell asleep.

Naeri came half-awake when Cathra crept in from the watch, pulled off her boots and jerkin and slid in beside her; then she drifted back into a dream of an old woman who was growing mosses in a garden of bones.

Soon after dawn Naeri put her head out of the tent and glimpsed blue sky through the laced oak branches. It was one of those rare cloudless late-autumn mornings that offers itself up like an unexpected gift.

"Come hunting with me," Cathra said, as she sniffed the damp fragrant air. Behind them, Fearnn—already dressed—was re-stringing her bow.

Naeri said, "If the ceremony is tonight . . ." She was remembering the complex day-long preparations her mother and sisters had made for the temple-rites.

Cathra shrugged. "So long as we bring this child back by dark, so they can wash her and dress her and chant over her—myself, I'd as soon stay clear of all the commotion."

They came out of the oakwood into hazel scrub and open pasture, following the rise of the land eastward. From the vantage point of a grassy slope they could see the Moon-Temple spread out across the valley floor on the edge of water meadows, in a landscape of low beech-plumed hills. Still farther west was the huge smooth-sided brooding shape that Cathra called the Mother-Hill, from which, each year at harvest-time, the Goddess was reborn.

Just above them, at the crest of the hill on which they stood, were seven barrows and two stone circles, one set within the other. From there, an avenue of standing stones snaked its way across the valley to the temple entrance: tall pillar-stones, and—partnering them—shorter broader shapes poised like dancers on a single foot.

With its huge surrounding earthworks, its large outer circle and two inner circles of massive stones, the temple seemed the work of gods or giants, built on a scale too vast for the human mind properly to encompass. But it was long past its days of glory, when it housed the ancient learned orders of sorcerer-priests: a secret temple-school of the Great Ones set on the edge of the high country, encircled and protected by forests and swamps. Now the enormous banks were half-overgrown, the great ditch choked with sodden leaves. From the edges of the forest, brambles and rank grass and hawthorn scrub relentlessly encroached.

Still, in these latter days the hunters of the hills and the witchfolk, the Mother's people, in their own fashion preserved the sanctity of the place. Tonight, Naeri knew, she must walk in the Moon Procession, among those ancient earth-rooted stones. There was a degree of terror in that knowledge, and with it a curious excitement.

"If you have seen enough . . ." she heard Cathra said. She emerged from her own thoughts, to see that the sun had climbed halfway up the sky. She followed Fearnn and Cathra down the slope through the long dew-soaked grass to the edge of a beechwood.

"Look," Cathra whispered, pointing into the tall bracken. Browsing quietly in the undergrowth was an immense twelve-point red stag. He was sacred to the Horned God, who was the Moon's consort, and could not be slain until after Winter's Eve. Naeri was glad, remembering that. He was a splendid beast, and her heart would have cried out to see him brought down in all his grace and pride. Still, remarked Cathra, the sight of him must be a good omen.

Somewhere nearby in the bushes Fearnn gave a small satisfied cry. They went to look: she had brought down a woodcock with a single stone from her sling. They watched her half-running, half-dancing ahead of them, with the bird bouncing against her thigh.

"She is a deadly shot with that sling," said Cathra fondly. "When she grows into her full strength, she will be as good with a spear and a bow as I am myself." She chuckled. "I know—that sounds like boasting. But it's no more than the simple truth. The Mother, who gave all of us our gifts, chose that one for me, and for Fearnn."

"Is she witchborn?" Naeri asked. This pale-skinned, bright-haired sprite of a girl had wakened her curiosity.

Cathra shook her head. "She comes from the forest-folk. Though when I am annoyed with her—as I often am, for she is strong-willed and does not listen—then I tell her she is a changeling brat, left by the Others." She laughed. "Maybe it's true, too, for a flint-smith raised her, and nobody seems to know who her mother was."

Just then the sound of her voice startled a pair of pheasants out of the brush. Before Naeri could blink Cathra had fitted a chisel-edged fowling arrow to her string. One of the birds landed with a small thud in a tangle of beech roots.

Toward noon they headed down to the river meadows to look for duck. The sun rose to the top of the sky, as warm now as at summer's end. Naeri's jerkin felt heavy and hot on her neck; she undid the laces to let the air reach her skin.

The only warning they had of danger was a brief glint of bronze in sunshine; and it did not come soon enough. The horsemen rode out of the hazel scrub where the forest thinned along the slope. There were five of them, in full fighting gear—helmets, bronze-edged leather shields, heavy thrusting-spears. The three women, armed only with throwing-spears and light bird-arrows, were caught in the open, with the steep riverbank behind them, and the horsemen cutting off retreat into the woods.

Naeri could hear the faint creaking of leather, a shrill neigh, the clink of metal, a voice shouting something she could not understand, except to know that it sounded surprised and eager. From Cathra, just behind her, came a soft monotonous cursing, like an incantation. For her own part, Naeri felt a great rage at the injustice of the thing. She was not ready to die on this bright noontime, with birds singing and the sun warm on her shoulders.

The horsemen rode in on them fast, so there was no time for anything but in-fighting; though Cathra was using a throwing-spear to fend off the axman bearing down on her. She saw Fearnn darting sideways out of the way of a spear, then sliding like a fish under the arm and shield of her attacker to strike with her flint knife at his unprotected groin. The man screamed and dropped his spear.

Naeri caught a sudden, startling glimpse of Cathra's face. It was slit-eyed, glazed with sweat, inhuman—the face of some ancient goddess-figure carved in stone. In that instant, as Cathra's eyes met hers and as quickly jerked away, a savage, choking terror overwhelmed her. This was no ordinary battle fear, but a rending horror, like a wolf tearing at the throat. It was the mindless pack fear that sends herds plunging over chalk cliffs to destruction; the terror-wind that bends before it the will of armies, scattering their spears like barley-straws. Naeri stood rigid, rooted to the earth, her fingers loosening on her spear shaft: willing herself to stand fast, while every nerve in her body shrieked for flight.

Then she saw what was happening to the horses: mad with terror, foam-flecked lips drawn back over their teeth, they were rearing, plunging, flailing out wildly at the air.

The three women had the advantage now. Naeri bit down hard on her own fear and moved in beside Cathra and the girl. She put her spear through one man's throat while, cursing and shouting, he dragged desperately on the reins. A great fountain of blood spurted as she wrenched out the spear, and he toppled sideways without a sound.

Two riders died at Cathra's hands, and Fearnn took the fourth when his horse threw him headlong into the grass. But as Fearnn stood up with her flint-knife dripping, the fifth horseman, who had had the wit to wrap the reins around his wrist, reached down from his rearing mount and caught her by her red curls, hoisting her writhing and kicking into the air. He threw her across in front of him, and they bolted away into the woods.

Cathra was kneeling beside one of the dead horsemen, in the trampled, blood-smeared grass. Her face under its tan was drained of color. When Naeri bent down and put an arm around her shoulders, Cathra turned her head and gave her the thin ghost of a smile.

"Forgive me, sister," she said through chattering teeth. "It is a double-edged weapon, the Horned God's magic. But you did not run, as most would."

Then, like a sleeper suddenly wakened, she lifted her head and stared wildly around. "Fearnn?" she called out. And again, her voice rising, sharp-edged with apprehension, "Fearnn?"

Naeri went down on her knees beside Cathra. There was a sick hollow feeling in her belly. She held the other woman tightly, offering what comfort she could. With her lips close to Cathra's cheek she said, very softly, "She is gone, sister."

She could feel Cathra's shoulders jerk, as though she had taken a spear thrust between them. Otherwise she did not move or make a sound. But the hard, narrow body Naeri held in her arms seemed, now, as cold and rigid as a statue's.

At length she felt Cathra's breath escape against her cheek.

"The horseman?"

"Yes."

"She was my spear-daughter," Cathra said. She used the old hill word *fidais*, which meant a bond between a seasoned hunter and one who had lately come of age. It could imply many things—

chosen pupil, foster-child, comrade-in-arms, friend, bedmate—or all those things together. It was a tie sworn in blood, closer among their people than a marriage contract, and unlike a marriage, rarely broken save by death.

With her two hands on Naeri's shoulders Cathra braced herself and struggled to her feet. When Naeri held out her spear to her, she leaned on it, chalk-faced and gasping for breath.

"Sister, will you help me?"

Naeri stood up. "What must I do?"

"Come with me. Help me track Fearnn to the horseman's lair."

"On foot?" Naeri asked gently. "Exhausted as you are now? Look—you are so weak and dizzy you can hardly stand."

"It is only the spell-sickness," Cathra said. "It will soon pass."

"In a day, maybe. Listen, sister. The horseman has ridden back to his camp. If we knew where Fearnn was, we could do nothing to save her. Remember, I have lived in one of those camps."

Cathra's face took on a stubborn, angry look. "Then I will go alone."

She took a few ragged steps; then, overcome by the sick dizziness that follows spell-making, she swayed and would have fallen if Naeri had not reached out for her.

"Weep, sister," Naeri whispered. "We will keen for her now, and then we will go home."

She knelt in the long grass at Cathra's side, and she wept for Fearnn, as once she had wept for her dead sisters. She knew that grief would stay with Cathra like a cold stone in her breast, until her own death severed the blood-bond. But Fearnn was gone—at peace by now, if she was lucky. There was nothing to do but gather up their spears and wash their wounds, and accept that which could not be altered.

After a time Cathra ceased her anguished rocking, and the sound of her keening faded.

"It is time to go back," she said in an almost steady voice. Her nails had left long angry furrows on her cheeks.

"No, wait," she said, as Naeri turned to leave. "There is one task yet."

With one of their sharp-edged axes she hacked off the four heads of the fallen horsemen and held them up to drain the blood. Then she tied them together in pairs by their long plaits, and each with their grisly burden, she and Naeri started back to camp.

• • •

All through the afternoon and evening the cooking pots bubbled slowly over the fires, sending up a moist smell of boiling meat. By evening the sky had clouded over, and in the moonless dark a thin mist began to rise. Close to the midnight hour the Mother's people made their way to the Hill of Seven Barrows, where the ceremonial way began. There, at the hill's crest, within the double circle of standing stones, the torches were lit and the procession began its slow progress to the temple.

The Old One went first, moving with a stiff-limbed, brittle dignity, like some ancient leafless thorn. At her mother's side, supporting and steadying her, was the First Daughter, Grania: a dour graceless woman, well past her middle years, with a lined humorless face. Then came Naeri, in her place of honor. Cathra walked with the hunting-band, and Daui somewhere behind, among the priests who served the Horned God, the Lady's consort.

Like the others Naeri wore light sandals and a thin white linen robe. She shivered and hugged herself against the cold and the rising damp; trudging through the wet grass, her feet were soon chilled to the bone.

As they passed along the avenue, torchlight fell on the ravaged surfaces of the stones. Gaunt, wrinkled, hollow-sided, lichen-encrusted, they seemed to Naeri like the faces of the ancient dead. Close to the southern entrance the way narrowed and the stones grew taller, looming over them. A final abrupt twist of the avenue brought them before the broad, grotesquely weathered stone that guarded the portal.

The long weaving line of torches crossed the causeway, entered the vast southern enclosure and approached the Mother-Pillar.

The people formed a circle now, facing the Mother-Stone; the men dressed in the skins of the red deer, crowned with the Horned God's antlers, the women in their white robes, their long unplaited hair held back with bands of silver. Beyond, the mist writhed and billowed, red-stained by torchlight. Drums throbbed, a piper played thin, distant-sounding music.

High and eerie-seeming, the moon-chant drifted away into darkness.

> Lady of wolves
> dweller in dark places.
> Thrice-white
> lady of many faces.

> Death-bringer,
> in your hand is the knife of flint
> and the spear of darkness.
> Life-giver,
> out of your deep womb
> the new life springs forth.

The Old One stepped forward. Proudly erect, head lifted, she went to take her place before the Mother-Pillar. A dark sweet-faced woman of thirty-odd came to stand beside her; and then the pale nervous girl who had been chosen to take Fearnn's place.

Crone, matron and maiden, they held up their offerings to the Goddess: four smooth skulls, gleaming in torchlight, as round and pallid as the winter moon.

And Naeri realized with a small shock of horror what had been bubbling in the cook-pots all that afternoon.

Naeri struggled up out of an exhausted sleep. It was pitch-black in the tent, but her time-sense, always acute, told her that dawn was near at hand. It was Cathra who had woken her, tossing and turning restlessly at her side.

Naeri sat up in the tumbled bed. "Have you slept at all?" she asked Cathra.

"A little. But I kept waking, and then I would think, over and over again, 'She is afraid, and calling out for me. Why did I not follow her?'"

"You could not stand, much less track a fast horse across the downs," said Naeri, "and there's an end to it. Now listen." She yawned and rubbed her eyes, which felt heavy and full of sand. "Tomorrow, Daui says, I am going back to the horse-camp. The women there hear everything; it is as though they pick up tales from the wind blowing in the grass. I will listen closely to their gossip. If Fearnn lives and is in one of the camps, I will be sure to hear of it."

Cathra reached up and seized Naeri's wrists in a hard, painful grip. "Why are you going back there, into the boar's den, sister? Tell the minstrel you are staying where you belong. We will take you into the hills with us."

The idea came to Naeri with the force of a blow. It was true—why had she not thought of it? She would be safe in the hunters' country, among the high wolds and forests and limestone cliffs, with the far blue ridges of the west beyond. But she shook

her head. "Cathra, I must go back. I have made that choice freely.
I have given my promise." She thought of Nhiall and of Gwi; of
the ties that bound her to them. "I too am *fidais*," she said. It was
as close as she could come to an explanation.

∾ 12 ∾

Winter

In the space of a morning the fine weather broke, and the black storms of winter lashed down upon the hills. All night the wind howled dismally around the feast-hall, rattling the horsehides over the door and crying to be let in. The world beyond the camp was hidden in mist and driving rain; the roads were quagmires. Clearly, there was to be no escape for anyone until the skies cleared.

At Daui's insistence Naeri moved back into the small room overlooking the courtyard. Even though she kept a small charcoal fire burning all day, the damp and the winter draughts crept through the wicker walls. Huddled in her cloak, she drifted between loft and smithy and feast-hall like a pale unhappy ghost. Sometimes a warrior with nothing better to do would offer in passing a lewd grin, a blunt invitation. Then she would choke back her sick helpless rage and think, I am the minstrel's kinswoman and the smith's apprentice. I have been the Winter Queen. This much can he do, but no more.

She was content enough in those hours that she was allowed to work with Gwi. She practised new skills—raising, flat-chasing, embossing—and mastering them, basked in his praise. It was hard now to tell her hammerwork from Gwi's own. But he no longer talked of the future, of making her into a master-smith; and when she spoke of that other part of her life, that belonged to Daui and to Nhiall, and to the witchfolk, something closed in his face like a shutter.

Rain turned to sleet. The life of the camp centered on the two great hearth-fires that blazed in the feast-hall from dawn until after midnight. Already the men were bored and restless—and the longest part of the winter lay ahead. They could neither hunt nor raid in this weather; instead they drank, and afterward they fought. Sometimes the fights were over women, or horses, or old grievances; more often than not they were for their own sake, for the sheer enjoyment of the brawl. When two of his young warriors died in a quarrel over a hound, Ricca banned weapons from the hall. After that they wrestled, hurled curses and beakers, smashed the crockery and furniture. Howling, they attacked one another with gnawed ox-bones snatched from the hounds, or with fire-brands pulled smouldering out of the hearth. Many a warrior lost his white-toothed smile forever in one of those bloody melees.

The First Wife, Suais, presided nightly over the feasting and the uproar that inevitably followed. Her southern blood craved warmth; in winter she grew more languid than ever and seldom stirred from the hearthside. Wearing furs and amber and a small contemptuous smile, she would sit amid toppled benches, spilled beer and snarling dogs until sleep overtook her.

"So, witchwoman, you are back," said Ricca. He scowled down at Naeri, remarking to Gwi, "Do you think it's safe, smith, to pasture your pretty heifer with the bull?"

"Only if the bull is tethered," Gwi said calmly, "and only if the herdsman has eyes in his head."

Ricca shouted with laughter, and thumped Gwi between the shoulders. It was true what men said of him—crossed, he raged like a bayed boar, but once his fury was spent he seldom clung to a grievance.

"Listen, smith," Ricca said, "where can I find a hundred good stonemasons? Can you put out the word for me?"

"For that," said Daui, "you would do well to look to the Dark Folk, Ricca. They were builders in stone long before your people came to these shores."

"Witches," said Ricca, dismissing the Dark Folk with a snarl of contempt. "Tomb-dwellers, death-worshippers. They are ruled by women," he added. He waved for a fresh jug of mead and sat down. "I have heard of their temples, where bones and skulls are offered up to the Witch-Goddess. No, minstrel, this place I am building will be a place of light and air, open to the Sun's eye."

"Why stone?" Gwi asked, as though he were merely curious.

"Wood rots," said Ricca. "Stone lasts forever. Seeing my Sun-Temple, our children's grandchildren will praise the name of Ricca."

"And where will you find these stones?"

Ricca gestured, with a wide sweep of his arm. "The chalk valleys hereabouts are littered with them," he said.

Naeri saw the minstrel's mouth twitch in a half-smile, and his eyes flickered, meeting hers for an instant. She could read the thought in his head as easily as if he had spoken. In her mind's eye she saw the gnarled ancient stones of the Moon-Temple, drawing their terrible power from the earth's belly; she saw the Valley of the Rocks, where toppled sarsen boulders lay like sheep across the greensward, their formless diffuse magic shimmering on the air. Like rivets into bronze, another small part of the pattern slid into place.

"Still," said Daui, "wattle and daub and timber posts are one thing—and stone is another." He stood up and reached for his string-box, leaving that thought hanging in midair.

To the whine of the rising wind and the drumming of rain on the roof-skins, he gave them love lays and battle songs and histories of dead kings; a hush fell over the hall as they listened, though they had heard these songs a hundred times before. As the last notes faded, Daui got up a little stiffly from the harper's place and called for mead. The slaves, yawning, began in a halfhearted way to clear up the evening's wreckage. One of the women nudged Suais awake and led her away to her bower. By now most of the war-band were rolled up in their cloaks, snoring, with their women and their hounds beside them.

Daui sat nursing the last of his mead, with his face half-turned away from Gwi and Naeri. The ruddy light flickered on his steep brow, the sharp angles of jaw and cheekbone; his eyes and mouth were shadowed, secret. Then he looked round abruptly, and they saw that he was laughing, as though at some private jest.

"What a song this will make one day," he said. "I relish the irony of it. The Great Circle—where the powers of earth and sky are fused, where all things come together and are made whole— that in the end Ricca should build it for us, and call it a monument to himself . . ."

Gwi said quietly, "I am no engineer, but I can guess that it would take a thousand men to drag one of those stones across the downs."

"At least," Daui agreed. He spoke as though the figure were negligible—as though, if he wished, he could snap his fingers and conjure up ten thousand, a hundred thousand men. "I know what you are going to say. Yes—for us, the task would be impossible. We may have knowledge enough to build the Great Circle, but we have no manpower at our command. Now, if you will, consider Ricca—Ricca the all-powerful, the immortal chief, whom no earthly weapon can destroy. He has no sorcery, no science; yet all the tribes of the west have learned to tremble at his voice. If he is bent on building himself a monument, why should he not build it to our design? A temple of the Sun and the Earth, built by the Sun's and the Earth's servants. Like the Great Circle itself, it has a perfect symmetry."

Gwi said, "I would not be the man to tell Ricca how to carry out his schemes."

Daui hesitated for the space of a breath, and then he said, "Clearly, the advantages must be pointed out to him. And an alliance must be arranged."

"Between the Dark Folk and the horsemen? Daui, you are mad," Naeri said. "That hatred goes too deep for ax-truce."

Daui leaned forward into the firelight. His eyes shone with an intense gray light. "Not ax-truce, cousin," he said. "I had in mind another kind of alliance." He paused and glanced away, watching a shower of sparks fly up to the roof. "Shall we say, a bed-truce, cousin?"

Always, she had been quick to discern the thoughts that lay beneath the surface of words. All witchfolk had that gift, or curse, to some degree. Now she felt, like a flash of foreknowledge, a sick empty feeling in her belly. Only after did the sense of his words reach her, as news of disaster follows upon foreseeing. She sat and stared at him in blank numb misery, as though she had been told of some terrible bereavement.

"Minstrel," she said finally. She could not bring herself to use his name or call him cousin. "We are blood-kin. To betray your own blood is a sin against the Mother. Though I have forgotten much, I have not forgotten that."

He did not answer at first. She wondered that he should have fallen speechless—he who understood above all else the ordering of words.

Gwi made a small uncertain gesture as though he meant to reach out to her; but seeing the look in her eyes, the set of her jaw, he must have thought better of it. It was as well; this was a thing between herself and Daui.

"Gwi," Naeri said. "Please. Leave us for a while." Her voice in her own ears sounded high and unnatural. Her throat hurt.

Daui's voice, when he at last broke the silence, was very gentle, and so low-pitched she had to lean forward to catch his words.

"Why do you speak of betrayal, little cousin? Those are hard words, and thoughtless ones. Shall I turn them against you, and ask if you would betray your duty, the obligations of your birthgift? You have seen how your people are hunted down like beasts for the horsemen's sport. Have you so soon forgotten your sisters?"

"You would give me into the hands of my enemies. If that is not betrayal, you must find me another name for it."

"Cousin, how can you believe that? Not into their hands. I thought your wits were quicker than that. Can you not see—it is Ricca who will fall into your hands, your power. You will be the serpent in the nest, the agent of his destruction."

She asked, in the voice of one who wishes to have the worst over quickly, "Do you mean me only to lie with him, or be a wife to him?"

Daui raised an eyebrow. "Half the women in camp have done the first. I mean you to have influence with him—an acknowledged hearth-place. For that, there must be a marriage."

"Ricca has two wives already, besides Suais; and any number of brats. What need has he of another wife, with dark blood and no bride-price?"

She marveled at how calm she sounded. When the blade touches your throat, she thought, it is too late to be afraid, or struggle. This must be how the queens of the flint-people felt, in ancient days, as they went to their seven-year deaths. Like them, she had watched the pattern building slowly, had discerned its final and irrevocable shape. To pretend surprise or outrage now was self-delusion.

"Clearly," Daui said, "you do not pay as much heed as I to bower-gossip. Ricca has children, yes. But only three sons. And two of those are in fosterage with southern chiefs, in pledge of ax-truce. Barra the Fair and Clia have borne, between them, a string of daughters, which counts for little among the horse-tribes. Suais came near to death with her last labor; the babe, which would have been male, was stillborn—and she has sworn there will be no others."

"Girl," he went on, "have you forgotten the soothsaying when you were Winter Queen? That a dark woman of the hills would bring fortune to Ricca's house? If you have put it out of your mind, you may depend on it Ricca has not. There is as much ambition in his eyes as lust when he looks at you, little cousin."

Everyone had gone now, or was asleep. Shadows rushed in on them; the raw cold crept through the walls. In the near-darkness she could hear the gentle persuasive sound of Daui's voice—tired now, a little hoarse, but making a song of his words still.

He said, "How am I to make you understand? You, more than anyone, have felt the power of magic in the stones. Imagine if we were masters of that power, if we held it pent-up, contained, like the hawk on the wrist, the arrow in the bow. Once we have harnessed those dragons that live at the earth's roots, no war-band can stand against us. The ancient order of things will be restored, our people will rule again in their own land. Can you see, now, the perfect pattern it makes? What vengeance more just than this— that the horse-tribes are brought down, destroyed, by the temple they themselves have built to their own glory?"

She felt empty inside, like the wicker-women that—in these days—the flint folk burned instead of queens.

"So," Daui said. He got up, settling his cloak around him. His mouth drew up at one corner in a bleak half-smile. "The priest will approach me first, as your blood kinsman. What answer will I give him?"

"Tell him what you will," she said. Her voice was gray and hollow-sounding, like the dull steady drip of rainwater from the eaves.

Afterward, when Daui had gone out, she heard a voice shouting in the courtyard—a fierce one-sided argument; and she guessed that Gwi had been waiting all this time outside the feast-hall. Then the horsehides were jerked aside and the smith came into the hall. With the last of the torchlight she saw the pain and bewilderment in his face, and felt bitterly ashamed—as though she were more betrayer than betrayed.

He reached out and seized her by the shoulders. He looked as though he wanted to shake her, pound sense into her; but all he did was to stare at her in an odd intense way, as though he had never properly looked at her before. Finally he said, "Woman, the minstrel has put a spell on you. Or is it a plain lie, what he has just told me?"

"No," she said, still hearing in her own ears that flat, lifeless voice. "It is no lie, and I am under no spell. This is what I was meant to do from the beginning."

"By whom?" He seemed to realize that he was shouting at her, and lowered his voice. "Your life is your own. You are beholden to no one."

She shook her head. "A smith seeks out his art for himself, Gwi, and so it carries no obligation. Mine was a birthgift, and bears a duty with it."

"Then foreswear it. You have found another art that serves you better."

The last torch guttered out. In the darkness she found the courage to reach out and touch his face. His hand came up and closed gently over hers. She could feel the hard cold knot inside her starting to dissolve; she knew she could bear anything else, but not his pity. She got up awkwardly, without pushing the bench back, and hit her knee on the edge of the low trestle table.

"It doesn't matter," she said, with her teeth clenched against the sharp unexpected pain. She stumbled out, leaving Gwi to wonder if she meant her bruised knee, his love, or the hard duty she had chosen.

She woke near dawn, screaming, for she had dreamed of pale ghost-women with bleeding flesh and mouths that cried out to the moon for vengeance. They wore the faces of her mother and her sisters; all but the smallest one, who had red hair and long green terror-stricken eyes.

In the morning she met Ricca leading his rough-coated brown stallion from the stable. He said nothing, but as he passed she felt his eyes upon her. Her hatred was like a snake that writhed and twisted in her belly.

～ 13 ～

Temple-Ground

Old Magha cast his auguries, and so decreed that the marriage-rites should take place at Spring-Feast, when the herds were driven to summer pasture and the clans gathered to celebrate the Sun's rebirth. But day after day the cold rain beat down upon the hills, and spring still seemed a long way off.

Naeri's place, now, was among the bower-women in the upper palace. It was not proper that the Great Chief's betrothed should spend time alone with the smith, or wander aimlessly about the camp. In any case, Gwi seemed to be keeping out of her way; or maybe his time was taken up with the gift-goods he must finish in time for Spring-Feast. Already he had taken on two apprentices, the women said.

Neither was Ricca much in evidence; bower-gossip had it that most of his time was spent in Council, laying plans for the great work of temple-building. Now when his path crossed Naeri's he greeted her in a ceremonious way, as custom demanded, though the hint of irony in his eyes did not escape her.

Daui came to her chamber with sheepskin scrolls and scraps of vellum marked in charcoal ink with geomantic lines and symbols. He showed her how certain alignments of the standing stones with the pathways of the sun and moon and the forcelines of the earth would serve to focus and magnify the power that was in the stones. These were the patterns that must be woven into Ricca's monument.

"When spring comes and Ricca begins his temple-building, we will be ready," Daui said.

By lamplight, and by the gray watery light of early morning, Naeri pored over the charts and formulae. They were the straws to which she must cling to keep from drowning.

But now that she was to have a place in Ricca's household, other duties demanded her attention. She spun and wove, and made bride-clothes of pale supple leather, oak-tanned and softened with cattle brains. With colored threads she stitched into these garments the golden symbols of the Sun-God and the emblems of Ricca's house.

While she worked she listened to the women's chatter, hoping for some word of Fearnn. But now that travel had ceased between the horse-camps, there was talk only of small hearth-scandals. The greater world no longer existed for them.

Toward midwinter the rains slackened, and high winds scattered the dense cloud cover. A fortnight of dry blustery weather followed. Now the war-band rode out every morning, their spears glistening in the cold sunlight, and there was fresh meat in the cooking troughs every night.

One morning, awakened at sunup by the drumming of hooves and jangle of harness, Naeri found a bower-servant hovering at the end of her bed. The woman was holding out a new doeskin tunic, and Naeri's heavy winter cloak.

"The minstrel bids you dress warmly this morning, lady. He is waiting for you in the courtyard."

Daui was standing at the stable doors, harnessing a pair of ponies to a two-wheeled cart. He looked up. "Get some food from the hall," he told her, "and something to drink. They say the valley crossing is passable—while the weather holds we have much work to do."

They rode south over the bleak windy hills, the heavy-wheeled cart of wood and rawhide creaking and jouncing under their weight. The ponies were eager after the long weeks of rain; they ran at full stretch, their hooves thundering on the high chalk track. Naeri held on for her life as the wind grabbed at her hair and the world whipped by in a tawny blur.

Daui reined in hard as the track plunged down to the wet tree-choked valley bottom; soon after, the ponies were scrambling up the other side, the cart wheels slithering and spitting mud. Before them lay the Great Down, winter-stark in the shifting light, with all its distances vanishing in mist.

• • •

The blue-stone circle rose dreamlike, insubstantial from the high bare plain. Here was the world's hub, the pivot point, thought Naeri. In this still place all the lines of power came together, as the blood's channels flow inward to the heart, and outward from it.

Daui tethered the ponies and left them to graze. The day had turned dull again, as thin high clouds moved across the sun. Even the birds were silent; there was no sound but the low monotonous sighing of the wind, no color anywhere but a patch of furze blooming in a hollow and the gray-gold of lichen on the rocks.

Daui stood waiting for her inside the broken double circle; arms folded, half-leaning in that easy graceful way of his with one shoulder against a stone, as casually as one leans against a doorpost.

"Cousin," he said as she approached across the winter turf, "I had hoped the ride would put color in your face, but you look as wan as a ghost still. Is it the stones that frighten you?"

She nodded, trying by an effort of the will to slow her heart's pounding.

Daui smiled. "Forget the magic that is in them, cousin. Forget geomancy. Today I wish you to see their patterning as I see it."

As he spoke, a small rebellious voice in her head said, "For you it is easy, minstrel. For you the stones keep silent, there is no magic in them."

He reached out, a little impatiently, and drew her to his side.

"Naeri, think of the man who built this circle. Clearly, he knew astronomy, mathematics, engineering—something of earth-magic. And what courage he must have possessed, what strength of purpose. It was no easy thing to carry these great stones by land and sea from that far mountain in the west."

"All that for nothing," Naeri murmured. "I know the story too, remember. It was too late; he could not bind the Faceless Gods, and was destroyed by them."

She shivered, thinking what had become of that nameless architect—of all those wise, gentle, clever people. For in some strange way she had been a witness to it—watching, waiting, afraid as they were afraid, when the Old Gods woke, and the sea rose up like a mountain over their land.

But Daui was only half-listening to her. "See how the axis-line runs," he was saying. "If you stand here, in the center, and look out through the entrance way to the Sun-Stone, midsummer sunrise lies straight ahead and midwinter sunset is behind you. So also will the new temple mark the birth and death of the sun—Ricca will be pleased by that, I warrant; but it is our own purpose we will serve, not his."

He pointed out to her how the four stones set inside the bank formed a great rectangle, aligned to the risings and settings of both sun and moon. "Imagine," he said, "how many years of patient observation went into that simple pattern of stones." And he showed her the long-distance sightlines running unobstructed across the downs—lines by which the priests of ancient days had, from the center of this circle, observed the moon's journeyings.

"Once," he told her, "there was a great interlocking network of such circles, spreading the length and breadth of the Westland, each one a focus of power, a knot on the earth-web." A light leaped suddenly in his eyes as he turned to her and said, "Is it too much to imagine, cousin, that one day we may rebuild them?"

After a time she began to feel tired and light-headed. Her scalp prickled. It was a clear warning that she had spent too long among the stones, that their power was taking hold of her. She made an excuse to Daui and wandered off by herself to let her head clear.

Following the slope of the land, she came down into a fold of the downs that offered some shelter from the wind. All around her, the landscape rose in gentle, swelling curves. Featureless and colorless in the drab gray light, it appeared to her now as it must have appeared in the first days of the world, before men came to make their patterns of cairns and barrows and ridge tracks on the chalk.

Truly, she thought, the earth is *her* flesh—skin, bone, blood, tissue of the Mother. In the rise and fall of the land she could see the graceful curves of back and thigh, valley crevices and slopes of limbs, the round uplifted shoulders of the hills. At this moment, all that she had been taught to accept, to understand, reached to a deeper place below the level of thought. There was purpose and pattern in the land, as there was pattern in the bones, nerves, arteries, sinews of her own body. Nothing was random, haphazard—nothing came there by whim or accident. Every mound, pit, stream, stone, every hollow of combe and slope of hill had its place in the vast harmonious order.

She came to herself with a start, and turned back to the blue-stone temple: seeing in its broken, toppled stones a great tear in the world's fabric—a wound that only she had power to heal.

That she must lie with Ricca as his wife, must open the secret places of her body to him—that was a small matter in the enormous scheme of things. What storms, blights, floods must the Mother have endured, what upheavals at the world's roots had rent her flesh? Yet how quietly she slept now, this dreaming goddess.

Naeri glanced up, to the south. Someone was approaching along the hill track: a tall gray shape against the paler gray of the sky. As the traveler drew near, she recognized his long downsman's stride. "Nhiall!" she called out joyfully, waving her arms to catch his eye; and she raced up the grassy slope to meet him.

Breathless, she took his hands and touched her forehead to them; then raised her chin to smile at him. He smiled back, with as much warmth as ever, but his face was finer drawn than she remembered, and his eyes were somber.

"It goes well with you?" she asked, the commonplace question hiding a sudden apprehension.

"Well enough." Then seeing her doubting look, he added, "Though perhaps last night I did not sleep as well as I should have."

"Did Daui send you a message?" it occurred to her to ask.

"No," he said. "Not Daui." There was an edge to his voice that made her glance up sharply.

Nhiall said, as though finishing a thought aloud, "He is a quiet man, the bronzesmith, not easily roused to anger. But he wore a face like a thundercloud when he rode up to my door last night."

Her breath caught in her throat. "Gwi sent for you?"

"Indeed. He told me I should find you here today—and hoped I could talk some sense into you. Those were more or less his words, as I recall."

She smiled a little at that.

Nhiall put both hands on her shoulders, and looked hard at her. "He is right to be angry," he said. "This is not what I would have chosen for you—this ill-considered marriage. You must believe that Daui acted without my knowledge or consent."

"I know," she said, and felt, curiously, that it was she who must offer comfort. "From the beginning, I knew that."

"You could have refused. You are not bound to do Daui's or anyone else's bidding."

"And yet it was you who spoke to me of my duty," she reminded him.

"Perhaps I did. But if you remember, I spoke only of your duty to yourself. It is Daui who places this greater obligation on you."

"What obligation is that?" Startled, they both looked round.

Daui's footsteps on the yielding turf were so quiet that even Naeri's quick ears had missed them.

The minstrel waited, one eyebrow raised, and returned Nhiall's greeting as coolly as it was given. They might have been strangers meeting for the first time at some rite of ax-truce.

Nhiall said quietly, "You have overstepped your rights in this matter, Daui. Remember, she is my kinswoman as well as yours. I should have been consulted."

Daui gave him a thin smile. "She is not a child, Nhiall. She makes up her own mind."

Naeri caught the sudden lightning-flicker of rage in Nhiall's eyes. "Does she indeed, minstrel?" It was not a question. Nhiall took a step or two forward. She could see the tension along his jaw. There was no gentleness in his face now; it had a hawk-fierce resolute look that frightened her.

She put her hand on Nhiall's sleeve. "He is right," she said. "I have decided for myself. There was no other choice I could make."

"At what cost?" His eyes were still dark with anger as they met hers. "Naeri, I think I know you better than you know yourself. To live as Ricca's wife—can't you see that it will destroy you?"

She said, "Instead, should I stand by and watch our people be destroyed? Remember, in the old songs, the battle that goes on to world's end between the Lords of Chaos and the Lords of Light? Nhiall, I have seen Chaos, and it wears a horseman's face."

He reached out and touched her cheek, and the anger in his eyes faded. In a tired, quiet voice he asked, "And you, Naeri? Will you be the one to challenge the dark lords?" There was no irony in his tone, only sadness and a faint surprise. "You have changed, these past months. You were not always so sure of your powers."

"Remember," she said, "how you told me I was the copper blade that draws the lightning down? That is how we will defeat the horse-lords—not through any power of mine, but by the power of earth and stone that passes through me."

The ghost of a smile touched Nhiall's mouth. "Well," he said. "It seems it must always be thus with the witchfolk—we are a race of dragonslayers."

He bowed his head—a little stiffly after his morning's journey—and touched her hands. He did not look at Daui, who was waiting with ill-concealed impatience.

She said, "Must you go?"

He nodded and smiled, somewhat ruefully. "Old men should

not stray far from their hearths in winter. The chalk wind is bitter when the sun drops—it gnaws my bones. Only remember there is a place by my fire if you find you have made too hard a choice."

"I will remember," she said, and sent him away with a daughter's embrace.

"Now," said Daui, with more than a trace of irritation, "I would like to finish what we came to do." And he led her back to the temple-ground, where he was plotting sightlines with two posts and a length of cord.

~ 14 ~

Spring Feast

That year spring came early to the chalk lands. The sap rose and the beech trees budded, the blackthorn put forth its fleecy spikes. Above the sloping fields where cowslips and violets blossomed, larks sang in gentian-colored skies. All these things were clear signs, said Magha, that the Sun-God smiled on Ricca's marriage.

In the close, narrow rooms of the women's quarters, Naeri awaited her bride-rites. Every morning, as she leaned out over the rampart walk to catch the early sunlight, she could see the chalk hills, tender green under a gauze of mist, fading into blue distance, and her heart ached for her half-remembered freedom.

In the courtyard below, hammers clanged and rang on metal. Gwi and an army of helpers were working against time to finish the feast-goods. Once again the horse-lords moved along the chalk roads, riding down from the windy hills and moorlands, inland from the fens and sea cliffs, up from the rich downs of the south. In these days all the chiefs of the Westland paid Ricca fealty, and kept his ax-peace.

Feast-day came. In the early morning the young men and women went out into the fields to gather whitethorn branches, the men riding, the women, with cloaks thrown over light warm-weather garments, racing in sandals through the dew-soaked grass. The manes and tails of the ponies were braided with brightly colored rags; the women wore violets and anemones wound into their yellow plaits.

They returned near midday, grass-stained and disheveled, carrying great armloads of white-foaming branches. They piled them in a circle, making a flowering hedge at the crest of the hill where that night the Spring Fire would burn. Then they went off to the horsefair outside the camp to amuse themselves until night fell and the rituals began.

Just before sunset Magha walked out of the feast-hall and through the gates in his red ceremonial robes. The elders of the tribe followed, then Ricca and his warrior-lords, aglint with gold and bronze in the slanting light. After them came Suais and the young wives Barra and Clia, dressed in soft embroidered doe-skins, with amber at their wrists and throats. Their many daughters, small copies of themselves, trailed after them.

Last of all came the bower-women, with Naeri in their midst. It was the first time in a fortnight that she had been out of the camp.

They climbed to the hilltop, to take their ritual places inside the circle of thorn. Clansmen, chalk farmers, slaves and children streamed up the slopes, summoned by the sound of drums and bullhorns, until the ridge was black with people.

The fire of oak and rowan wood had already been laid, with straw and furze to kindle it. Magha stepped forward, carrying the ceremonial fire-drill that called down the Sun's own fire from heaven; and birch-agaric to make the sacred spark leap quickly into life.

There was a silence as the whole camp held its breath. Magha was an old man; each year his hands lost a little more of their strength and suppleness. Suppose this year all the magic was gone out of his fingers, and the fire would not come?

The last rays of the sun slipped behind a western ridge; in that instant the tinder caught and blazed. Tongues of fire licked round the logs, then with a sudden roar leaped skyward. A sigh ran like a soft wind around the circle and was lost in the hiss and crackle of the flames. All was well in the world. Once again the Sun-God had sent down his sacred fire. Barley would grow tall this summer, and the herds would thrive. Many strong warrior-sons would be born to the horse-tribes.

In the warm dusk the women were passing out the choosing-cakes. Only the warriors took and ate the small hard barley-bannocks. One of the cakes had a lump of charcoal baked inside; the man who bit down on that bitter portion would be the fire-dancer. Before this night was out he must leap three times over the highest part of the flame.

There was a shout, and laughter. Young Ket, son of the

horsemaster, had bitten into the charcoal. He held up a piece of it, crumbled between his fingers, and grinned. His face was pale under its tan, and beads of sweat stood out on his forehead. Suais was watching him from her place on the woman's side; he must have felt her steady gaze on him, for he glanced up, and she smiled.

According to custom, Ket waited to let the flames burn down just a little. It was not as it had been in ancient days, when living men, children, animals, all were thrown as sacrifices into the fire. Now it was only a ceremony. He who danced well, and leaped high, might live to boast of it.

To the shrill of the pipes and the quickening beat of the skin-drums Ket danced three times round the fire, loosening his long limbs and summoning up his courage. Then he leaped, straight through the highest part of the flame. He was quick and agile; once, twice, he soared like a young stag, and came through unscathed, though the flames licked greedily at his bare legs and his tunic hem. As he leaped for the third time, a sudden gust of wind sent the fire roaring up; he shouted as he touched earth on the other side, and then they saw him rolling frantically in the grass.

He got to his feet quickly enough, looking sheepish; his tunic was scorched black along one side, where the fire had caught hold, and one foot was starting to blister, but he had taken no serious hurt.

The bower-women clustered around him, fussing and tut-tutting. One of them smeared unguent on his burn, and another bandaged it with a strip of linen.

When the fire had burned down nearly to embers, the herdsmen would drive the sheep and cattle through it, to make them fruitful; but few of the young men and women would remain to watch. Naeri saw from the corner of her eye that Ket had already disappeared, and Suais with him. Soon others drifted away to dance and make merry, and to share the pleasures of the fields on that warm spring night.

Naeri stood at the edge of the dying fire, savoring the sweet night air and this short-lived interval of freedom. She knew that Ricca would not approach her; it would be ill-omened for them to lie together on the night before their marriage. But there would be many another woman hoping to catch Ricca's eye—to lie with the Great Chief at Spring Feast meant good fortune, and strong sons for her husband.

The wind changed, and smoke drifted into her face. She

coughed and moved back, nearer the hedge of whitethorn. Close to, the blossoms had a sickly fragrance, an odor of decay. She remembered that among her people they were a flower of misfortune. To bring whitethorn into a house meant a death within the year.

She heard footsteps behind her, and swung round.

"It's not too late to change your mind," Gwi said. He still had on the scuffed leather tunic he wore for forge work.

She gave him a wry smile, and shook her head. "Why are you not out there in the fields with the others?" she asked.

"The grass is wet. Anyway, I wanted to see you, this last time."

Surprised, she said. "You will still see me afterward."

"Only as Ricca's wife. There'll be small pleasure in that, my girl." He looked at her, rather wistfully. "I've missed you, Naeri. The work has gone more slowly than it should, without you."

"Are you finished, then?"

"The last goblet, the last shield-boss. Ricca will make a fine show tomorrow. He doesn't know that I have put a small discreet curse into every feast-gift."

She laughed. Gwi picked up one of her hands and examined it gravely. "Look, those chapped fingers of yours are as smooth as a bower-woman's. Ricca has done what I never could—he has made a lady of you." He glanced up. "Your wedding headdress is finished. And your necklace."

"I know," she said. "One of the women saw them on your workbench—she said they were fit for the marriage of a southern queen."

He shrugged. "Well, I would not have you ashamed, with all the Westland looking on . . . You're shivering," he said suddenly, and put an arm around her shoulders. "Are you cold?"

"I'm afraid," she said. "More afraid, I think, than if I were riding into battle tomorrow."

"Well," Gwi said, "it will not be much different for you than it is now. You will continue to spend your days in the women's bower, spinning and weaving like any dutiful clan-wife."

"And my nights?" she asked. She had not meant to say that—the words slipped out unbidden.

"Yes, well." Now he looked as miserable as she herself felt, and she was ashamed.

"Walk with me a while," she said. "We may not have the chance again."

They wandered down the hillside and across the dark sloping

fields. The moon had not yet risen. The wind was quiet tonight, no more than a light air that brought with it a smell of turned earth and fresh new growth. Around the myriad small fires that had sprung up in the level places, the pipes and drums still played dancing music, though few remained to listen. In the shadows among the beeches and the small-leaved rowans, in the thickets along the meadow's edge, they could hear whispers, muffled laughter.

Naeri linked her arm through Gwi's. He turned, drawing her nearer to him, and kissed her hair. She longed desperately to hold on to this moment—to trust, friendship, tenderness—to Gwi's solid, comforting presence. And to this aching sweetness she felt, as she stood close to him in the dark. Like a warrior on the eve of battle, she was learning how fear sharpens all the senses, and against logic, stirs desire.

She felt Gwi hesitate, pull back, was aware that an awkwardness had sprung up between them. She guessed that his mind, as always, was standing guard over the instincts of his flesh. He had been her friend, her brother, her teacher for too long; for her sake, he had set that other part of his love aside. It was up to her, now, to speak.

She swallowed, and came straight to the heart of the matter. "I don't think," she said in an oddly matter-of-fact tone, "that Ricca knows he is taking a virgin to his bed."

"No," said Gwi dryly. "I dare say it will surprise him a good deal, that."

There was a silence. "Gwi," she whispered, finally. "Must I say it straight out? Well then. The witchfolk believe that when a maid first lies with a man, there should be fondness. On her part, anyway. And patience and gentleness on his." She looked up. His face was a vague glimmer in the darkness. "The new field, they say, must be furrowed with love, else the corn will not flourish."

There was an odd catch in Gwi's voice as he answered, "And my people say that it makes a bond between a woman and a man that is not easily broken."

The warning was clear enough, if she wished to heed it. Instead, she put both arms round his neck and laid her cheek against his. He kissed her temples, the hollow of her throat, and then, unhurriedly, her mouth. As surely as though he had the witchsight, he knew what would come of this; and it no longer mattered.

~ 15 ~

Bride-Rites

In the chill gray hour before dawn the bower-women came with lamps to dress her in her wedding finery: the long doeskin skirt and overtunic stitched with colored threads, the soft boots with catskin cuffs. They brought the necklace that Gwi had made for her, giggling and whispering and clicking their tongues at the splendor of it. Naeri looked at it with a craftsman's eye, seeing the long hours of close work that had gone into its making. It was made up of hundreds upon hundreds of amber beads threaded on linen, interspersed with golden plaques. The amber was the color of red honey, and warm to the touch. Sun-jewels, the horsemen called them, and believed there was magic in them.

And then the headdress, aglitter with gold and amber sun-discs that swayed and spun and clashed softly together, with two large coils that came down over her ears, helping to keep the whole in place. The entire elaborate structure was built upon a leather cap that tightly gripped her temples and the back of her neck; already she could feel a film of sweat gathering under it.

Underneath, they had brushed her hair down loose and straight, unbraided and unadorned. That was how she would go to Ricca when this long day ended.

The sky was lightening, the dawn mist rising off the damp fields as the Westland tribes assembled, marching in full ceremonial dress from their clustered tent-camps.

Thin ribbons of rosy light lay across the sky to the east above the downs. The undersides of the clouds were flaming gold, like molten metal; as light gathered below the horizon, the sky turned dull red, then violet.

Naeri walked slowly through the gates and across the causeway, down to the ritual-place at the bottom of the hill. She held her chin high and her head very steady. As she moved, her headdress made a chiming, jangling music. A thin trickle of sweat worked its way from under the cap and down her cheek.

She had had no proper rest, only dozing a little toward dawn—a broken, dream-wracked slumber. Her head hurt, and she had that slight feverishness that comes with too little sleep. Everything that was happening had a faint air of unreality, as though she were still caught somewhere between dreams and waking.

Now she was moving between the women's lines, while they beat their small ceremonial drums and chanted,

> Lord of the Sky, Life-Giver,
> let your seeds of fire
> make fruitful this woman.
> From her womb
> let strong warriors spring forth,
> tall sons for Ricca . . .

The bullhorns snarled; she could see Ricca approaching between the long lines of chiefs and war-lords. With his left hand he held the great golden shield that Gwi had made for him, in his right hand he carried the Great Chief's stone-headed scepter. His stiff bullskin cape and stallion-crested headdress exaggerated his girth and stature—made him seem a giant among men. His torque was of red-gleaming twisted gold; he wore on his breast the great golden face of the Sun-God.

She could hear the warriors' song, the dawn-hymn:

> Lord of the heavens,
> mighty hunter,
> whose bright spear scatters the herds of night,
> warrior in the swift-horsed chariot—
> Chief among chiefs, undying Father,
> let your face shine this day upon Ricca,
> let your mighty strength be in him.

She stood quietly in the ritual-place, staring up at Ricca. He put a hand under her elbow, quite gently, and turned her to face the east.

There was a thunder of drums and a wailing of pipes, a bright flash on the horizon; and then the golden wheel of the sun rode up the sky.

From the south side of the ritual-place the women watched; on the north side stood the ranks of warriors. The low light glinted and dazzled on their gorgets and buckles and breastplates, their brightly burnished weapons.

Naeri felt the weight of many eyes upon her. Most were curious or merely indifferent; but there was open hatred in the cold dark eyes of the clan-chief Uigh. She remembered the bower-gossip: that Uigh had a marriageable daughter with an eye to Ricca's bed, and a place for her father at Ricca's right hand.

Ricca reached down and took Naeri's left hand, holding it across his own, palm upward. While the high voices of the women made a wordless, flutelike music, Magha drew his little sharp flint-knife, and in the old way of the horse-tribes, cut a quick slash across Naeri's outstretched wrist, then Ricca's. He held them together to let their blood mingle, so that their flesh became one.

She scarcely noticed the sting of the knife—feeling, through it all, that same odd sense of detachment, as though she were dreaming this, or viewing it from a long way off. She stole a quick curious glance at Ricca, seeing beneath the waving stallion-crest the broad flat high-colored cheeks, the deepset eyes under their heavy brow-ridges, the strong mouth and heavy jaw. It was a face of enormous pride and arrogance; and wore, at this moment, a look of overweening self-congratulation.

Magha held out the golden marriage cup filled with fermented mare's milk. Under the wide yellow eye of the Sun-God they drank, and it was done.

The spears of the war-lords, raised together in salute, threw long thin shadow stripes across the grass. Afterward, each man came forward and laid his spear at Ricca's feet in pledge of loyalty.

It took a long time, that oath-making. The sun climbed up the sky. Naeri's neck had begun to ache under the weight of the headdress; her skin prickled and itched under the clinging doe-skins.

She was thinking how little any of this had to do with her. For Ricca she was the spice in the honey-mead, nothing more. What mattered was that great heap of burnished weapons piled glittering at his feet.

At last it was finished. She was Ricca's wife, in the Sun-God's eyes and before all the tribes of the Westland. Unless Ricca should set her aside in anger, she would remain so to the end of her days.

It was not yet midmorning; a full day of games and feasting lay ahead.

In the hearth-hall, where weapons and ornaments were once again stacked high, the clan-chiefs and their allies met to await the gift-giving and to hear Ricca speak.

Ricca said, "The Sky-Lord smiles upon this day, and upon my marriage. This dark woman brings fortune to our undertaking." He grinned at them. "It is a good omen, Magha has told me, that this woman of the earth-people, the Goddess-worshippers, should lie beneath the Sun's warrior, as the earth spreads itself beneath the Sun."

The chieftains and their warriors bellowed with laughter at that, and banged their dagger handles on the tables.

"Tomorrow," said Ricca, "the work begins. This I ask of you, you who are chiefs of my clans, and the Great Chiefs who have sworn truce with me. I bid you go back to your lands and raise an army in my service. Bring me men with strong arms, strong backs, who are no more afraid of hard work than warriors are afraid of battle. Slaves and free-folk, bond-servants, hostages. They will do this great work for me, and your warriors will see that it is done. Take these tokens of my trust, and return in a fortnight with your men."

There was a mutter of protest, starting among the men of the North Chalk and quickly spreading. Rudra of the River called out, "If we send the slaves from our hearths to work for you, and also the freemen from our lands, and our war-bands to oversee them, who then will tend our crops and herds? Who will protect those crops and herds from our enemies?"

Ricca said, "Rudra, you yourself have complained that the Westland reeks of too much peace and the young men are restless, now that my ax-truce reaches from the western to the southern water, and no tribe dares to raise its spears against me. If I told you that some wild tribe of the north were marching down upon us—or that ships of the east were landing on our coast—would you question me then, if I asked you to raise me a war-host?"

"No," roared the answer around the hall.

"And while you cursed the enemy, you would be glad in your hearts, seeing the young men burnishing their spears.

"The roads are dry, the barley is planted, the herds are in summer pasture. After the long winter, it is time to sharpen our axes and ride to battle. But where is an enemy that will stand against us? So. I give you an enemy. I give you these great unwieldy stones that lie to the west of us. I give you the rough down country across which we must carry them. These are your enemies. Raise me a war-host to defeat them, to impose the will of Ricca upon the land."

They stood as one man, shouting their ax-pledge. The feast-gifts were distributed; fresh mead jars and beer casks were broken open.

Suais left the women's circle and came to sit among the war-band, in the First Wife's place across from Ricca. Naeri—who for this night only had a seat at Ricca's left hand—flinched under Suais's hostile gaze. The First Wife's eyes were the color of dark amber in the torchlight. Eyes like that should have had the sun's warmth in them; instead, they were cold and hard as stones. After a moment those eyes moved restlessly on, dismissing Naeri. Suais had caught sight of young Ket, who was limping across the feast-hall on his blistered foot. She looked up at him from under her heavy lids, and flashed her white teeth at him. Naeri saw Ket's mouth twitch as he tried, for Ricca's benefit, to pretend he had not noticed.

The wedding-feast ended, like all feasts before it, in fighting and dancing and drunken revelry. Tired past the point of exhaustion, Naeri allowed herself to be led away by the bower-women.

Ricca's sleeping-place, which looked out over the gates of the camp, was as large as two ordinary rooms together. The women had been in to ready it for the marriage-night: taking up the stale straw and spreading fresh bracken on the floor, sprinkling herbs and shaking out the sleeping-rugs. They had made up a charcoal fire, though the night was warm; had trimmed the oil lamps, and set out small cakes and a jar of mead.

Two of them helped Naeri to undress, and folded away her wedding garments; another brushed her hair and smeared sweet-smelling oils on her breasts and stomach. Finally they put her into bed, under a vast rug of joined marten skins; and giggling behind their hands, they left her to herself.

Soon after, Ricca pushed aside the horsehide curtain. He was not sober, but neither was he as drunk as she had expected. She decided with faint surprise that he must have left the feast early, before the mead was finished. Huddled under the marten skins, she waited with grim resolve.

The old terror was clutching at her, like sharp claws under her ribs; ruthlessly she fought it down. Nor would she think of the sweetness of last night, lying in the warm dark with Gwi. She locked that memory away so it would not be spoiled, as lime-mead is spoiled by the taste of sour beer.

Unsmiling, Ricca met her gaze; she saw a flicker of something in his eyes—amusement, maybe, or irony. He tossed aside his cloak; pulled off his bracelets and brooches, his torque and bronze-buckled belt, dropping them clinking and jangling onto a chest. He unfastened his golden breastplate and set it carefully in a corner; then casually, as if he were alone in the room, drew his tunic over his head. A mat of blond hair covered his chest and shoulders. When he had rid himself of leggings and boots and breechclout, he pulled back the rug and lay down beside her. He smelled of drink and of sweat and woodsmoke.

He was not deliberately brutal; that too surprised her—she had thought there might be old scores settled tonight. He seemed merely indifferent to her pain, or unaware of it. But he was a large man in all ways, and impatient. Her inexperience and fear, and the mead he had drunk, made the whole business awkward and difficult. Cursing softly in her ear, he finally succeeded in entering her. She bit her lip hard, for she had vowed to herself that she would not cry out whatever happened.

Finally it was over and he fell abruptly asleep, with the full weight of his body on her. She squirmed out from beneath him, and slid over as far as she could against the wall. She lay in the darkness with her eyes wide open, listening to Ricca's snores, until fatigue overcame her.

~ 16 ~

Witch-Wife

It was too fine a day to bide indoors; the women of Ricca's household had moved their looms and spinning wheels into a quiet corner of the courtyard near the granaries, where they could enjoy the late spring sunshine. Their small daughters played and quarreled around their feet.

Naeri had set up her loom so that she could work in the shade, with her back against the granary wall. Having thus distanced herself from the other wives, she watched them covertly through the weighted warps.

Outside the walls she could hear the creaking and groaning of ox-drawn supply wagons, the drumming of hooves and clatter of two-wheeled horse-carts. From all over the Westland, the hosts were gathering.

All day the smoke of their cookfires had hung like autumn haze over the fields, and at night the sky was stained with crimson. As word spread, smiths, peddlers, minstrels—all the wayfaring folk of the chalk—streamed in from the hill-camps and villages. It was as though an enormous horsefair had sprung up, out of season, at Ricca's gates.

Suais was absent this morning—sleeping late, said Barra, with a knowing smirk. What she knew, but did not say aloud, was that Suais had come in at dawn on dew-soaked feet.

Barra was the second of Ricca's wives, a tall slender blond young woman with blue eyes and delicate rose-flushed skin. She might have been beautiful, were it not for a thin beak of a nose that gave her an oddly predatory look.

The other, Clia, was darker, plumper, softer—by far the sweeter-tempered of the two, but lacking Barra's quick intelligence. When Suais was not there, Barra the Fair would queen it over the easy-going, empty-headed Clia, ordering her about and excluding her from the bower-gossip as though she were a servant. With Naeri's arrival at the hearthside, there was a subtle shifting of power; now, more often than not, Barra and Clia were allies, united in their scorn of the shy, inept, incommunicative new wife.

This morning, Clia was distraught over the loss of her best gold brooch. She had been going on about it since daybreak, her voice as tirelessly repetitious as the flick-flick of her shuttle.

"I cannot think what I could have done with it," she moaned for the twentieth time in an hour. "It was part of my bride-price, and I set it down on my chest only last night at bedtime."

"You know very well what happened," snapped Barra. "The clasp broke, and you dropped it somewhere."

"No, no," poor Clia protested. "Only last night I had it. I set it down on the top of my chest, as I told you."

"Well then," said Barra, in a voice clearly meant to end the discussion, "one of the bower-slaves has taken it; so you must tell Ricca, and he will discover the thief and punish her."

At this suggestion Clia dropped her shuttle and burst into tears. Naeri decided that the matter had gone on well past the limits of endurance; and besides, she felt sorry for Clia, who was a warm-hearted girl at bottom, and could not help her silliness.

She put her head around her loom and spoke for the first time that morning. "Clia," she said, "shall I see if I can find it for you?"

Two pair of eyebrows shot up. "You?" said Barra.

Naeri held out her hand. "Give me something else of yours," she said to Clia. "That gold earring will do very well."

"What do you want with it?" Barra demanded, when Clia, docile as always, reached up to unhook the ring.

"I mean to let like seek like," Naeri said. "Don't worry, Clia, you shall have your earring back. And maybe your brooch too, if you are lucky."

She cut off a piece of linen thread and fastened the earring to it, winding the extra length around her fingers. Closing her ears to the small noises of the courtyard, she watched the pendulum weave its patterns in the air.

"Is Clia's brooch in the women's bower?"

"No," responded the pendulum.

"In the camp, still?" Yes, was the reply.

"Did a slave take it?" No.

"A woman?" No.

Naeri wrinkled her brow for a moment, then light dawned.

"A child?" The pendulum circled moonwise.

Naeri glanced up at Clia, who was watching wide-eyed. "Besides your bower-slave, who was in your bed-place last night?"

There was a long pause, while Clia searched her always unreliable memory. Then her round pretty face lit up. "Barra's Pisca came in while I was undressing."

This brought a scowl and a quick protest from Barra. "My Pisca would not touch your brooch."

"She is not yet four," Naeri reminded her. "Small children love glittery things." She was thinking that the child was aptly named Pisca—"small mischievous one." She seemed to be everywhere at once, and had the instincts of a fera, or a jackdaw. Had Clia been cleverer she might have solved the mystery herself.

"Come here, Pisca," Barra said. The child appeared, dragging a tattered corn doll through the dirt. She regarded her mother with large, solemn, slightly tip-tilted eyes.

Severe though she might be with others, Barra was an indulgent parent. She picked the child up and set her in her lap. Pisca clutched the front of Barra's saffron-dyed gown in a grimy fist and peered inquiringly at her.

"Tell Clia you have not seen her best brooch."

Pisca smiled dazzlingly at Clia. "The big round gold one? With the bumpy bits?"

Clia nodded encouragement.

"I dropped it in the midden heap," Pisca said.

There was a silence. Naeri clapped a hand over her mouth to stiffle her laughter.

"I didn't mean to," Pisca added, with no sign whatever of contrition.

A deeper flush had risen in Barra's rose-petal cheeks. "Of course you did not, my lambkin," she said. Her voice was soothing; though, thought Naeri, no child ever looked less in need of comforting.

"Show me where," suggested Naeri.

Obligingly, Pisca led them to the big kitchen midden behind the feast-hall, reeking and fly-ridden in the midday heat.

"There," she announced, pointing vaguely toward the center. Clia's face crumpled, and fresh tears sprang forth.

"Stop crying," said Naeri irritably. "Pisca, where were you standing when you dropped the brooch?"

Pisca shrugged her small bony shoulders. "I forget."

"May the Black God take the child," Naeri muttered under her breath. She began gingerly to skirt the midden-pile, letting the pendulum lead her, and holding her nose against the ripe stench of rotting entrails.

"There," Naeri said, pointing, as the pendulum began to swing in a strong, unequivocal circle. "Go fetch a slave with a shovel. Someone has dumped a fresh load of offal on top of it."

A few minutes later, Clia had her brooch and her earring back, and was wreathed in smiles.

Barra's pale blue eyes narrowed. "Sorcery," she said, spitting the word out. She looked at Clia. "I told you, they are all witches, these Dark Folk."

"But," said Clia complacently, "I have my brooch back." She wiped it on the sleeve of her gown, leaving a long dark streak.

With her mouth set in a thin hard line, Barra turned and stalked off, pulling Pisca along at a trot. Clia smiled at Naeri, a trifle uncertainly, behind Barra's back, and looked as though she would have thanked her if she dared.

By evening the tale was all over the camp. In the days that followed, Naeri used her art to find a ring for the stablemaster's wife, a mislaid awl for the harnessmaker, a prized bronze knife for the armorer's son. Then the horsemaster sent his apprentice to say that a mare due to drop her foal had strayed and was lost somewhere in the oakwoods. If it pleased her, could the Lady Naeri find it? That puzzled her—until she thought of taking a sharp stick and, with the apprentice's help, drawing a map of Ricca's fields and woods in the courtyard dust. While the boy stared, she searched over the map with her pendulum. With an animal's sure instinct, the mare had given birth in a benign place where two forcelines spiraled and crossed. The foal and its dam were recovered, and the fame of Ricca's witch-wife spread.

There had been a time, long ago, when the witchfolk served the commonfolk of the downs as priests and teachers. No man, in those days, would think to build a house or plant a new field without first consulting an earthwitch. But that was before the horsemen came to harry the witches and drive them into the hills. Now children, born in houses built over black streams, came pale and sickly into the world, while their parents were plagued with fevers. Crops, planted in fields without harmony, refused to flourish.

Word spread across the downlands, among the steep hill-steadings and sheltered hamlets: "There is an earthwitch in Ricca's camp." Day after day the chalk farmers and herdsmen arrived on foot at the gates, begging Naeri's services.

"Lady, the barley in my new field grows sparse and small; will you use your art to seek out baleful currents?"

"Lady, it is in my mind to build a house for my daughter and her new husband; will you help us to choose the site?"

As her reputation spread beyond the camp, so did ill-will within the household. Barra, who could smell power as others smell snow upon the wind, was the first to speak.

"I saw you this morning," she said, "sneaking out of the gates without a by-your-leave. What would our husband say, seeing you wander off every day or so, with some village lout, to perform who knows what mischief?"

Naeri said, "He knows. Daui has explained to him."

Barra's eyes narrowed. She snapped off a thread as though she wished it were Daui's neck. "Does he know that your loom stands idle? That your tasks are never finished? Does he know that we must spin the wool and dye the cloth, and see that the meal is ground and the bread is baked without your assistance?"

"You managed before," said Naeri, reasonably enough.

Clia said, all in a breath, "My bower-slave's kinswoman says the witchwoman found a black stream under her hearth, and that is why her babe was born sickly, and so they moved their house, and now their babe is thriving."

"Be quiet, goose," said Barra. "What business is it of Ricca's wives, what happens to some chalk farmer's brat? Her place is here, at her loom, and so I mean to tell Ricca."

Suais glanced up. She was sitting on a deerskin in a patch of sunlight, eating honey from a comb. She said, "Why make such a bother about it, Barra? How long do you think Ricca will keep her—this thin sapless stick of a girl?" As always, she spoke as though Naeri were deaf, or feeble-minded. "Three of such creatures would not be enough to warm his bed." Her tongue flicked out and gathered a drop of honey from the corner of her mouth. "And look, what space is there in those narrow hips, to bear him sons?"

Naeri bent to her spinning and pretended not to hear. How shriveled their spirits are, she thought. Barra, who was blessed with hair like moonlight and skin like apple-bloom, had a soul as sharp and bitter as a milkweed stalk. And Suais—she was like a soft ripe fruit with a rotten core.

That night Ricca sent for her. He had thrown open the outer door of his bedchamber, which looked onto the rampart walk, to let the warm night breeze in. Still the smell of leather and horse sweat hung in the room, along with a faint aromatic odor of dream-herbs. She could see a thread of smoke curling up from the incense burner by the bed.

He was wearing a light woolen tunic edged with beadwork— not the coarse cloth woven in the camp, but fine eastern stuff brought in by merchants. His heavy brows gave him a scowling look even when, as now, he was in a good humor.

"You have been making use of your witch-gifts," he said.

"When I am asked. I do no harm."

Ricca grunted. "No—no harm, if it is true, as Daui says, that you help the cattle to thrive and the crops to grow. That means more meat on my table, more grain in my corncribs."

"Why have you sent for me, then? Did Barra complain to you?"

His eyebrows drew together. "Does Barra ever cease to complain? But if you want to know, yes—she has been to tell me that a witch in the house sours the milk and spoils the cheese-making, that the spring will dry up and the ducks will lay no more eggs. So—I will say to you what I said to Barra—what happens on the women's side is between you and them. I want no part of it."

He leaned forward, his ice-blue eyes intent upon her face. She flinched a little under that sudden hard scrutiny.

"Listen, and I will tell you why I sent for you. Daui says that an earthwitch has knowledge of . . . what? The lines of power within the earth?"

She nodded. "And the sculpturing of the land, and the patterning of stone. It is called geomancy."

He grunted. "So—you see where I am leading. Tomorrow I meet with Magha and the elders, and with my war-lords, to choose the temple-site."

"Among my people," she told him, "that is the geomancer's task."

"So then. That is what Daui said, also." He was treating her, she realized, with a certain wary respect, like a falconer come into possession of some half-trained, unpredictable hawk. "Tomorrow you will sit with us in Council." He cleared his throat. "You understand. This is a matter for the Great Chief and his Council to decide. But Daui tells me that the women of the Dark Folk are used to having a voice in Council."

He paused to pour himself mead, then held up the jar with a questioning look. Surprised, she nodded, and he filled a beaker for her. "Tomorrow," he said. "Tonight there is no need for you to talk." And he reached out a gold-braceleted arm and drew her down to the bed.

The servants whispered behind their hands when next morning she followed Daui into the feast-hall. This was an unthought-of circumstance—that a woman, who was only a Fourth Wife and tainted with dark blood besides, should sit with the lords and elders in the Council-Circle.

The war-lords gave her some dark looks as she entered, but Ricca only grinned, as if this were some sly joke of his, and waved her to a bench. Seghed Red-Ax moved over to make room for her. Her stomach was clenched like a fist, and her throat felt gritty.

Ricca said, "Don't look so scared, woman, you are not here to be flogged; so far you have given me no cause for that."

Several of the men chuckled, and heads swiveled in her direction.

"The minstrel has said that I should seek the help of the Dark Folk in my temple-building. There are few of your race I can trust not to put a knife in my ribs when my attention wanders. You, maybe. Anyway, I have trusted you in bed and so far have not suffered for it."

There was more laughter. She opened her mouth to reply, but Ricca scowled her into silence.

The Council turned back to the matter in hand. Picking up the loose end of the discussion, the war-lord Vingi said, "The temple should be built on that barrow-hill just to the east, in sight of the camp. In the morning we would look out over the ramparts and see the sun rising above the stones, and so each day would begin with the Sun-God's blessing."

Several others grunted their agreement. "This plan has merit," Magha said.

"The ground there is not level enough for building," Daui pointed out. "The hilltop slopes quite steeply to the north.

Remember the size of this temple, Ricca. This is no barrow-cairn you are building, but a place for giants."

"Just so," said Ricca. "And what do you suggest, minstrel?"

"Let the Fourth Wife speak," Daui said.

Naeri coughed, out of nervousness, then said, "Not far to the south, on the Great Down, there is a temple-ground. It is very old, and was in use as a sun-temple when the flint-folk ruled these lands. There are some stones already there, from an unfinished circle, and one tall stone over which the midsummer sun rises."

Ricca said, "We cannot see this place from my rampart walk. How then would men know that it was Ricca's temple?"

Naeri replied, "It lies in the center of all the lands you hold in ax-truce. Since time's beginning men have called it the hub of the wheel, the Westland's heart." She finished simply, "It is a place of power."

Ricca pushed back his bench. "You will show me this place."

Her eyebrows lifted. "What, today?"

"Of course today. The levies have been raised, the tribes are waiting. We must decide, so work can begin. Take me to this place of power." And so saying, he called for his cart and ponies.

Though Ricca handled the team as one born to it, he seemed to take little thought for his own neck. Naeri clunged to the sides of the cart and mouthed a prayer to the Mother as they rattled and swayed along the ridge track, with the sun beating down on their shoulders. Rolling away below them were yellow barley fields, and steep pastures splashed with vetch and speedwell; in the low distance was the darker blue of wooded valleys.

The broken circle lay shadowless in the noonday sun. Scowling with concentration, Ricca paced off the circumference of the bank and ditch, peered down the length of the avenue, over the Sun-Stone.

"This processional way—where does it finish?"

"At the river.

Ricca tugged at his beard, thinking. "And the midsummer sun?"

"It rises straight over the Sun-Stone."

He turned to her. "These forcelines—where are they?"

The question made her smile. "They are everywhere. They are under the earth and above it, radiating outward, crossing and recrossing, spiraling, coiling like serpents around the stones."

Furrows appeared in the smooth brown expanse of his brow. "But you cannot see them?"

"No more than I can see the wind. But I can feel them, as I feel a strong wind blowing. There is power in the stones, also—the one intensifies the other." She saw that he did not understand. "Put your hand against that stone—there, behind you."

He shrugged, and did as she asked.

"Do you feel anything?"

"I can feel the sun's heat on the stone."

She shook her head. "It is more than that. You would know if you felt it."

But he had lost interest. He looked bored, restless—a great dangerous boy grown impatient with childish games. He said, "I know if I feel a spear in my ribs—an ax splitting my skull. That is the kind of power a warrior understands—not this woman's magic. Nonetheless," he said, "this is a good place. You spoke the truth. It stands at the very middle of my lands, and there is room here for many huge stones. Next year at midsummer dawn my warriors and all the chiefs of the Westland tribes will march up from the river and along this avenue in a great ceremonial procession. All men will bear witness then to how tall Lord Ricca stands in the Sun-God's eye, how far his shadow stretches."

"Come," he said. "We will go back now, and tell them the choice is made."

~17~

Dragon-Fire

Clia's youngest, a babe of nine months, had fallen ill—first running a high fever, then, when the fever had broken, lying pale and listless in its mother's arms and refusing to rally. Magha came in and tried various small wizardries, to no avail. A healing-woman was sent for, but her potions and nostrums accomplished nothing.

"This is witch's work," said Barra; and Clia, beside herself with grief and worry, believed her. "Everyone knows that a witch in the house spreads noxious emanations, so that the very air is unwholesome to breathe. It is no wonder your babe is pining."

Suais yawned, and stared at Naeri with her hard, copper-colored eyes. "Look at how her face has filled out, this witch-woman, how much more color she has than when she first came here. Clearly, she is using sorcery to drain the strength out of your babe. She is feeding on its very life-blood. We have such women in our country."

"And what do you do with them?" asked Barra, curious.

"We put them in a wicker cage and burn them. That lets out the life-force, and maybe it will find its way back to the child."

Naeri shivered, and went on teasing the wool in her lap. But that night in the women's bower, when they thought she was asleep, she heard them talking again.

"What would Ricca say?" That was Clia's voice, high-pitched and querulous as a frightened child's.

Suais replied, "How should he know? We will seize her in her sleep, and take her out into the fields. It will be just a little fire, and nobody will notice it. Afterward, we will say that she ran away when the gate was left open, and went back to the witchfolk."

Naeri fumbled in the darkness for her knife, and lay with her hand upon it. She did not sleep the rest of the night; but when dawn came, Barra and Suais still lay snoring softly, while Clia cuddled her whimpering babe.

All that day Naeri dozed over her work, and through the night kept vigil; on the third night she decided it had been Suais's notion of a joke, and fell fitfully asleep.

And so she was still weary, and not on her guard as she should have been, when she left the camp next evening to look for watercress. She remembered that she had seen some growing in a hillside spring. One of her small cousins had fallen ill with a blood-weakness and had been cured with calf's liver and cress. It was worth trying, she thought—if only Clia could be convinced she meant no harm.

Tonight the fields around the camp were deserted. At dawn the tents had been struck, the fires stamped out; the ox-wagons and pony carts had rumbled westward behind the horse-lords, followed in their turn by packhorses and beef cattle; and then a great host of men, women and some children traveling on foot. Soon now the stone-harvest would begin; but first they would go to the oak forests to cut great logs for sledges and rollers. Isla the master-carpenter; Gwi, who in his travels had picked up some knowledge of stone masonry; and Daui, who as a youth had studied the builder's art as eagerly as he had studied the patterns of the stars—these three had planned what must be done. The Council of war-lords and elders had listened, and seen the sense of it, and Ricca had given the orders.

Gwi and Daui had gone to the oak forests with the others. Till they returned she was without friends in the camp, and must look out for herself. Her hand brushed thoughtfully against the pommel of her knife.

Her shadow stretched out long and thin beside her; the chalk hills were washed in the soft rich evening light. Her footsteps on the warm turf stirred up scents of thyme and agrimony, and brown clouds of butterflies.

At the crest of the hill above the spring was an old, still-unbroken stone circle. She knew that there was a strong above-ground forceline running through it, and lately she had discovered another, underground current that curled around it like the tail of a snake. At this time of the waxing moon, the power in the stones was strong. Even at this distance she could feel it in her nerve-ends as a low monotonous humming.

She knelt by the spring and began to gather watercress into a wicker basket. As she worked, the sun dropped behind a ridge, and the warmth went quickly out of the air.

The tightly woven turf muffled sound like a carpet. The women were nearly upon her when, finally, her ears picked up the faint noise of a footfall, the swish of a linen kirtle hem through the grass. She dropped the basket and whirled to face them, with her hand on her knife.

"Witch's herbs," said Barra, not looking to see what was in the basket. "See, as if she has not done enough, she is gathering noxious plants to poison Clia's child."

Suais did not answer. She was out of breath from the climb, her face flushed and her bosom heaving under her saffron-colored robe.

They had brought with them four of the bower-women, who pushed and jostled one another in their eagerness to see what would happen next.

Barra looked at Suais. The First Wife nodded, and at that signal they all began to move in upon Naeri like a pack of she-wolves. Naeri stood her ground, taut-muscled, half-crouched, feeling the balanced weight of her knife-hilt in her hand. Meanwhile a small cool voice in the back of her head was saying, "Draw blood if you must, but if you kill them, there is nowhere you can run that Ricca will not hunt you down like a hare."

She sidestepped, showing them the knife, playing for time. As she did so, she felt a kind of glow within her flesh, a tingling warmth, as though she had stepped suddenly into a shaft of sunlight or a warm sea current.

She began to back slowly up the hillside, letting the strong tidal flow of the forceline draw her into the whirlpool currents of power that eddied about the stones.

The women followed her. She saw a thin gleam of bronze half-concealed in Suais's skirt. Now she could feel a more intense warmth, an almost painful prickling of the nerves, in her nape and down the length of her spine.

As her shoulder blades touched the nearest rock face, there was a faint crackling sound; a flicker of blue witchlight darted around the circle, from stone to stone. With her back against the rock and her right arm bent sharply behind her, palm flat against the warm rough surface, she raised her left arm and held it straight out before her, fingers spread. She felt the sudden terrible surge of earth-power, rock-magic, jarring her hand, wrist, shoulder; coursing like flame through nerves and arteries, arcing, dancing, leaping—showering fountains of sparks from her fingertips into the blue-gray air of evening.

The bower-women huddled in the grass, shrieking, as though they had been flung there; one of them pulled her skirt over her head. Barra and Suais stood open-mouthed and staring. Too shocked to make a sound, they clutched one another in superstitious terror. Suais's dagger dropped with a small thud at her feet.

Naeri slumped back against the stone, leaning her weight upon it. The power of the circle was spent now, discharged through bone and blood and flesh. Nhiall's words came back to her, from a summer night that seemed, now, half a lifetime distant: "You are the copper blade through which the lightning passes. The power of earth and the power of stone flows through you, and does not change you."

She was not changed or harmed; yet was so weak and drained that she could hardly stand. If they wished, they could kill her as easily as one snaps a sparrow's bones.

For a long time no one moved. Then Suais shook herself, like a sleeper waking. She snarled something in her southern birth-tongue, a curse perhaps, and turning in a flurry of skirts, stalked off down the hillside. The bower-women got up awkwardly, without once taking their eyes off Naeri. The one who had put her skirt over her head went on wailing in a high-pitched hysterical fashion until Barra elbowed her sharply in the ribs and bade her be silent. They trailed down the slope after Suais, now and again glancing nervously over their shoulders.

Naeri started to laugh, as much from sheer relief as anything else; her laughter died in her throat when she turned to look at the stone, and saw that all down its near face the lichen was charred black. A patch of it crumbled away to ash at her touch. Suddenly she felt chilled to the bone, and her teeth were chattering. She gathered up the scattered watercress and put it into the basket; then, hugging herself against the cold and swaying a little with dizziness, she started back to camp.

On the darkening ridge behind her, the standing stones loomed black against the sky: silently renewing their ancient power from some hidden place at the world's roots.

Naeri stopped by the cistern in the outer court and drenched her head in cold water. Then, dressed as she was in deerskin tunic and jerkin, and still carrying the basket of watercress, she put on as bold a face as she could and marched into the feast-hall. She drew a deep breath, seeing that neither Barra nor Suais were in the women's circle. She sat down; and when Ricca glanced over his beaker-rim and raised his brows at her rough garb, she stared defiantly at him.

Much later, as he left the table, he beckoned her to follow him. On this night, for the first time, she went willingly.

⤜ 18 ⤛

Stone-Harvest

By morning the story had spread like brushfire through the camp. When Naeri came down to the feast-hall in search of breakfast, the hearth-slaves stared at her with eyes as big and round as shield-bosses, and gave her as wide a berth as they dared.

Suais and Barra were nowhere in sight; only Clia was there, looking sad and tired as she nursed her baby by the fire. Catching sight of Naeri, she clutched the child against her breast to shield it from witchery. Then, as Naeri timidly held out her peace offering of limp stems and shriveled leaves, Clia's good nature overcame her fear. She had, after all, only the word of Suais and Barra that the new Fourth Wife was a sorceress, that she meant to burn them all in their beds with witchfire. Naeri had always been kind enough to her. And so, thinking these things through in her slow plodding way, and seeing in Naeri's hand that ridiculous bouquet of dead watercress, she began, in spite of everything, to laugh.

"Naeri, Naeri, how little you know—the child cannot eat those, she will choke on them, or spit them out." But she agreed to try the calf's liver, mashed to a soft pulp and mixed with gruel. By the time the full moon rose, the baby seemed to rally a little; or maybe after all it had been a lingering fever that, given time, had burned itself out.

On the first day of the full moon Daui and Gwi rode back into camp. Hearing that they had returned, Naeri slipped out of the

126

gates and down to the women's bathing-place: a hazel-choked hollow where a dammed-up stream made a warm shallow pool. She washed her hair, and worked the tangles out of it with a little bone comb she had bought from a peddler. Then she put on a clean tunic and her best kirtle, fastened her string of blue beads at her throat, and, feeling unaccountably light-hearted, as though it were a festival-night, she started back to camp.

She found Daui sitting on a bench outside the hearth-hall, tuning his string-box in the warm air of evening. He raised a hand in greeting as Naeri approached.

"Where is Gwi?" she asked, trying to sound off-handed, while she swallowed the lump of disappointment in her throat. "They said you had ridden back together."

"So we did." Daui looked thoughtfully at her. "He won't be long—he's in the smithy." He moved over to make room for her, and she sat down to wait. Her heart was thumping so loudly that she felt sure Daui must hear it.

Presently Gwi appeared. His face lit up when he saw Naeri, and crossing the courtyard his steps quickened. His hands lifted as though to reach out to her, and then dropped to his sides. He stood gazing down at her with an air of uncertainty. It was as though someone had drawn a line in the courtyard dust that he dared not cross.

"Naeri," he said, and added with gentle irony, "my lady."

She made a face, and laughed, and the moment's awkwardness vanished.

"What is there to eat tonight?" asked Gwi, with a nod toward the feast-hall door. "I've had nothing since morning."

"Lamb," said Naeri, who earlier had been in to look. "Roast pig. Honey-cakes. Blood-pudding. A brace of ducks."

"Ricca does himself proud," remarked Gwi. "This summer, every night is a feast-night."

"This whole year the land has been bountiful," Daui observed. "Magha says it is a gift of the Sun-God. Shall we go and see if this woman speaks truth about the dinner?"

"It's sweltering hot in there," said Naeri. "The fires have been going all day. Tell them to bring a platter out to us, and a jar of beer."

Gwi smiled to himself and said nothing. Perhaps he was remembering the scared starved waif he had sheltered by his smithy fire not so many seasons ago.

He found a bench and sat down across from her. She tried to

keep her eyes from his face, where they kept straying unbidden. She ached to sit close to him, to touch him; to rest her face in the hollow of his shoulder as she used to do when she was grieved or frightened. She stared at the ground, making lines in the dust with the edge of her sandal.

"When must you go back?" she asked, not looking up for fear that Gwi would see her heart in her eyes.

"Not until I am sent for. Until the logs are cut and the sledges built and the stones chosen, there is nothing for me to do. As soon as we saw the size and weight of those stones," he added, "we knew it would be a tedious business. To begin with, we don't have enough rope. Now we have sent men out to all the camps and steadings for a three-days' journey around, to buy up hides and borrow women to plait them."

"I am a good ropemaker," Naeri said rather wistfully. "My mother taught me. There is nothing I cannot make into rope at a pinch."

"If it's work you want, you'll soon enough have your chance," Daui said. "Tomorrow, if this weather holds."

She looked round at him, surprised.

"Did I not say? That is why I came back with Gwi, to fetch you. I need your earth-magic to choose the stones. Can you be ready at sunup?"

She nodded. The prospect of the journey excited her, even though it was Daui and not Gwi who would be her companion.

A hearth-slave came with a laden platter and barley-beer. When they had eaten, Daui played a new song for them, an eastern tune he had learned from a wayfaring harper. And so they sat, until the blue summer twilight deepened into night, and the stars came out.

They traveled by pony cart on this second journey westward, taking the longer, easier road across the chalk. The perfect midsummer weather showed no signs of breaking. A warm wind, smelling faintly of salt, soughed through the gorse and the short dry grass, bending the bright blue heads of the sheepsbit on their slender stalks. Among the fallen stones and the humped shapes of ancient barrows, wild roses were in bloom.

As they jounced over the summer-hard track Naeri smiled to herself, thinking what hard words Barra would have for a Younger Wife who cast off her kirtle and her necklace of rank to dress like a half-grown boy, in bare legs and sleeveless tunic with a dagger on her belt. But neither Barra nor Suais had had any words at all for Naeri since that evening on the hillside. When she approached they turned their backs on her and flounced away. That first night, coming back from Ricca's chamber, she had discovered her bed-place torn up and scattered, her few belongings dumped outside the bower-door. And so she had gathered them up, with scant regret, and reclaimed the small room over the courtyard that had been hers as Winter Queen.

Daui reined in; they had come to the lip of that wild valley where juniper scrub and yellow grasses straggled over the sacred stones. It looked, now, like the encampment of a war-host. Everywhere—on the valley floor and scattered across the slopes— were tents, cattle, ponies, carts, children, cook-fires, and huge chalk-dug pits where whole cattle roasted. The hushed quiet, the sanctity of the place, was broken, perhaps forever. Yet the sarsen stones had lost none of their terrible power. Even at this distance she could feel the flickering, prickling storm-tension burning its way along her nerves.

There was another presence in this place—unseen, yet perceptible to Naeri as the faint odor of sunwarmed thyme. She knew that Cathra's hunters—outcasts now in their own country—had retreated to the hills; but something of their spirit and their magic lingered. She could almost believe she saw them watching, waiting, in the hazel thickets on the valley's rim.

Daui watered the ponies at a spring, and tethered them; and they started down the juniper-covered slope.

The work was well begun. Woodcutting crews had dragged massive oak timbers out of the nearby forest, and the carpenters had half-finished the first of the transport sleds. Other logs, to be used as rollers—greater than a man's girth and more than twice a tall man's height—were stacked nearby. Meanwhile women, old men, youths—anyone who lacked strength for wood-cutting and log-hauling—sat plaiting cowhide in the shade of tents and hawthorn bushes. The sweet smell of cut wood was overlaid, where they worked, with the stench of fresh-stripped skins.

The hide tents of the warriors, each with its cluster of smaller shelters for body-slaves and womenfolk, were scattered across the level floor of the basin. The carpenters and masons, wainrights and harnessmakers, teamsters and beast-tenders, foreseeing a long sojourn, had built sturdy shelters or had brought their own tents with them. Those without rank or power, who were neither warriors nor craftsmen—the flint folk and half-folk, the shepherds and poor chalk farmers, slaves and bondservants—slept rough, wherever they could, under the trees or the stars, with their cloaks thrown over them and their sandals for pillows.

"Let us make a beginning," Daui said. Opening his pack he took out his charcoal sticks and measuring cord, and unrolled his sheepskins.

In places the huge stones were so thickly strewn that a child could leap from one to another. Approaching one such place, Naeri caught her breath and staggered, as the raw power of the rocks leaped out at her. She took a quick step back and felt Daui's hands under her elbows, steadying her.

After a time she learned to move and work within the field of power, as one learns to swim in a strong current, or breast the wind on the high chalk. Some of the stones drew her to them with an overpowering attraction; others, when she touched them, thrust her violently away, so that more than once she was knocked off-balance and nearly fell.

She used her bare hands to test the strength of the force within each stone, and her pendulum to determine the pattern and direction of the flow. Once her choice had been made, Daui measured the stone and marked the cutting lines with charcoal.

She sensed a kind of feverishness beneath the deft precision of Daui's movements, as he measured, checked, remeasured. He worked methodically and without haste: it was not in his nature to be slipshod or impetuous. Yet she felt a vague anxiousness, a tension in him, as though he had one eye always on the sun.

As soon as the first stone was chosen and measured, a crew of masons moved in with mauls and wedges to begin the work of splitting and rough-shaping. The first stone, as chance would have it, had a natural crack running down the middle, which speeded up the work. She watched the men pecking at the crack with their stone hammers and chisels, opening it up so that they could drive in wooden wedges. Then, Daui explained, they would soak the wedges in water so that they swelled and forced the crack still wider, until in the end the huge slab split in two.

Where there was no break in the stone's face, they would make fires of fat-soaked twigs along the charcoal-line in order to heat the stone, then cool it quickly with cold water. If they were lucky, a crack would start. Then, working in unison with stone mauls and wedges, the masons would begin the laborious task of breaking apart the rock.

Soon the first sledge was ready; the first sarsen pillar, still gray-green with lichen on its outer side, was levered up with poles and packed underneath with timbers, so the men could slowly and cautiously raise and as slowly lower it into place. As they were lashing down the stone—an immense unwieldy slab nearly three times a man's height—one of the clan-chiefs turned to Daui and said, "That is a task for giants, not little men—they will never move it."

"Little men have moved such stones before," Daui said. "My ancestors moved stones like this, and raised them to the sky, when they built the Moon-Temple."

"But they were witchfolk," the man said. "Surely, they called upon their powers of magic."

"I know no magic," Daui said, "to make those stones lighter. Then, as now, it was done by craft and skill and careful planning, and many strong arms to haul on the ropes."

Naeri had a tent to herself, with furs and rugs for her bed-place, and two women to tend and cook for her. She was weary at day's end, but restless with it, and found it hard to fall asleep. She took to walking out over the downs in the long summer twilights. Daui forbade her to go alone—not only for appearance's sake, but for fear she might meet some horseman who failed to recognize her as Ricca's wife. She chose for her companion young Coran, the master-carpenter's son, a sturdy copper-haired lad of twelve, about to begin his warrior's training. He was in awe of her, and would not spoil the evening's quiet with pointless chatter.

She had marked his skill with a bow and spear when the boys of the camp were at target-practice. His mind was as keen as his aim, and she enjoyed his company. At first, he was too afraid to speak at all. Clearly, the tales of Ricca's witch-wife had reached his ears. She showed him how to use a sling, which was a hunter's weapon, not a horseman's; and after they had killed a few partridges and hares together, he lost his terror of her. In return, he taught her to ride his shaggy-haired good-natured pony.

As they roamed with slings and throw-spears through the shadowy combes and up the shoulders of the downs where the last light still clung, Naeri told the boy of her childhood—of deer-stalking in the wild hills and waterfowling in the river marshes. She recounted fireside tales of wolf hunts, boar hunts, bear killings, as vividly painted in her mind's eye as if she had seen them for herself.

Sometimes, not often, he remembered her rank, and called her "my lady." For the most part she was simply Naeri to him—a skilled hunter and warrior-in-training like himself.

Before the full moon rose again, her work in the stone-fields was finished. All the stones were chosen, measured, marked for splitting and rough-shaping. The longest and hardest part of the labor remained, for the carpenters and masons, the ropemakers and drawers of sledges. Her task now, and Daui's, was the laying out of the temple-ground.

She went to make her good-byes to Coran, and to his gentle-eyed pony. She had become fond of them both and would miss them. Coran looked crestfallen when he knew that she was leaving.

"I wish we could go hunting again," he said.

"We will," she assured him. "Do you think it will be over in a week, or a summer, this stone-gathering? We will see each other again. But," she reminded him, "soon you will be a man grown and a warrior. You will have to tell me your name when we meet again, for you will have grown so tall I may not know you."

He grinned. "And it may be I will be chosen by Lord Ricca for his war-band . . ." His fancy caught fire then, and he went on, "and I will rise to serve in his War-Council; and you will sit in feast-hall with us . . ."

"And I will ask who this tall warrior is, that sits on my Lord Ricca's right hand, and you will say, 'Naeri, have you so soon forgotten young Coran, the master-carpenter's son?' and I will throw up my hands in astonishment." And they broke off the game in laughter.

As she was turning to go, a thought came to Naeri. "Coran," she said, "it is in my mind that you can help me, if you will."

"Gladly . . . my lady."

"When you are in the youth's house, learning to be a warrior, do you see boys from other camps?"

Looking puzzled, not seeing where the question led, he nodded. "Often. They are sent to train with us, under Ricca's war-band."

"So then. Since I am a woman and cannot enter the youth's house, will you be my ears, Coran? Will you ask if in any of the clan-camps there is a red-haired girl-slave—a little girl of maybe fourteen, who looks younger—with a mop of curls, and leaf-green eyes?"

"If you like. But if the answer is yes, what then? I cannot enter the bower or speak to any woman while I am in the youth's house."

"You will send a message to me. Look, I will show you." She bent down and snapped off a piece of bracken frond; then pulled a bit of red-dyed thread from the stitching on her jerkin. She wrapped the thread around the leaf and gave it to him. "If you hear tell of her, send this to me with one of the men-slaves. That will be half the message. I will send someone—a man—to seek you out in the youth's house and hear from your own lips the rest of the message—where she is, at whose hearth she sleeps. Will you do this, Coran?"

His eyes were wide and owl-solemn as he replied, "On my honor, lady." She knew that he was delighted, in his heart, to share this secret with her. She touched her forehead to his hands, in the old gesture of farewell between friends. "Till we hunt again," she said.

～ 19 ～

Earth-Magic

The outer ditch of the blue-stone temple, built by men of forgotten times, followed a huge loop of earth-current, one end of which wound off in a double serpent-coil around the Sun-Stone. Within the circle was a labyrinthine pattern of loops and spirals and radiating lines of force.

Patiently, painstakingly, she mapped the maze; charting it with charcoal ink on a roll of sheepskin. Crouched beside her, Daui traced with a forefinger the intricate web of lines, and taking the stick from her, made heavy black marks to show where the stones would be placed.

As they worked together, Naeri began to recognize the enormous complexity of the task they had undertaken. Much of what they did still lay outside her narrow understanding. In spite of all that Nhiall had taught her of the mind's art, her true powers of magic were intuitive, instinctive; she understood with the flesh, the blood and nerves. She was an instrument in Daui's hands, working by half-comprehended formulae to a vast purpose, the shape of which she had yet to grasp. Like the chisel in the mason's hand, she did as she was directed, seeing the parts but not the whole.

She knew that the spiraling flow of magic in the stones waxed and waned and sometimes changed direction with the moon's phases, and that the lines of force within the earth could wander or disappear. All these things must be taken into account, made rational and predictable, charted into the plan.

When the pattern was completed, each of the stones in the great outer circle, each of the stones within that circle, would be driven like a dagger blade, like an arrow shaft, into a loop of current, and between the nodes of the intersecting currents; would become rivet-rocks to fix in their place the erratic energies of the earth. Thus, with stones within circles within greater circles, would this vortex of wild power be pent-up, controlled, like a raging river between high banks—like a dragon harnessed.

The mighty archways and doorways of stone would frame the rising and setting of the sun at the year's turnings. The great circle of stones would mark the moon's phases, and the nineteen-year cycle of its sky-journey. So would the Pattern be completed, the unbroken wheel of power linking earth with stone, stone with sky, and sky again with earth.

But it was no simple task. The forcelines twisted and turned, crossed and recrossed, merged into one another and reappeared. Naeri's head ached, her stomach churned. Each time, after she rested, the giddiness and sickness returned more quickly than before. She left off in exhaustion each day at sunset; slept in a shelter of skins and thorn branches on a bed of bracken—and rose at dawn to begin the work again.

Daui sighed, and sat back on his heels. "It is done," he said. He sounded as bone-weary as she. "When the stones are in place, there will be power here that will bring the horsemen to their knees and make the witchfolk kings and queens again in this land."

In her mind's eye Naeri saw what might, should, come of this: the gossamer web of forcelines shimmering across the landscape, linking dolmen and cairn and barrow and standing stone, transfixed and focused and amplified by them; bringing order, pattern, a vast enduring harmony to the land.

But then she shivered in the warmth of the summer afternoon, for she had seen what else might come. She was remembering the dragon-fire that had leaped under her hands out of the small stones in a forgotten place. She thought how it would be to feel in her blood and bones the power that was harnessed in this place, the power more terrible than the sea's strength, the rage of the storm,

∽ 20 ∽

Omen-Fires

All that summer the Sun-God smiled on the people of the chalk. The crops flourished, the cattle grew heavy and sleek. In the high pastures the strong young foals ran after their mothers on their gangling legs, while the boys who tended the sheep dozed with their flocks on the sun-drenched slopes, among the gorse and harebells.

All summer the great stones lumbered on their creaking sledges down the chalk slopes to the ford of the river west of the Moon-Temple, then onto the trackway that crossed the tree-choked vale at its narrowest place.

Day after day the long lines of workers strained and sweated at the ropes, cursing as they dragged the sledges dogleg by dogleg up the steep southern scarp of the vale; never seeing the bright drifts of summer flowers on the chalk, or the clouds of small blue butterflies that were the same rich color as the sky; seeing only the knotted, sunburned, sweat-glazed muscles of the men who were next in line.

Five men died on that climb, one glaring summer's noon, when a rope snapped and the sledge slipped back on its rollers, crushing them as they bent to lift and move the hindmost log.

Once across the vale, on the ridgeway, it was easier going; on the level track teams of oxen could be used to take up some of the cumbersome, dragging weight.

Harvest-time came, and the work slowed, as the farmers went

back to their own fields for the barley-reaping and the harvest-rites. Then it was hazel-month, with warm yellow days, mist rising over the chalkhills, and a bite in the air at sunset. The lowland forests turned gold and bronze and copper-hued, but still the warm, dry weather held and the stone-harvest went on. Only the men remained in the stone-fields now. With berries and nuts to gather, grain to be winnowed, flax to be retted, warm cloaks to be stitched against the coming of winter, the women were needed in their own house-places.

Naeri turned to these tasks with listless resignation. For the other women, gossiping by the hearth to the rhythm of spindle and shuttle, the days went quickly enough; but Naeri had no part in that sisterhood of shared work, small bickerings and easy chatter. She did as she was bidden, as custom and duty demanded, but few in the household dared to offer her as much as a kind word or a smile. She saw a wary distrust in their eyes as she approached: the fear of the alien one, whose thoughts cannot be guessed at, whose every act is therefore suspect. Clia alone might have been her friend; but Clia feared Barra, and feared Suais more.

In-gathering came, at winter's edge, and then the Feast of the New Year. Old Magha would need no magic this year to see the shapes of ill-omen that flickered among the rowan-flames.

The stacks of feast-goods were no less high, no less glittering, though perhaps there was more copper and stone and jet this year, less bronze and gold. No one left the feast-tables hungry, or sober either. There was plenty for all—though a sharp eye might have discerned, for the first time, a less than lavish hand in the replenishing of the mead jugs and the great wooden meat platters.

The autumn had continued mild and unusually dry. This meant that work could go on until the time of in-gathering and the autumn slaughter. It meant, as well, that the roads from the north remained open. Travelers from the forests and moorlands, dealers in wolf and bearskins, jet and western river-gold arrived at Ricca's gates. They brought word that one of the horse-tribes of the hills, not bound by Ricca's ax-truce, had swooped down into Rudra's lands to reive his horses. They had chosen their time well. With the better part of his war-band away in the southwest, along with his bondsmen and herdsmen, Rudra's pastures offered easy pickings.

The news ran like grassfire around the New Year's fair, where the bondswomen heard it; and brought it back to the women's circle.

Rudra, counting up his spears and smelling how the wind blew, sent a messenger pounding over the high chalk to the stone-fields to summon back his war-band.

That was the first small chink, the weak place in the bank that would widen, bit by bit, until the whole gave way. The chiefs of the brother-tribes, and Ricca's own clan-chiefs, began carefully, each in his own head, to reckon what spears he had left to defend his own herds and his own ramparts. Black Uigh was the first to speak out.

He rose in feast-hall, his usually slow and sullen tongue made fluent with mead. "Never in memory," he said, "has the Sky-Lord given us such a summer. Yet when our farmers should have been in their fields reaping the God's bounty, they have been harvesting rocks for Lord Ricca, and leaving their proper work to lads and house-slaves. Who can say what vast stores of grain we might have put in our cribs, if the men had been there to reap the harvest? Foals have died—mares and stallions, too—for lack of tending; with raw boys to watch them, sheep have tumbled over chalk cliffs and the wolves have eaten them. Maybe the tribes of the rich south country can afford such losses, but in my lands the winter is long and harsh, and I can stand to waste nothing."

Without any particular hurry, Ricca got to his feet. The firelight turned his yellow beard to russet, struck sparks from his torque and golden arm-rings. He set his mead cup thoughtfully on the table, and his gaze met Black Uigh's. He wore that scowling, fierce-visaged eagle-look that had power to silence bolder tongues than even Uigh's. But when at length he spoke, his voice had none of its usual bluster; it was grave and measured—the voice of a conciliator.

"Gently, my cousin," he said. "As you are oath-bound to serve me, so also am I oath-bound to you. While you live under my ax-pledge your corncribs will not go empty, nor will your byres nor the bellies of your children. No kinsman and no war-companion of Ricca's will suffer in his service. If your grain runs short, why then, ask, and I will give you more. If your foal falls over a cliff, I will give you two more to take its place."

"So then," said Uigh with sour irony, "is there no bottom to Ricca's generosity? Or to his treasure-chests either?"

"Magha," Ricca called out, abruptly turning away as though he saw no more point in this discussion. "It is time, old man." As the sorcerer tottered forward, Ricca said, "Throw the rowan branches on the flame, and tell us whether this year bodes well or ill for us."

When the flames had burned down to a gray frill of ash, Magha looked up, and muttering so that in spite of the hush they had to strain to hear, he said, "The flame bodes well. The tall stones will stand at the center of the land, and the land will prosper. All men will sing great Ricca's praises."

Naeri wondered what else he might have seen in the leaping of the rowan-flame: what shapes that, like the good servant he was, he thought it was wiser not to reveal.

Emar, daughter to one of Ricca's war-lords, was Winter Queen this year: a fair, full-fleshed, pink-cheeked enchantress. Naeri had seen Ricca's gaze following her as she was led, in her white linen, into the feast-hall, and brought before Magha to receive the corn-babe. When they brought her to sit in the war-circle at Ricca's side her large blue eyes lifted with innocent boldness to return the Great Chief's stare.

They danced that New Year in beneath clear skies; though the bare fields glittered with frost in the starlight, and the air had a raw bite to it, promising early snow.

Naeri went with the other household women, wearing her amber ornaments and a new wool kirtle woven with red and violet stripes. She had no wish to dance, but to stand apart and alone would cause comment—and perhaps Ricca might notice and be angry. She wondered what man would claim her as a partner and lead her from the dance-ground; and she wondered, when the time came for bedding, by what ruse she might elude him.

The drums throbbed and the pipes shrilled; the flames leaped up as yellow as autumn beech leaves. Naeri stamped and whirled with the rest as the two great circles spun about the fire, one turning with the moon and one against it. The heads of horse and stag, wolf and bear threw long fantastic shadows across the ground.

The black bull leaped past her, but he had no eyes for her tonight; it was the little pink-cheeked Winter Queen that he would choose for his one-night bride.

Now the circles were starting to break up, the couple-dance beginning. Naeri danced alone at the rim of the firelight, thinking she could escape soon and would not have to be chosen. Just then a man in a badger mask caught her two hands and whirled her away, beyond the firelight's edge and into the shadows. He spun her wildly one way and then, when she was dizzy enough to fall, the other. They swayed, and leaped, and pounded the earth with their heels; matching step to step as though their two minds were one in the wild rhythm of the dance.

They spun to a stop, gasping. If she had not already recognized the smith by the breadth of his shoulders and the touch of his hands, that narrow band of coiled bronze on his wrist would have given him away. Out of breath and laughing, she reached up and stroked the black and white striped badger fur. It had been painstakingly glued in strips to a wicker form, in semblance of the living animal, with dark holes where the eyes should have been.

He lifted the thing away from his face, and grinned. "It is the totem-animal of my tribe," he said. "A creature fond of bees' honey and his warm den in winter; fierce at need, but much preferring to make himself invisible."

Naeri giggled. "I have never seen you dance before," she said.

"And you thought I could not? Ah, Naeri, you have not known me long enough. I have danced in eastern courts with black-eyed princesses to the jangle of tambourines. I have danced with the Horned Hunter of the Wood, and with the faerie folk on the hilltops of the Western Isle." He paused in this flight of fancy to catch his breath, and said, laughing, "I thought I had grown too old for it. But I swear, I have never danced as I did this night."

She leaned against his arm, wiping her flushed face with her sleeve. She had not drunk much mead tonight, thinking she would need to have all her wits about her. All the same, she felt warm, easy in spirit, filled with a reckless, leaping excitement. She tilted up her face to Gwi's—they were very nearly of a height—and he pulled her close, and kissed her.

"Will you come back with me to the smithy?" he said in her ear. For answer she tightened her arms around him. Something within her was unfolding, flowering—a place that, when she lay with Ricca, was like a clenched fist, a lump of stone.

"It will be safe for us tonight," Gwi said to reassure her; and she smiled to herself, thinking how, with Gwi, even such a reckless act as this was tempered with a certain native prudence.

She woke just before dawn. This one night, Gwi had forgotten to bank the smithy fire, and it had burned down to coals. Sitting up, she could see her breath faintly smoking on the gray air.

The badger mask lay on the floor beside the bed-place, staring up at her with its empty eyesockets. Something in the look of the thing made her laugh. She remembered that this was the first day of winter, and she wished that like the badger she could stay in this warm snug place until spring came. She yawned and slid back under the covers, curving her body into the warmth of Gwi's back. After a while he rolled over, pulling her into his arms, and they made love again.

"Now you have to go," he said. "As soon as I have made up the fire." He got out of bed and pulled on his tunic and leggings. She watched, with the bed-rugs hauled up under her chin, as he struck spark to tinder and made the fire blaze up.

In a small voice she said, "Ricca will not ask me where I have spent this night. 'Let no man seek out his own wife, or ask where she lies, on Winter's Eve.' That is what the horse-people say."

He looked around at her, and she thought she saw a shadow pass across his face. "No, he will not ask. All the same, I would sooner no one tells him. I am thinking, he would heed it less if you had lain under a thorn bush with any of his warriors than if he knew you lay with me."

He came over to the bed-place and looked down at her for a moment with his heart in his eyes. Then he gave the sheepskin cover a sharp tug. "Anyway, get up now. Though it saddens me to say it, the feast-night is over."

The first open break in Ricca's ax-peace came not in the feast-hall but in the campground, as the clans were striking their tents and making ready, while the weather held, for their homeward journeys. There was a promise of snow in the cold breath of the wind—not today, nor for a week perhaps—but soon.

Naeri was in the marketplace that day, looking for bargains among the last of the peddler's booths. The easterners were anxious to sell what they could and return to their own lands before the winter gales roared down across the Narrow Sea.

She had a few bits of bronze in her pouch—armbands, earrings and the like that she had worked herself and which Gwi had told her to put by for market-time. She knew how to haggle, and how to use charm if she had to. When the shouting broke out, she had just acquired a wristguard of banded jasper worth a good deal more than the studded buckle and the smile she had traded for it.

No one could say for sure, afterward, what had sparked the quarrel. Someone said—though it was no more than a rumor—that one of Black Uigh's warriors had seen Naeri walking in the marketplace and made a rude jest about Ricca's dark-haired witch-wife. He had called her a usurper, and worse, for lying in the bed that should have belonged to Uigh's daughter; and one of

Ricca's war-band, deciding that an insult to the Great Chief's Fourth Wife was an insult to the Great Chief, had come at the man with drawn dagger. Most agreed later that Ricca's man, Eoan, whom even the horsemen considered a hothead, and Uigh's second spear, Keeva, had been the first to draw blood.

Neither Ricca nor Uigh nor their war-captains were in the marketplace that morning, so there was none who might have stepped in to stop the carnage that ensued.

When Naeri heard the shouts and curses and the excited barking of dogs, both she and the peddler ran to look; keeping a pair of juniper trees between themselves and the fight in case of ill-aimed spears, and an easy line of retreat behind them. Most of the trading-folk were already there, and having placed their wagers, were loudly cheering their favorites.

The high, cold sunlight danced on burnished metal. By now there were at least two dozen men locked in hand-to-hand combat. They fought close in with daggers, going straight for the throat like hounds or striking upward for the heart. Watching, Naeri sucked in her breath. She was both appalled and fascinated by the sheer savagery of the fight. Her eye was not sharp enough to pick out Ricca's men from Black Uigh's; they were, after all, one tribe, with only the colors of their clan-feathers to distinguish them. What she saw was utter confusion: bodies twisting and dodging; blades feinting, thrusting, stabbing; feet starting to slip in the blood that was soaking into the thin turf and the chalk beneath, turning it to red, treacherous mud.

Already there were three men down: one writhing and moaning with a knife in his ribs, another with blood running down his shoulder as he struggled to sit up; and a third not moving at all.

By now the women's bower had caught wind of the fight, and there was a great shrieking and calling out of names from the sidelines. One girl crouched with her kirtle over her head, sobbing and keening for her fallen favorite.

There was a warning shout from an onlooker which, at first, was given little heed. Then all at once Ricca and Uigh were wading shoulder to shoulder into the midst of the melee, bellowing out orders. Ricca had a bullhide whip that he cracked over the heads of the combatants as though he were breaking up a hound-fight.

It was all over, as suddenly as it had begun. The snarled knots of men fell apart, shame-faced, and sheathed their weapons.

They slunk off to see to their dead and have their wounds tended before they faced the wrath of Ricca and Black Uigh. The two chiefs, stalking from the scene, parted without words; but Naeri had caught the black dagger-look that passed between them. Though fights were common enough at any horse-gathering, this thing had gone further than hot words between warriors. Too many men were involved, and the clan-lines were too clearly drawn. It would take more than a bandaging and a burial to hide the damage that had been done.

∞ 21 ∞

Map-Magic

There was a hard frost the fortnight after Winter's Eve, followed by the first dry powdery snowfall. Counting on an open winter, Ricca had made plans to continue the stone-harvest until well after the turning of the year. But at midwinter the white wind came shrieking down from the northeast, scattering both farmers and clansmen back to their own lands. The cattle were brought into the byres and the horses stabled. The sheep were folded in the winter pastures, and the people of the chalk huddled close beside their hearthfires. The snow came again and stayed, turning the chalk lands into a silent world of white hills and hummocks and purple-shadowed hollows.

With no grazing, fodder ran short; soon there was nothing left but leaves and barley-straw, and the ribs of the cattle began to show through their starved flesh. Lambing time came while snow still lay thick upon the ground. In the cold and the driving wind, many of the lambs died before they had time to draw a breath.

Men muttered among themselves that Black Uigh's warning had come true—that Ricca might have done well to pay more heed to Uigh's words and less to Magha's.

In Ricca's own household, folk suffered less than elsewhere. The Great Chief had always begun the winters with overflowing corncribs and an ample supply of hay and tares. Still, among the weak, the very old and the very young there were many that perished. Before that long winter was over, Clia mourned her own small, sickly daughter.

At last the icicles lengthened on the eaves and the mild gray rains came. With alder-month the sun returned, drying the winter-sodden roads. Catkins dripped beside the streams, the blackthorn blossomed, and green shoots stirred in the winter-weary earth. But with the rising of the sap and the opening of the high tracks came the first rumblings of trouble in the north.

One morning in the middle of alder-month Naeri received a summons. She had been working since sunup with the rest of the women, hanging the bedclothes to air in the outer court. Hearing one of the women call out, "Have you come to give us a tune, harper?" she peered around a corner of a rug to see Daui's dark-clad figure beckoning to her.

"Ricca wants you" was all he would say as he hurried her into the hearth-hall. She knew that the War-Council had been closeted there since early morning; and that the night before a messenger from Rudra's camp had ridden in on a sweated, worn-out pony. It seemed reasonable to assume that these events were in some way connected.

The war-lords turned to stare at her as she entered, though without any show of surprise. Clearly, her presence was a thing already agreed upon. They might distrust this strange, dark wife of Ricca's, or fear her; there was not a man among them dared to mock her.

Ricca gave her a long, considering look. Conscious, suddenly, of how she had changed over these last months, she glimpsed herself as he must see her: a tall, spare, sinewy woman, lean-flanked and hollow-bellied, with a face that was all eyes and mouth, sharp angles and shadows.

Ricca said, "They tell me you can find stray cattle with that witch-bauble of yours."

She nodded, feeling the eyes of the war-lords intent and curious upon her.

"So then. Could you find a raiding party, tell us where to track it, if we knew where it had last been?"

She blinked. "Maybe—I don't know." She thought quickly. "If I knew the country . . ."

"Or had it charted for you?"

"Perhaps."

"Daui says he can do that—make one of his charcoal maps of the land." Ricca took a long swallow of barley-beer and shifted his bulk on the bench. His face looked thinner than she remembered; there were faint shadow-smudges under his eyes. He had not suffered this winter past as others had suffered, and perhaps a stranger would have seen no change in him. Still, last summer he had been a young man, at the peak of all his powers; and now his thirty-odd years seemed to sit heavily on him.

He said, "Listen, then. This is the way of it. Yesterday a reiving party rode down out of the woods overlooking the Summerbourne, into Rudra's winter pastures on the lower slopes. They made off with the cream of his cattle herd and a dozen colts.

"Rudra has had his herds raided before," he added, "and he will again. There is too much wild country to the north of his lands, too much forest to the south and east. But he is my kinsman, and when he asks for my help I will send it. I need no witchery for that, only good axmen to ride with me."

He emptied his beaker, and glanced at his war-captain, Gruah. "There is a rumor that has reached my ears, and I want to know the truth of it. One of the herdsmen lived long enough to say this: that he had seen in the plaits of these reivers the black crow-feathers of our tribesman Uigh. Clan against clan, that is an ill-omened thing."

"We have no proof," put in Gruah. "They have taken only yearling ponies, not yet branded, and they will slaughter the cattle."

"Unless," said Ricca, "we can catch them while they are still on the road. A war-band moves faster than a cattle herd. But there is more than one road back to Uigh's camp." He beckoned to Daui, who spread out a sheepskin and began to sketch quick black lines on it.

The war-lords looked on curiously as he worked. This was a kind of magic—this making of lines on sheep's-hide that looked like random marks, a child's scratching in dirt with a sharp stick; yet represented hills, forests, chalk roads, river valleys; and could be followed by a man who understood their meaning.

"Here is the river," Daui said, "and here is Rudra's camp, lying in a bowl surrounded on all sides by hills, with tracks leading off in all the wind's directions . . ." He drew lines to the west, north, east and south. "As you see, it is not a well-chosen site, and is difficult to defend. The Great Ridgeway rides above it, following the escarpment of the chalk. The Lower Way curves off to the northeast into Uigh's wooded chalk hills. That is the straight and broad way, that a man would choose on honest business, but it offers scant concealment. There is a forest track here to the south, that takes you to the edge of Uigh's country. If I had stolen a man's herds, that is the way I would choose. But there are others."

"And," said Ricca, "while we sit here pondering how Uigh's mind works, Rudra's cows and colts are disappearing into the hills."

"Wait," Naeri said, as she felt in her pouch for the small shale bead and the skein of thread she remembered hiding there.

She sat for a while staring at the network of black lines. In those marks Daui had captured the essence, the spirit, of the landscape. Under her slow, patient searching it could be made to give up all its secrets.

She fixed in her mind an image of the real country that the lines described, seeing vividly enough those bleak, rock-studded hills north of Ricca's camp that for five years had been her hunting-grounds. She imagined that she was walking in willow shade along the banks of the Summerbourne, then climbing the smooth flanks of the downs through a fringe of hawthorn and juniper scrub. She explored at random, watching to see how the bead responded, following the eastward line of the broad green ridge-way running high and lonely beneath the sky, with the rivers and the far blue hills and all the Middle Lands lying in a haze below. She fashioned in her mind a picture of the reivers on their long-haired chalk ponies; the yearling horses, foam-flecked and wild-eyed with terror; the cattle bellowing and stamping and tossing their horns. Uigh's men would be driving them hard, whichever road they chose.

She let the pendulum draw her south, into low country, following the axis of its swing and marking the sheepskin as she went with the sharp point of a cloak-pin. Now she was surrounded by the gloom of deep woods, amid crowding oak trees, holly thickets, the black brooding shapes of yews. At last, with a small thrill of triumph, she saw the bead begin a strong steady circling.

"There," she said, marking the place and standing back so Ricca could see. "There on the forest track, moving east to the ford of the Great River. You must catch them quickly," she said, for once they are over the river they will be into Uigh's hills, and you will have lost them."

Ricca said, "With luck, if we ride now, we may stop them this side of the ford. The road will be wet and treacherous where it goes down to the river—not an easy track for cattle-herding."

The war-lords were peering at the sheepskin chart, turning it and examining it, muttering among themselves. She sensed their uneasiness. Herb-healing, the weaving of a charm into a cloak, the finding of a lost trinket—these were women's tricks, not real magic, and if they could not understand such things, they could accept them, even in a woman of their own race. But this thing that Naeri had done came from a darker place. It was battle-sorcery, and—if it proved true magic and not a dark woman's trickery—men would die of it.

Ricca looked down at the sheepskin, tracing the route with his finger. He gave orders to his war-captain, then said, "Have them bring out my chestnut. It is in my mind to ride with you."

Gruah raised his eyebrows. Ricca said, "If it is Uigh who has done this thing, has cut the ties of kinship and broken my peace, then it is my ax that should exact the price."

They rode out in full battle-gear, armed with war-axes, javelins and heavy thrusting-spears. The reds and blues and greens of their cloaks and riding-blankets, the saffron-yellow of Ricca's sun-cloak, made bright splashes of color in the noonday sun. Into their blond plaits were twisted the sun-gilt feathers of the yellow-hammer.

The horses snorted and stamped and danced, as battle-eager as their riders. The war-band had chafed too long in the bridle of Ricca's ax-peace.

The wives and the bower-women leaned over the rampart walk, calling out jests and promises. Suais, as plump and languid as ever, flashed her white teeth at young Ket's salute. Then the war-band was gone, thundering over the chalk road to the northeast, and a waiting silence lay heavy over the camp.

The men were back next day at noontime, having slept overnight and licked their wounds in Rudra's hall. They were mud-smeared still, and blood-stained, their ponies stumbling with weariness. Three of the war-band had suffered wounds, none grievous; there were no heads taken among Ricca's or Rudra's men.

That night in the feast-hall, with the door thrown open to the warm spring wind, Ket the horsemaster's son recounted the battle-story. One day Daui, who sat listening intently, would put his own words and music to the tale.

On Ket's eager tongue it became a battle in truth, a great meeting of war-hosts; yet Naeri knew—they all knew—that it had been no battle at all, only a small skirmish on the river's edge, and quickly over. The dozen or so reivers, exhausted from a day of driving cattle through dark, twisting forest paths, then floundering through the marsh and mud of the rivershore, were no match for Ricca's and Rudra's handpicked warriors. They had reckoned on stealth and surprise to escape unhindered; and Naeri's arts had turned those very weapons against them.

"We caught them at the ford, on the far side of the river," Ket said. "An hour more and they'd have been clean away into Uigh's lands. As it is, we have all the cattle and the yearlings safely back, though a weary task it was, herding them through that churned-up mud. And three men escaped at most, to tell Black Uigh that the heads of his warriors will watch the victory-feast from Ricca's roofbeams."

Naeri's glance slid upward to the smoke-blackened ceiling, and she saw six fresh heads grinning there, some with crow-feathers still wound into their plaits. Lord Ricca himself had taken no less than three, Ket said, with his great ax that smote like the Sky-Lord's thunder; and three more had gone to Rudra's feast-hall.

She had never laid eyes upon the living men who had so lately worn those heads. Now they were dead in the red mud of a river-ford, and she had killed them, as surely as if she had driven her copper knife into their hearts. She found that thought both puzzling and disturbing.

When the torches burned down Ricca put out a hand to Naeri, and she walked from the feast-hall at his side, like a bride or a First Wife. It crossed her mind to wonder if Suais were watching; and if she were, what black thoughts might be festering in her head.

～ 22 ～

Blood-Treaty

Heavy rains fell at the end of alder-month, miring the stone-sledges in mud. Then, just as the whitebeams were flowering, the skies cleared and the chalk roads hardened. After Spring Feast and planting-time the call went out across the Westland, summoning the horse-clans back to the Valley of Stones. Fewer warriors answered the call this year; in the lines of men and beasts dragging their ponderous loads across the chalk, there were fewer farm-folk, fewer ox-teams. There was much grumbling, some cursing—and more news of raiding on the borderlands.

With most of the men gone, a drowsy peace settled over Ricca's household. Women dreamed over their looms in that soft spring weather; the clatter of tongues and the flick-flick of the shuttles slowed. As often as she could, Naeri slipped out of the gates to wander aimlessly on the downs; and no one seemed to notice or care.

In the feast-hall one night Naeri felt a light touch on her sleeve, as though someone had brushed against her in passing; and before she could look round, some small weightless thing was dropped into her lap. It was done so quickly that none of the other women looked up from their gossiping. She turned her head briefly, in time to catch a quick eye-flicker from a tall young warrior. She thought she recognized him as one of the new spears, just come from the youth's house at last Winter's Feast.

Without looking down, she closed her hand over the thing in her lap, and slipped it into the pouch on her belt. Though she had guessed what it was, still her heart began to pound when, in the quiet of her bed-place, she held in her hand a scrap of bracken frond tied round with a bit of red-dyed thread.

She lay awake till nearly dawn wondering whom she could send to the youth's house in answer to Coran's summons. Any manservant she knew well enough to trust had gone west with Ricca to the stone-fields. And something, some half-unconscious hesitation, kept her from approaching Daui. In any case, one did not send the Great Chief's minstrel on an errand to the youth's house—unless one wished to stir up fresh gossip in a camp that these days had little to do but talk, and little enough to talk about.

Gwi, she thought. Though she had not seen him in Hall, she knew he was back from the stone-fields. There had been sounds of hammering in the smithy all the day before. No one would wonder if the smith went to the youth's house, where there were always weapons needing to be sharpened, dinted and battered shields to be hammered new.

Before long the gray murk in her bedchamber brightened, and she heard faint sounds that meant the camp was stirring. She got up, dressed and crept down to the courtyard, long-shadowed and empty in the cold light of dawn.

The door of the smithy stood ajar. Gwi was already up and eating a bowl of barley-porridge while he waited for the furnace to grow hot. She could see his broad back in its worn brown jerkin, his brown hair, close-cropped for warm weather, curling a little on his neck.

She spoke his name softly and he turned his head. His eyebrows lifted a little, and his eyes smiled at her as he stood up. There was a long silence, that Naeri felt no need to break. It was enough to be near him, in the peace and homely comfort of this place.

Finally Gwi said prosaically enough, "Have you broken your fast, Naeri? I think there is some porridge left in the pot."

He lifted the copper kettle from the hot stones and set out a bowlful of gruel for her, breaking off a piece of flatbread to scoop it with. "I make my own now," he said. "The hearth-women have enough to do, with all the men gone."

She knew he was using words to bind her, as though if silence were allowed to fall between them she would vanish away like smoke. So did folk in the old songs try to hold the dwellers of the Bright Land in the world of ordinary men.

She said, "I came to ask a favor."

He smiled, and put his hand over hers. "Anything."

She sat looking at his large, square, scarred hand covering her smooth, narrow one. And then like pent-up water over a bank, the whole tale spilled forth. When she had finished, Gwi said, "It is an old story, the horsemen raiding the hill-tribes. If they can find no cattle or stores, they seize the women instead. But Daui knows that; he should not have led you into such danger."

She shook her head. She said, "I went hunting with my kinswoman, that was all. I would have gone even if he had ordered me not to."

Gwi's mouth twitched. "Yes, I dare say you would have."

"Anyway, it is all in the past now. Will you go to the youth's house for me?"

He nodded. "I'll go now, while they're at their morning chores. This shield has to be returned in any case."

"I will wait here," she said.

She saw the question in his face. "No one cares what I do these days," she said.

While she waited she tinkered with an embossing hammer and a scrap of copper. She was pleased to find that her fingers had not lost their sure touch. Finally Gwi pushed through the doorway with an armload of weapons. He grinned, and at once she felt a great weight of tension lifting from her.

"You spoke to Coran?"

"I did. It seems that young Kirith, who earned his spear this spring, rode with the war-band after Rudra's cattle; and he could not resist the chance to boast to his old comrades in the youth's house. Coran made up some tale or other of a red-haired runaway slave from his father's steading, and asked Kirith if by any chance he had seen her, the night he spent as Rudra's hearth-guest. Sure enough, Kirith remembered a thin little green-eyed girl with red curling hair."

"There cannot be two such," said Naeri softly. "Did he say if she fared well or ill?"

Gwi shook his head. "She was alive. Kirith said she was skinny, but a horseman thinks that of any woman of the Old Tribes."

He knelt, sorting through the pile of broken spears and axes. "So there it is. What will you do, now that you know?"

"What can I do, but bide my time? Cathra must not be told

yet—she would ride straight into Rudra's camp, to her certain death."

"Sometimes bargains can be made," Gwi said, and left the thought hanging.

She did not answer at first. Her mind was racing ahead, thinking with what coin she—or Cathra—might hope to buy Fearnn's freedom.

"Tell me," she said with what must have seemed a sudden change of thought, "what of the temple-building? I have heard no news for a fortnight."

"It goes slowly," Gwi told her. "Even now, in this fine weather, it is back-breaking work. Ricca had no idea of the strength, the sheer weight of numbers he would need, just to drag those stones out of their sockets in the chalk."

"As though their roots were fastened in Underearth," Naeri murmured.

"Yes—I remember, one man used those very words. Most of the stones have yet to be moved, and after that comes the whole business of setting them in place. Daui says he has planned how that is to be done. But ideas in a man's head are one thing, and raising those great pillars of rock may turn out to be quite another."

He got up, and tossed a cracked ax-head into the heap by the forge fire. "In the meantime," he said, "men remember how it was this winter past. Is it any wonder their minds are more on their own fields and herds, and their children's bellies, than on temple-building? It is not by love that Ricca holds the clans, but by strength of arms, and the wealth in his treasure-house. Now they can see both of them dwindling before their eyes; and the ax-truce crumbling away at the edges like stale bread."

She looked down, not wanting him to see in her eyes the sick despair she felt. She thought, it has all come to nothing. Nothing. Daui should have seen from the start that the thing was impossible. An odd memory came to her, from childhood: a cold winter in the hills, and Daui—a boy of twelve—crouched on his heels in the snow, too intent upon his task to feel the cold. He was building a white city of towers and temples, palaces and columns, like the drowned city of the Great Ones. And when the sun came out and in the space of a morning melted it away, Daui stood chalk-faced and trembling with rage, refusing all that day to speak or eat. A small thing; but it came to her now as vividly as though it had happened yesterday.

She felt Gwi's hand touching her hair, and she leaned against him. Just then they heard the creak of the great gates swinging open, the clatter of hooves on hard-packed dirt. Gwi drew back abruptly, holding her at arm's length and smiling ruefully at her.

He said, "That will be Daui—he was expected back today. Go quickly, Naeri. It is better that he does not find you here."

She waited inside the smithy door until she saw Daui leading his pony into the stable shed; then she slipped out across the empty courtyard to the feast-hall.

Presently Daui came into the hall. Chalk dust powdered his cloak hem and clung to his soft boots. Naeri fetched beer for him and ladled broth from the cauldron beside the hearth. These days, as a matter of course, they all fended for themselves.

She sat down in a cool place beside the open door. A shaft of dusty sunlight lay across the trestle board between them. Daui's eyes looked pale as rainwater in his gaunt, dark face.

"It goes badly, still?" It was not really a question.

He lifted one eyebrow, gave her a sour grin. "Does that surprise you?"

"No—but I suppose I still had a little hope."

"That was before you talked to Gwi."

She shrugged. "Is it as bad as he says?"

"Maybe not as bad as that. But it is not going as I would wish. Those who can count the stones, and the holes that have been dug at the temple-site, and the passing of days, can judge for themselves that the work must drag on for a long time yet. They can see Ricca's hold loosening as the war-lords ride back to their own lands and never bother to return. Now they say around the watch fires, when Ricca is not listening, that this temple will be built with the blood and bones of the horse-clans, a cairn to mark the death of Ricca's ax-peace."

"Then," she said with bitter irony, "maybe we will have what we want, after all. We will have succeeded in bringing Ricca to his knees."

"Don't talk like a fool," he said sharply. "If Ricca goes, another, maybe worse, will take his place. Once the truce falls apart and war breaks out among the tribes, you and I, my girl, will be like a pair of grouse caught in a grassfire. Only the Great Circle can give us strength. At all costs, Ricca must hold the reins of power until the Circle is finished."

But, she thought sadly, it will never be finished. For all their scheming and striving, it had never been more than a mad dream, that was melting away like snow-towers in the sun. And now it seemed the land would fall into a greater darkness than any it had known since Flood-Time. That small inner voice, that was like another secret self, said, "There is nothing more to keep you here. A smith is free, not tied to any man's hearth." She could go with Gwi to some far southern country where the Moon-Goddess still ruled the sky.

Daui's voice broke into her thoughts. "There is something that I must tell you. They say that Rath Wolfslayer is raising a war-host from among the clans of the northern worlds. He has chafed too long under Ricca's rule, and sees his chance come at last to be overlord of the chalk. And Black Uigh, who once thought to have a place at Ricca's right hand, now rides with the Wolfslayer."

"And Ricca knows this?"

"He knows. So you see, little cousin, how the Pattern is working itself out. If we are clever, we can hold Lord Ricca in our grasp like this." And he held up his lean dark hand, palm upward, making a cup of it. His eyes glittered, as gray stones glitter when they are touched with frost.

She waited. "You see," he said. "As we need Ricca, so he has need of us. Unless he can find new allies, new spears for his war-host, he stands to lose everything."

She caught at his meaning. "And you want the Old Tribes to go to war for Ricca?" Bitterly she added, "As soon ask the roe-deer to save the wolf."

"Cousin, you have not considered what we can ask in return. Make no mistake—with these tidings from the north, Ricca is ready to talk terms with anyone who can raise an army for him."

Naeri opened her mouth to speak, then closed it suddenly; it had occurred to her what one of those terms might be. She pushed back from the table and stood up. Now she could look down at Daui, and that small advantage gave her courage.

"You must go to the stone-fields," she said, "and tell Ricca that I will meet with him. Alone. I must have a promise from him, that I will hear only from his lips."

Daui grinned. "What shall I tell him—that his Fourth Wife orders him home?"

"Tell him if he means to save his temple—and his ax-peace, and his chiefdom—he will meet me. And I will not be his Fourth Wife when we meet, but a woman of the witchfolk."

A rider pounded over the causeway next day at sunup with a

message from the Great Chief. When Naeri came down to the hall that evening Ricca was there, sitting on a hearth-bench with his legs sprawled out before him. He turned to her with that heavy-browed glowering look of his, but she thought she could see a glint of amusement in his eyes.

He had not bothered to change his dusty, sweat-soaked riding-shirt. She saw that it hung loosely now, over a tautened belly.

"So," he said, "the little witchgirl sends me orders, like a queen." He did not gesture to her to sit down, so she remained standing. Even looking awkwardly up at him like that, and dressed in rough warrior's garb, there was a power in him, a harsh domineering strength that nothing could diminish.

She started to speak, but he held up his hand, cutting off her words. "Not here," he said. "Come to my chamber as soon as I have finished eating."

She found Ricca stretched out on his bed, naked under a loose robe. The air in the room was pungent with herb smoke. He had washed his hair, and it stood out around his head, unplaited, like a horse's mane. Naeri saw that there were broad streaks of gray in his beard, and wondered that she had never noticed them before.

Ricca waved her to the small stool beside the bed-place and poured mead for her. Other times, she had sat crosslegged on the floor-rug and served him. Perhaps it amused him to carry on this jest of her queenship. "Well?" he said, and waited.

Her heart was thudding against her ribs. Not for fear of Ricca—she had lost that terror a long time ago—but for fear of what hung in balance in this room, the certain knowledge that a wrong move, an ill-considered word, could destroy it all.

She had thought this man cruel, ruthless—a half-tamed beast, a great blustering dangerous child. He was, she supposed, all those things—yet none of them served to define the man who now lay watching her with that emotionless, faintly mocking ice-blue gaze. He is no fool, she thought. Dangerous, but no fool at all. He is as good at kingship as I am at witchery—better, maybe.

It needed more than wealth or simple strength of arms to bind these proud, fractious, quick-tempered chieftains to his will; to impose a peace, however uneasy, on such men. In Ricca, pride, honor, intelligence, low cunning, cruelty and single-minded self-interest were so closely woven that one could never hope to distinguish warp from woof. So it must be, she thought, with any man who is born to kingship. He had looked into the hearts of the men he ruled, and knew that if their bards remembered him in a hundred years, it would be for the battles he had fought, not the peace he had maintained. And so he would risk all, if the stakes were high enough. These were the rules she must learn, if she meant to play the game of chiefs with him.

And then she thought, I am bound to this man. That knowledge, taking sudden shape in her mind, startled her. I am his wife. What fate befalls him, befalls me also.

She said in a sudden rush of words, as though she must force them out before they stuck in her throat, "If I said I would raise you a war-host, help you to put down the rebel tribes and afterward finish the temple-building, would you listen to my terms?"

His eyes narrowed very slightly. "Tell me first where you mean to find this war-host. Then tell me your terms."

"I will bring you the hunters of the hills," she said, "and the people of the forest. The Old Tribes, the Mother's people. All those that the Horse-Lords have driven into hiding. They are fierce in battle, and once they have given their word they will not break it."

"And in return?"

"A truce," she said. "Your word, as Great Chief, that from this day on, the horse-tribes will leave the Mother's people to live in peace. There will be no more rape, no more killing, no more slave-raids. And beyond that, I want your word that all the Dark Folk who have been taken into slavery in the horse-camps will be set free unharmed and sent back to their own tribes."

There was a silence. Ricca said, "How shall I trust these people? They are silent and sly; their knives are quick, and they deal in sorcery."

"You will trust them," Naeri said, "because I am one of them, and I say they will repay your trust. I give you my word, and it is their word."

"Go then," said Ricca, and all at once she was aware of a great weariness in his voice. In those two words was the tired despair of a drowning man who grasps at a root or branch, knowing it is too frail to bear his weight.

"First," she said, "I must have your pledge."

"What, woman? Is my word not enough? Do you demand a blood-swearing?"

Dumbly she nodded, and held out her wrist for the knife.

He stared at her. "There is not a man in the Westland who

would ask more than my word in pledge of faith. Do you know that, girl?"

She thought, now I have taken it, that one small misstep that will cost me everything. But suddenly Ricca threw back his head and laughed.

"Well, it is not the first time we have crossed wrists, witchwoman—and now it seems my chiefdom hangs on it. Give me your knife," he said, "and let us have done with it."

"Go now," Ricca said. "I must leave again at sunup, and I need to sleep."

That surprised her a little—but she was glad he had not asked her to lie with him. She was spent, exhausted; realizing, suddenly, how taut-strung her nerves had been through this long day.

She went into the feast-hall, and found it full of shadows and silence. No one was there but a hearth-slave and a few graybeards and unblooded youths who had been left to guard the household in the war-band's absence.

Seeing Daui's drawn, haggard face, she guessed in what an agony of impatience he had waited and watched for her. Out of sheer malice, she let him wait a moment longer while she fetched a cup of mead and settled herself on a bench.

"Well?" said Daui. His eyes were restless and impatient. "Will you never speak, cousin?" He seemed a little drunk, which was a strange thing for him.

She drained her beaker, and calmly returned his stare. "Rest easy, cousin. The thing is done. Ricca has met our terms."

"All of them?" His voice seemed too loud in the quiet room.

"All. Are you so surprised, Daui? Did you doubt I could do it? You said yourself we held him in the palms of our hands."

A faint, chill smile touched his lips. All that he said was, "In the morning we will ride to the hills, to Cathra's camp."

Gwi had not appeared in the feast-hall that night, but she could see the forge light flickering through the smithy door. She put her head in, and halooed. Gwi set down his tools and looked round inquiringly. She pushed aside a clutter of spears and stepped inside. A round of barley-bread, the remains of Gwi's supper, was lying on a bench. Suddenly ravenous, she reached for it.

"Well," said Gwi, "the whole camp, what is left of it, is abuzz with gossip tonight. You have summoned home the Bull of the Westland, they say, and he has come running to your side like a favorite hound."

She grinned. "Just so. I have offered him my terms, and he has agreed to them."

"You have offered him . . . Naeri, lass," said Gwi, and he burst out laughing. "You never cease to astonish me."

And she admitted to him a thing she would never have confessed to Daui. "This time, I astonished myself."

"So," she said, "That is only half the battle. Now I must seek out my kinswoman Cathra and through her the elders of the Old Tribes."

Gwi said, more soberly, "You are not going alone, I trust."

"Daui will go with me."

Gwi responded to that with a grunt, which could have meant anything.

"Anyway, I have come to ask for a good, light throwing-spear and a buckler."

"Gladly. The best that I can lay my hands on."

He rummaged through the storeroom and found her a fine ashwood javelin, newly sharpened, and a bullhide buckler rimmed and bossed in bronze.

"Will those serve?" Gwi asked, watching as she put her arm through the shield straps and hefted the javelin with her right hand, testing its weight and balance.

She nodded. "Well enough. I wish I had had such a spear, when I lived by my wits on the chalk."

"I have something else to give you," Gwi said. "I bought it from a peddler at the last Spring Fair. He thought he was cheating me, but I got the best of the bargain in the end."

He drew out of its leather sheath a long narrow-bladed dagger with hilt plates of horn and an ivory pommel. She could put no name to the pale, cold gray metal of the blade. It was not copper, or bronze, or flint, or even darkened silver, which it somewhat resembled. She ran a finger over the flat of the blade—she could see that the edge was very sharp—and looked inquiringly at Gwi.

"It is made from what you would call sky-stone. There is a country beyond the great eastern plain where they can build forge fires hot enough to work this metal; you rarely see it this side of the Narrow Sea. I bought it as a curiosity—also thinking I could resell it for a higher price. But it is doing no one any good hidden away in a corner of the storeroom. And I have never given you a proper gift, as a friend should."

"You have," she said. "Have you forgotten? You gave me a

buckle for my belt once—instead of the beating I should have had for prowling around your hut."

He laughed, remembering. "And it was flawed," he said. "I thought at the time, I should have found you something better. Take this knife, Naeri. It should serve you well. It is harder by far than bronze, and will keep its edge. Only mind you burnish it well and keep it dry—the damp will ruin it."

As he held it out to her, her hand brushed his, and a small pleasant shock ran through her. She put her belt through the sheath loop and buckled it around her waist. Experimentally, she drew the knife. It slid silk-smooth out of its sheath, and lay in her hand like a thing that belonged there.

"It's a fine weapon," she said, feeling suddenly, unaccountably shy.

"Yes. Though I pray to the Mother you'll have no call to use it."

He put his hands on her shoulders, as though for a comrade's farewell. And then without knowing quite how it happened, his arms were fast around her and she was kissing him a way that had very little to do with comradeship.

He said into her hair, "Beloved, it is not safe. Ricca is in camp tonight." But his arms did not loosen their desperate hold.

She said, "He is burning dream-herbs in his room tonight. And I left him with a jug of strong mead, three-quarters full. I doubt he will stir before sunup." She hoped this were true—but it did not seem greatly to matter.

They lay together in the dark afterward, and Gwi said, in a slow, drowsy, contented voice, "When the temple is finished, then will you come away with me?"

She turned on her side and looked down at him. "If you will have me still."

He put up a hand and stroked her tumbled hair back from her face. "You have never told me how all this is to end."

"Gwi, I don't know how it ends." For the first time the full meaning of those words struck home to her. She said, with a kind of horror in her voice, "Truly, I do not know." Then slowly, shaping thought into words, she went on. "I am like a spearman creeping through a dark wood, with all the torches extinguished; trusting that my captain has his battle orders and will tell me what to do when the time comes." She dropped her head against his chest; there was something oddly reassuring about the slow, even rhythm of his heart. "Maybe it is better I do not know," she said.

"It is not the way that I would choose to go to war," Gwi told her. "I would rather fight, if I must fight, in the full blaze of noon. I like to see where my arrows go, and know my enemy's face."

There was a silence. Then Naeri said, "Tell me where we will go, Gwi, when we leave this place."

"Where? Anywhere the wind blows. We could go overwater to the Western Isle. Every riverbed there has gold glittering in it—we could live like chieftains. Or we could go south to the summer lands, and I could show you ancient cities, full of palaces and towers and marketplaces. Or," he said, "we could go north to amber-country, to the pine forests that go on to world's end, where the giants live." He propped himself up on an elbow and looked down at her, smiling. "Or maybe I will take you eastward across the grasslands and over the Ice-Gleaming Mountains. We will seek out the man who forged that knife, and learn his secrets."

She laughed. "You speak like a minstrel, Gwi. I did not know you had such poetry on your tongue."

"Well, when you have heard as many minstrels, good and bad, in as many camps as I have, after a while you pick up the rhythm of it."

They were quiet for a time, and Naeri dozed. When she woke, the small, high window overlooking the courtyard showed gray against the blackness of the walls. She lay warm and drowsy and contented while the dawnlight grew and brightened. In his sleep Gwi had flung his arm across her. Just above the inner elbow was a small puckered burn scar, where molten metal had splashed up. For some reason, it aroused in her a sudden heart-wrenching tenderness.

"South to the summer lands, north to the world's end," she repeated softly to herself. "East over the Ice-Gleaming Mountains." It was pleasant to imagine such things, though she could not see how there could be room for them in the Pattern.

~ 23 ~

Spear-Truce

The chalk road to Cathra's hill-camp curved north through the wild upland pastures divided by the River of Mists: a harsh lonely land softened into beauty on this spring morning by flowering gorse and pale clouds of crabapple bloom.

They came up over a windswept ridge where not even gorse or juniper had managed to take hold, crossed the Ridgeway, and descended into a broad green plain. By afternoon they were riding through flat meadowlands at the headwaters of a southward-flowing river. From this green river country a myriad small streams rose, some flowing south and west into the Hefryn, others wandering eastward to join the Great River that emptied into the Narrow Sea. Beyond, to the north and west, the gray-green steeps of the wold country rippled into distance.

All that day Daui had been in a strange somber mood. Puzzled, she tried to draw him out of his brooding silence, but his thoughts seemed to be in another place, and she got no more than a few words from him. Then, as they stopped late in the afternoon to water the ponies, he turned to her suddenly, and as though giving voice to what had been churning in his mind all day, he said, "Cousin, it is a dangerous game you are playing."

She stared at him, baffled for the moment; then, understanding, she felt the blood rush to her face.

"You and the smith . . ." The words stood like a drawn dagger between them.

Flustered and angry, she said, "Suais lies with many young men, and Ricca turns his head away."

"Girl," Daui said, "will you use the wits the Mother gave you? Suais will bear no more sons for Ricca. She is free to do as she pleases. But a horse-lord leaves his name, his shield and spear and his gold to his own sons, the seed of his own flesh. It is not as it is among the Old Tribes, where the name and wealth of the house passes through the woman's side. It matters much to a horseman that his own seed grows in his woman's womb. The more so for Ricca, who hopes when the time comes there will be a son of his loins to stand before the Council as Great Chief."

She looked at the ground. Then, stubbornly, she said, "At feast-time . . ."

Daui said impatiently, "A child conceived at feast-time is no man's child, it is the Sun's seed. There is no shame for any man in giving it a place at his hearth, or treating it as the child of his own flesh. But cousin, it is no longer feast-time."

"Well," he said, as his pony lifted its nose from the stream and he bent to gather up the reins, "that is all I have to say. Only consider what you do, and what the cost is. It is madness to risk all for a whim of the flesh."

She mounted, stiff-necked with rage, and dug in her heels, startling the pony into a canter. She rode ahead of Daui in an angry silence all the way to the beginning of the hills. For you, minstrel, she thought, such words come easily. You sing of love, but it has no power over you. For you it is a whim, an itch in the loins, a tune on the harpstrings; not this cruel sorcery that locks two spirits together, branch and root, so they cannot be torn apart and live.

They rode up the winding wooded valleys, while the light thickened and grew honey-colored. Cathra and her hunting-band appeared to them suddenly as ghosts out of the green shadows of the woodshore. Naeri threw the reins over her pony's neck and slid to the ground into Cathra's embrace.

"So," Cathra said, as she held Naeri away from her and, squinting into the low sun, scrutinized her face. "You are as skinny as a hazel rod, but I suppose it looks well enough on you."

To Daui, she remarked with a grin, "You made better speed this time—I had your message barely two hours since." She opened her hand and showed him a bundle of tied leaves and twigs.

Naeri bent down and broke off a scrap of frond from the bracken-clump at her feet. She reached out, took Cathra's hand, dropped the fern leaf into her palm and gently closed her fingers around it. "Here is the rest of the message," she said.

She saw Cathra's eyes widen with a fearful and reluctant hope. "Surely," she said, "after so long . . ." She could not seem to finish the thought.

Naeri seized both Cathra's hands and held them tightly. "She is alive. That much is all we know."

Cathra said, on a long outrushing breath, "The Goddess be praised." She sat down abruptly on a stump and turned away her head. Presently she wiped her sleeve across her eyes and said, "Well, sister, for sure you have caught me off guard with this news. But if you know that much, then you must know where she is?"

Naeri shook her head, hoping that the lie, when it was found out, would be forgiven. "Listen, sister. We have brought other news. Hear us out, for the one is part of the other. Have you heard the rumors that have come down from the north?"

"That Rath Wolfslayer means to be Great Chief, and is raising a war-host to challenge Ricca? It is more than a rumor. A party of ax-traders came through here a fortnight ago and brought the tale. They think that Rath has gone mad, believing he can win out over all the southern clans that Ricca holds in spear-pledge."

"A year ago," Daui said, "that might have been true. But now . . . Ricca's people have just come through the worst winter in memory. Men say that the Sky-Father has turned his face away from Ricca."

"I have heard," said Cathra, "that this temple-building of his has cost him dearly."

"Too dearly, it seems. The ax-peace is crumbling."

Cathra said, "It is in my mind, cousin, that it is not your voice I hear speaking to me, but the voice of Ricca. And that, I am thinking, is a very strange state of affairs."

Daui replied, "These are strange times. What it comes down to, in the end, is that it suits me best if Ricca wins."

Cathra shrugged. "Either way, it is no concern of mine. One horse-lord is as bad as another. Let them slaughter each other for a change, instead of hill-folk."

They were like two knife-fighters, Naeri thought—dancing this way and that, feinting and dodging, testing one another out.

"Let us say," added Daui, "that one horse-lord may be worse than another—depending on the circumstances."

Cathra gave him a shrewd look. "What circumstances?"

"Ricca has never been known to betray an ally. He has many faults, but he would cut off his right arm before he would break the terms of a truce."

"So," said Cathra. "Now that he has done his best to wipe us from the face of the earth, he finds a use for us. Spit it out, then, minstrel. What are the terms of this ax-truce?"

"From the Old Tribes, spearmen and archers to swell the ranks of Ricca's war-host. Help to put down the rebel tribes, and afterward, labor to finish the temple."

Cathra scowled. "And in return?"

Daui said, "These are Ricca's terms. Send him warriors, and Fearnn will be returned to you."

Naeri heard the quick catch of Cathra's breath. "You must believe *me* mad," she said. "Do you ask me to lead my people into battle, into a horseman's war, to risk their lives for the life of one woman, because she is my friend? Tell me where she is, and I will go after her. But it is my neck only that will be offered to the ax."

Naeri said quietly, "That was only the first condition. Sister, will you hear us out? Fearnn will be set free; and every other slave of the Old Tribes from every camp in Ricca s lands."

Cathra's eyes narrowed. She waited.

"And no more slaves will be taken from among our people. There will be no more raids, no more rape, no more burning."

"And Ricca has sworn to that?"

Naeri said, "He has sworn." She held out her wrist, where on the pale inner flesh a faint red line still showed.

"And if we do not agree?"

"Then I think there is not much chance that Ricca can win this war. If you thought him a bad enemy, you may find Rath Wolfslayer a worse one."

"Yes," Cathra said. Her eyes darkened. "The ax-traders have brought us those tales. There is a savagery in him, a black cruelty that goes beyond the limits of Ricca's skill, or his imagination."

A slanting shaft of sunlight, filtering through the laced branches, was warm on the back of Naeri's neck. The beech forest whispered and rustled around them. Wild hyacinths washed in deep blue drifts against the gray smooth massive trunks. How strange, thought Naeri, to sit with friends in this flower-scented wood and talk of death.

Daui said, "There is another thing. It is necessary, above all, that Ricca should finish this Sun-Temple he is building."

Cathra remarked with sour amusement, "So we must first fight his battles for him, and then we are to build him a monument."

"Just so. And you must trust me when I ask you to do these things."

"We share the same blood, minstrel," Cathra reminded him. "We both serve the Goddess. There should be no secrets between us."

Naeri saw Daui hesitate, knew that he was debating how far Cathra could be trusted to keep silent; weighting the advantages against the risks. In the end, caution won out.

"Not secrets, cousin. But sometimes, between friends, kinfolk, brothers even, there may be things held back for a little, not revealed before their true time. As the sorcerer may not speak of his magic, for fear the power will dissipate like mist rising off a field."

Cathra gave him a dubious look. "Like the fog of words you are throwing up to hide your meaning," she said acidly. "Never mind, let it go—if it is sorcery you mean, I will ask no more questions."

"This much," Daui said, "I will tell you. That this war of Ricca's is only the beginning—the means and not the end."

"Well," said Cathra, getting up, "You have had your say. It is not for me to decide alone. I must take this to the Old One, and to the Council."

Naeri said, "Cathra . . . the old woman lives, still?"

Cathra nodded. "We thought sure this winter would be her last, but she clings to life. Though I think her mind dwells more in the Bright Land, now, than in our own. One day soon the door between the worlds will slide shut, and then only her empty husk will be left behind."

The camp clearing, set in the midst of a beechwood, was well protected and well concealed. The platted bramble-covered brush of the outer wall made an almost impenetrable stockade. The long low huts, sunk part way into the earth, their turf roofs overgrown with vines and bushes, looked more like barrows than dwelling places for the living.

Today the compound was nearly deserted. Most of the young folk had gone off with their skin tents to the summer hunting-grounds, leaving the old ones and the children to guard the livestock and tend the garden plots. Grania, the First Daughter, sat outside one of the huts, weaving an osier basket. She glanced up, her dark face expressionless, as Naeri approached.

"Come with me," Cathra said. She beckoned to Naeri. "The Old One has been asking for you."

Naeri ducked her head under the lintel, going down into the dark, herb-smelling, cavelike interior of the hut. A little dusty sunlight filtered through the smoke hole. She could see the edges of bed-stalls along the walls, the cold hearth in the center of the long, low room.

"Old One," Cathra called out softly. There was a stirring, a whispering of cloth, the faint noise that arm-rings make when they clink together. Naeri's eyes were growing accustomed to the gloom; she saw the Old One, a pale upright shape against the darkness of the wall.

Cathra said, "Old One, why do you sit in darkness? It is a fine warm evening. Come out into the forecourt. The sun will melt the stiffness from your bones."

The old woman's voice rustled and crackled like dry branches. "Let me be, girl. I am perfectly content. Who is that with you?"

"It is I, your kinswoman Naeri."

"Come closer, child."

A hand, dry and light as a drifting leaf, touched Naeri's cheek. "I have missed you, child. It has been . . . how long?"

Naeri thought back. "A year and a half, Old One."

"As long as that? Yes, I remember, you came at winter's beginning, and they say another winter has gone and it is spring again." She turned her head so that the dim light from above shone full upon her face. Something flickered in those sunken shadowed eyes like fires in deep shaft bottoms.

Cathra said, "Old One, Naeri has come to ask for our help—and maybe offer help to us."

"Tell me, child." As Naeri spoke, the Old One held the younger woman's hands lightly cradled in her own. Feeling the frail grasp of those gnarled, twisted joints, the bones that were like dry sticks under the skin, Naeri thought that her hand was a last link holding the old woman to this world. If she let go, the Old One might drift away like sea wrack on the outward-rushing tide.

Naeri sat in the half-light of the long room, calmly setting forth her case, and the Old One listened. When Naeri had finished the old woman sighed, and rubbed her hands together as if to ease the pain that gnawed inside the bones. She said, "I recall how they spoke of Rath's father—even his own warriors spoke so, behind his back. The Demon-Lord, they called him—the Rider on the Gray Horse. No one kept count of the Dark Folk who died in his time—or those who would gladly have chosen death to what they suffered at his hands. Girl, this is an old battle—only the faces of the warriors and the weapons change. My people—the hunters of the forests and the fisher-people—have watched it all. It is we who are truly the Ancient Folk. These lands belonged to us before the witchfolk came to the Lost Isles, before the chalk farmers landed their little skin boats, before the first copper-maker came. We have watched them come, and shrugged, and made our peace with them, and gòne our way. But it seems there is no peace to be made with these horse-lords."

She fell silent for a while, and Naeri thought she had drifted into some unreachable place. Then suddenly she looked up with a bright, lucid, penetrating gaze, and said, "The choice of battle-leader is mine, still. Where is Cathra?"

"Here, grandmother."

"You, my fierce one, my warrior-daughter. You will lead the Old Tribes into battle."

~ 24 ~

War-Trail

Naeri had been dreaming of her mother's house; maybe it was the smell of peat smoke and skins, or the sharp-sweet fragrance of leaf mold, that had stirred old memories. When she opened her eyes and saw Cathra at her bedside holding out a cup of venison broth, she thought for one strange heart-stopping moment that it was her sister Lia kneeling there.

She sipped the broth, blinking sleep out of her eyes. Cathra squatted back on her heels and waited for her to finish, then said, "Well, it has started. Late last night a jet-trader wandered into camp. Three days ago when he left the moor country he saw Rath's war-host gathering. Word is that Rath Wolfslayer will march south to join Black Uigh with all the northern chieftains at his back."

"Then west," Naeri said, "along the Ridgeway."

Cathra nodded. "I am calling our hunters back from the summer deer-runs. It is time for the yew branch to go out."

For three days the lean shadows of Cathra's hunters moved along the forest tracks, carrying the yew sprigs into the high wolds and wooded hills, down to the coast, and across the ancient turf-and-timber roads into the marsh country. Swiftly and silently the people of the Old Tribes responded to the battle summons; at the end of three days a wide circle of their fires had sprung up around the walls of Cathra's camp.

They were tall, sinewy, fair-skinned people: blue-eyed, for the most part, with tawny or russet or nut-brown hair. If the horsemen called them the Dark Folk, it was because they were moon-worshippers, night-stalkers, dwellers in caves and hollow hills; though it was true that on many the witchblood of the Isles had left its mark of raven hair and sea-gray eyes.

They came in buckskin kilts and soft skin shoes that made no sound on the forest paths; carrying tall slender cross-webbed bows of yew or hazelwood, and arrows with delicate leaf-shaped heads. There were wolves' teeth and boars' tusks hanging against their chests, and their skins were battle-striped with mud and ochre.

Cathra moved among the campfires, greeting kinfolk and old hunting comrades as she called the chiefs and war-leaders into council. There was not much talk around the fires tonight—certainly none of the cheerful uproar of a hunt-gathering. Here and there a group of warriors huddled over the knucklebones, but most were intent on checking weapons and equipment—refletching arrows and replacing bowstrings, testing knots and sharpening spears—all those small tasks a warrior seeks out for reassurance on the eve of battle.

"Welcome, Caer, old friend," said Cathra, greeting a tall, fair-haired warrior, with a pattern of loops and spirals traced in clay across his chest. And, "Ethnai, it is too long since we have hunted together"—this to a little leather-skinned woman with heavily tattooed arms and face.

And so it went, with a joke, an embrace, an asking after absent kinfolk, until presently the clan-chiefs and captains moved off to Cathra's tent.

Naeri stayed behind, sitting near one of the fires to eat her supper of stew and flatbread. The night had turned cool; a small wind, fluttering through the beech trees, brought with it a pungent odor of damp moss and decay.

"You have done well, cousin." In that cat-silent way of his, Daui had come up behind her.

Naeri was feeling, at that moment, both apprehensive and dispirited. Now something in Daui's manner, a certain air of self-congratulation, annoyed her intensely, and she swung round on him.

"Have I done well, Daui? You may think so, but I am thinking, maybe all I have done is send these people to their certain deaths."

He shrugged. "That is a risk, surely, in any battle. It is neither the first risk we have taken, nor the last." He tossed a log onto the fire, sending up a shower of sparks. "Anyway, I only came to say you'd best make your farewells tonight."

She looked at him with feigned surprise. Now it was his turn to be irritated. "We have done what we came to do. I want to make an early start in the morning, get you safely behind Ricca's walls before the war-host moves off."

"Do you indeed?" she said. "Then maybe you should have consulted me."

His eyebrows drew together. "What do you mean?"

"I mean I am not going back with you to Ricca's camp. I am marching with the Old Tribes."

He looked hard at her to see if she were joking, saw to his dismay that she was not. He said, on a rising note, "Do you imagine I would let you risk your neck like that?"

She replied with a cool obstinacy she knew very well would infuriate him, "It is not your choice to make, cousin. Did you imagine I would send these people into battle, maybe to their deaths, while I ducked back into my warm safe bolt-hole? Go back to camp, Daui. Tell my lord Ricca that his Fourth Wife is serving him in the best way she can. Tell him I think I am more use with a spear in my hand than with a spindle."

She saw the baffled rage in his face and bit her lip hard, fighting a crazy urge to laugh.

"What use is the Great Circle," Daui asked her, in a carefully reasonable voice, "what use is anything we have done, if you are lying in a field with an arrow through your throat?"

She said, deliberately echoing his words, "It is only one more risk, and maybe the last one. I leave it in the Goddess's hands. If she means us to succeed, I will live. If not . . ."

She broke off as he took a step towards her—for a moment she thought he meant to seize hold of her, carry her back to Ricca by sheer force. She stood her ground, wordlessly defying him. Something wavered in his eyes. He gave her one last furious thwarted look and abruptly turned away.

Before sunrise Naeri and Cathra loaded Naeri's pony with food and gear and set out on foot, leading the animal. With them marched Iohna, Cathra's chosen lieutenant, a silent woman of twenty-odd with a look of witchblood in her dark solemn face. The long winding snake of the war-host followed them as they went along the dim forest paths, their feet on the damp moss and leaf mold making no more sound than a fox might have. Then they

were out on the open downs with the early sunlight in their eyes
and the tall flowering summer grasses brushing against their legs.

They crossed that desolate high country where the great rocks
break through the sparse thin turf; then turned down through
rolling hills to Rudra's valley. Along the way Naeri passed
familiar landmarks. There was a cluster of barrows where once
she had spent a long uneasy night, fearing the wraiths of dead
warriors that her imagination conjured up in the windblown mist.
Farther on was the thorn copse where she had killed her first
partridge with a sling. Then she had been alone, without kinswoman or comrade, thinking she would perish in these empty hills
like a lost colt, a wounded fawn. Now Cathra strode beside her;
and if she turned her head she could see, streaming out behind her,
a great river of men and women who shared her blood and were
prepared to die with her.

They crossed the Great Ridgeway, leading east along the chalk
scarp straight into the heart of Black Uigh's country. Broad and
green it stretched away through the high, bright air, its margins
edged with summer flowers. Somewhere eastward on that pleasant highway her own death, and all their deaths, might at this very
moment be approaching.

Now, as they crested a ridge just to the north of Rudra's valley,
she could see Ricca's war-camp: a clustering of tents, cook-fires,
horselines, near the shallow valley bottom on the edge of the
Summerbourne Stream.

Ricca himself rode out to meet them. With him was his brother
Finga, his war-captain Gruah, Ket the horsemaster's son, and
several of his household warriors. They were already stripped for
battle, in loincloths and thick bullshide belly-straps, with the
golden feathers of the sun-bird twisted into their plaits.

She saw how much harder, leaner, Ricca was, than he had been
a year ago. The winter had melted away the extra flesh so that his
muscles stood out sharply under the brown skin of his chest and
shoulders. Naked, he was not diminished as some men might have
been. He still seemed to occupy more space than any of the big,
fair warriors around him: a man born and shaped for kingship,
wearing that kingship on his shoulders like a bullshide cape.

Now that he was mounted she had to tilt her head back to look
him in the eye. He gazed down at her with lazy good humor. If it
angered him to meet his Fourth Wife marching at the head of a
war-host, certainly he gave no sign.

"So, witchwoman," he said, "you have kept your part of the

bargain." And he shot his brother Finga a private look, as much as to say, "You see?"

Cathra stood tense and tight-lipped, idly stroking her spear shaft. She whispered to Naeri, in the hill-tongue, "Sister, is this him?"

Naeri grinned. "In the flesh." To Ricca, in horseman's speech, she said, "Here is my kinswoman Cathra, captain of the hunt, whom the Old Tribes have chosen as their war-leader."

Finga snorted, and spat. "It is as I told you, brother— they are commanded by women, and will fight like women."

She felt Cathra bristle suddenly like a hound at the scent of trouble, saw her knuckles whiten on her spear shaft; and guessed that she knew something at least of the horsemen's tongue.

"Be silent, my brother," said Ricca in the mild tone of one who knows he will be obeyed. "These are our sworn allies, and you will accord them that respect." Meanwhile his gaze rested on Cathra, taking her measure. She looked, at that moment, both formidable and dangerous.

Finga contrived, with a lift of his shoulders and a sidelong grin, to show what he thought of this alliance; but he fell silent all the same.

The War-Council had gathered in the shade of some alders by Ricca's tent. Ricca's own war-circle was there, and the clan-chiefs, among them Tighern Longbeard, Derga One-Eye, and Rudra of the River; as well as the Great Chiefs of the allied tribes. Cathra took her place calmly enough between Garech the Red and Aithra of the Long Spear. Behind the War-Council, Ricca's household warriors leaned upon their spears.

"A scouting-party has just come back," Ricca told them. "Rath's war-host, and Uigh's, are camped on the Ridgeway, about half a morning's march east of here, on the far side of Sheep Hill. Their intention is clear enough—to come west along the high track, straight up over Blaghnor Height."

He took a swallow from the beer jar Finga handed him, and looked at Naeri from under his heavy brows. "Tell your captain that is the hill scarp that marks the northernmost point of my lands." Naeri translated this quickly into the hill-tongue, and Cathra nodded.

"At all costs," Ricca said, "we must stop them before they take the Height. From there, they can command the whole of the upper valley of the Great River to the northwest—and with it, those hills where your people take refuge, Naeri. South and west they will have clear passage straight through my lands and on to the sea.

"Listen well," he said. He broke off an alder wand and began to trace his strategy in the dirt. "I will lead my warriors east along the Ridgeway, to meet Rath's war-host before it comes to Blaghnor Height. Rudra's men will take the trail from the south, past the Vale of Tombs, up over Hazelwood Down. It comes out on the Ridgeway close to Sheep Hill, and with the Sky-Lord's help he should be able to slice through their flank."

"And our warriors?" Naeri asked.

"How many are there?"

"Three hundred," Naeri guessed. She glanced at Cathra, holding up three fingers. Cathra nodded.

"That many?" Ricca raised his eyebrows. "So then. Here is a southern track, winding through the folds of the hills, well screened by hawthorn brake and juniper. I am thinking that if you take your war-host by this road and circle well to the east behind Sheep Hill, that will be another surprise for Rath and Uigh. While my axmen make their main thrust head-on, and Rudra moves in from the south, your archers and spear-throwers will be well placed to harry them from the rear. Thus we will catch them between us, with no easy retreat save up the hillsides.

"You, Naeri." She looked up at Ricca, vaguely surprised to hear him use her name. He jerked his chin in Cathra's direction. "How well does this warrior-woman know these hills?"

It was on the tip of her tongue to answer, "It is no matter, I will be marching beside her, and I know every height and hollow as well as my own hand." But there was time enough on the morrow for Ricca to know that she meant to fight. She would leave the telling of it to Daui, when it was too late to stop her. She had heard stories enough of mutinous wives who had been beaten senseless, or shackled to roof-trees, until they saw the error of their ways.

"Never mind," Ricca said. "I will send a scouting party with her." As he spoke, a pair of foot scouts appeared at the circle's edge. They were breathing hard, and there was a fine sifting of chalk dust in their hair. Ricca gestured, and they came to squat beside him. Someone passed them the beer jar.

"Well?" said Ricca as the second man, with a sigh, set down the jar.

"Lord Ricca, we have been to the top of Sheep Hill and have looked down on their war-host. We have seen Uigh's crow-feathers and Rath's eagle-feathers. But now other tribes have joined them—wave upon wave of them marching out of the east along the Ridgeway."

Ricca threw back his shoulders and stretched, arching his back with his hand in the small of it, as though he had grown stiff with sitting.

"So," he said. "There have always been horse-tribes outside my ax-peace; but their runs are a long way off, beyond Rath's lands. They kept to their own borders, save for the odd horse-trader, and we had no quarrel with them. But now it seems that Rath has raised the whole of the north and east against us. Well," he finished, "there is no help for it. Go now, talk to your war-bands. Tell them, after tomorrow's work they will feast well. Tonight they will burnish their weapons, and see to the horses, and sleep."

As twilight fell, the watchfires sprang up as thick as crocus flowers across the valley floor. Naeri made her way through the gathering dusk to the circle of Cathra's fire; and when they had shared a supper of venison strips and hardcake washed down with river water, and she had tended her pony, she rolled up in her cloak in the shelter of a hazel copse. Cathra and her lieutenants slept nearby in the bracken, wrapped in their mantles of wolf and martenskin.

Sleep, which would have been more welcome to her than lime-mead, refused to come. She turned and twisted feverishly on the hard ground, lying still between times, listening to the faint rustle of grasses in the night breeze; the stamping and snorting of the ponies; someone coughing, a curse as someone else tripped over a hound or a tent rope, followed by muffled laughter. She heard Daui's voice, quiet and distant-sounding, singing a battle-song by Ricca's fire; and much later, when all other sounds had subsided, the harsh cry of a fern-owl in the wood. She saw a gibbous moon glimmer among the hazel boughs, then vanish behind a shoulder of the chalk. She saw the darkness pale to a thin gray ghost-light; and finally she dozed, only to be roused before sunup by the clatter of the waking camp.

Naeri got up, wondering if she had slept at all; stretched and moved about for a while to work the stiffness out of her joints, then went down to the stream's edge and splashed water on her face.

She watched the eastern sky turn rose and gold as the sun came up; and wondered, like all warriors before her, if she would see tomorrow's sunrise. Her belly was tight-coiled with tension. She felt hollow inside, and slightly nauseated. How easy it would be to take the pony from the horselines and ride back to Ricca's camp, to wait with the other women for the battle to be over. No one would think the less of her, except maybe Cathra—and she herself. She drew the storm-colored dagger out of its sheath, ran a cautious finger along the blade, watched it gleam fish-cold and deadly in the morning light.

She gnawed at a chunk of hardcake without much appetite, and for what was probably the hundredth time checked her buckler-strap, counted her arrows and ran a thumb over her bowstring.

Two scouts had gone out during the night to spy on the northern host; by midmorning no word had come back. Already the day was uncomfortably hot, like high summer, the sky hazy. Thunder weather. She could feel the faint storm-shimmer on the heavy air.

Nearby, hammers clinked and rang on metal. Gwi had ridden into camp with the armsmaster and the two apprentices he had taken on that winter, pulling a stone anvil in an ox-cart. There were always last-minute repairs to make on the day of battle; and would be more later, if the fighting continued.

She was experimenting with the grip of the heavy thrusting-spear she had browbeaten the armorer's boy into lending her, when Cathra came by and looked at her with her eyebrows raised.

"And what do you mean to do with that?"

Naeri glanced up innocently. "Kill somebody, if I can manage it."

Cathra snorted. "Not if I can help it. Have you ever used one of those things in close combat?"

Naeri shook her head.

"No more have I. But I know it takes both skill and more strength than we have between the two of us. This is not the time to learn the trick of it." She put out both hands for the spear, and Naeri yielded it up. "If I were wise, I should order you to stay in camp, for fear what Ricca may do with my head if you come to harm. Failing that, I want you well behind cover. You are a bow-woman today, sister. An honorable enough rank, in any army."

In late morning the scouting-party crept back into camp. At last, they reported, the enemy war-host was advancing.

The war-horns snarled, and the drumming of fists on shields, as the long lines of men moved up the slopes, grew into a noise like thunder.

≈ 25 ≈

Battle-Magic

Like an army of ghosts, that makes no sound or shadow in its
passing, the Old Tribes followed Cathra eastward, along stream
beds and cattle tracks, keeping always to the shelter of the combes
and wooded hillsides. Somewhere above and to the east where the
Ridgeway ran, they could hear what might have been the low
grumble of thunder—or the sound of a war-host on the move.

Near noon they halted, sheltering in beechwoods on a slope
beneath the Ridgeway, east of Sheep Hill. The sound was
unmistakable now—that heavy rapid thudding of feet on the chalk
track, the rhythmic drumming of fists on leather bucklers.
Looking up the hill flank between the trees, they could see the
dark mass of the passing host, with the sun glinting off shield-
bosses and spears. There were no horses—the lords of the High
Chalk rode to their war-camps, but they marched into battle on
foot. The fiery, unpredictable hill ponies were nearly impossible
to control in warfare; beyond that, they were far too valuable to be
wasted.

After what seemed like hours, the last of the rearguard vanished
westward. Presently in the near distance they heard the bellow of
war-horns, a clashing of bronze on bronze, and a great howling.

"Now," Cathra hissed, and raised her spear to give the signal;
the order rippled backward through the lines.

They broke from cover and ran up the bare chalk slope, through a low tangled bank of thorn and bryony, then out onto the high track that dipped and climbed beneath the skyline.

From here they could see all the wide north country spreading away below: pale tendrils of smoke that marked the scattered forest camps, the broad gleaming line of the Great River, and the dim blue outline of the northwestern hills.

Thousands of trampling feet had broken through the thin turf of the road, so that puffs of white dust flew up as the Dark Folk moved across it. The wind of the high downs, ceaseless even in summer, blew the din of battle to their ears in sudden gusts and eddies; between times, they could hear larks singing over a vast and breathless silence.

Sweat was pooling in the hollows of Naeri's throat and trickling down her sides under her light tunic. Her quiver-strap chafed her shoulder, and she was starting to limp a little on one foot. She shifted the heavy quiver against her shoulder blades, and ran a finger under one of her sandal straps where it was biting into her flesh.

Now, coming up under the shoulder of Sheep Hill, they could see along the Ridgeway's curve the outermost fringes of the fighting, could hear the battle-howls, and the cries of the wounded.

The warriors of the Old Tribes were strung out along the eastern incline, waiting for Cathra's signal. Looking up Sheep Hill, Naeri could see that Ricca had chosen his battleground with some forethought. The crown of the hill, overlooking the Ridgeway, was enclosed by an earthen bank and ditch, built by some long-forgotten tribe. Below were thorn spinneys and a few scattered clumps of beech and fir. As defenses, the earthworks were unimpressive, but they would afford a measure of cover to Cathra's archers while her slingers and spear-throwers crept down through the trees within closer range.

Cathra led them in a half-crouch up and over the hilltop. Now they could look down and see the main bodies of the two war-hosts spreading along the broad road in both directions, and over the verge and down the slopes. Where the two vanguards had met headlong, knots of men were boiling up the steep hillside, as water swirls up on the rocks in a narrow place.

The noise was appalling—an ear-shattering din of metal on metal, screams, curses, battle shouts. In that churning maelstrom of flesh there seemed no hope of distinguishing friend from foe.

Kneeling in the shadow of the bank, Naeri set arrow to nock and

took careful aim on a black crow-feather, letting fly down the
hillside with a volley of others on Cathra's command. At that
moment the battle lines heaved and surged, rolling over the place
where she had aimed; so that she would never know whether or
not her arrow had struck home.

Now, as the thick of the fighting swelled to the west, she could
more easily pick out the black and gray and dark brown feathers
of the northern host from among the yellow and blue and rusty-red
of Ricca's clans. At the same time, she discerned the true
hopelessness of their task. No one, not even Magha, could have
foreseen the sheer magnitude of numbers that Rath and Uigh had
hurled against them. In the face of those numbers, that endless
surging tide of men, their arrows and stones and spears could have
no more effect than hornet stings. The southern hosts were
faltering, crumbling; their battle-lines, under that ferocious onslaught, driven inexorably back upon themselves.

She heard Iohnna say, without any real enthusiasm, "If we
closed ranks and came straight down on them with our spears, we
might drive a wedge in and split off a part of their flank . . ."

"And have all our heads split for our trouble," Cathra finished
for her. "I will not throw away your lives in such a fashion. There
are too few of us against so many. We have neither the weight nor
the arms to carry such a charge."

She sucked in her breath, and shouted, "Hold," adding to
Iohnna, "Don't let them waste any more bolts." A swift glance
passed between the two women, which seemed to convey anything else that needed to be said. Cathra drew aside Fiacc, the
third in command, and the two held a brief, low-voiced confer-
ence. Then Fiacc raised his hand, fleetingly, and scrambled over
the bank. Screened by brambles and elder scrub, he slipped down
the hillside to the Ridgeway. Somewhere westward the battle was
raging; below, the road lay empty, save for the wrack the tide of
battle leaves behind it. Here and there, scattered along the
roadside and down the grassy slopes, the dead and wounded lay in
tangles of blood-soaked leather, torn flesh, white-gleaming bone.

Naeri swallowed hard and looked away. She saw Iohnna
standing beside her, her thin dark face shining with sweat.

"Where has Fiacc gone?" Naeri asked.

Iohnna turned slowly. She had heavy, rather drooping lids that
gave her eyes a hooded, secret look. "Wait," she said. "Listen."

Far down the hillside she heard one of the wounded men
screaming—a shrill inhuman sound that ended, finally, in a kind

of whimper. After that there was only the surf roar of battle, dulled by distance, and the monotonous sighing of the wind.

It came without warning, booming and echoing over the high chalk, a great hollow-sounding blast like the noise a conch shell makes, with all the sea's grief and fury in it, but magnified a hundred, a thousand times: a noise to shake the very earth's roots, and crack the hills.

An awestruck frightened murmuring ran through the ranks of the Ancient Folk. A woman said softly, "My mother told me of that sound. I never thought to hear it in my lifetime . . ."

Naeri seized Iohnna's arm. "Tell me what is happening," she whispered in bewilderment.

"It is the war-horn of the Goddess," Iohnna said. "Fiacc has sounded the Blowing-Stone."

The hair lifted on the back of Naeri's neck at the long-drawn echo of the ancient hollowed rock that had stood on the Ridgeway since the world's beginning: the battle-call that roused the Lady of High Places from her long slumber.

The tribes-people knelt silently behind the earth-bank, or waited in the thin shade of the thorn trees along the slope. Iohnna moved a little apart from the others, and her narrow face took on a closed, inward-gazing look. There was a lull for a while in the soughing of the wind; the air was breathless with heat and the threat of storm, charged with a nerve-prickling energy. There was a power here, as yet diffuse, unchanneled, like the raw power in unpatterned stones.

Naeri looked at Iohnna, and a cold shock ran down her spine, seeing that plain somber face transformed into a wild, perilous, inhuman beauty; seeing in those gray hooded eyes a wisdom that was older than the hills themselves, old and undying and implacable as stone. Lark song and battle clamor drifted up across the hills like faint messages from a far country. No one spoke or moved.

Behind Naeri, a murmuring rose. At first it seemed that nothing had changed, and she wondered what the hunters could see that she could not. Then she glanced down, and observed that her feet and legs had vanished halfway up to the knee in a white vapor, a ground mist, that appeared to be seeping up out of the hill's belly through the layers of chalk and turf. It had no business there, on this sun-drenched summer's noon; and it seemed thicker, milkier, more substantial than any ordinary hill mist. It was as though the very chalk of the earth had mingled with the humid air, thickening it to the consistency of gruel.

Tendrils of the mist climbed higher, coiling around their waists, their shoulders; glistening like frost crystals in their hair. For a while they could see the shapes of the trees and bushes as gray blurs in the luminous pallor; then even those vague shadows vanished, and it was as if each one of them stood alone upon the hill.

Then Iohnna, rousing herself as it seemed from enchanted sleep, called out to them. "Have no fear," she said. "The Goddess has sent her cloak to hide us from the eyes of the enemy."

Cathra said, "Keep together, each one with your hand on the shoulder of the one before you, and I will lead you down to the Ridgeway."

She moved forward, whistling a hunting song to mark her position, and led the three hundred of them in a long, wavering, stumbling line that groped its way over hummocks and tussocks, around briar thickets and through spinneys, down the grassy slope of the hillside to the flat ground below. Then they turned westward, with the din of battle, the clatter of spears and clash of shield-bosses and thud of axes growing louder, till it seemed they could smell, through the blanketing fog, the stench of blood and sweat-soaked leather and trampled grass.

And suddenly, by some queer trick of the wind, or maybe more battle-magic, the mist thinned so that they could see the road before them.

"Archers," Cathra called out, and gave the order to take aim. "Spearmen, be ready."

The fighting had spilled out sideways from its narrow field, leaving carnage all down the slopes below the road and up the hillside. As Naeri heard later, in the endless retellings of this battle, at first much had gone according to plan. Rudra's troops, pouring up over the road from the south, had driven deep into the left flank of the northern horde, splitting the war-host nearly in two. But the sheer strength of numbers remained with the north. They had managed somehow to regroup and close ranks, forming a wall of bucklers, and now were fighting hand to hand with Rudra's men, forcing them ruthlessly backward down the hillside. Farther west, where the vanguards of the two hosts were locked in bloody combat, the south was beginning to waver and give ground: their solid shield-wall parting and thinning under the fierce onslaught of Rath's heaviest shock-troops. The north was within a bowshot now of Blaghnor Height, and a final triumphant charge up its nearer slope.

But then, just as Black Uigh's axes crashed through the last of Rudra's crumbling defenses, splattering brains and blood across the greensward, the thing happened that was against sense and reason, and abruptly turned the tide.

It may have been that one man turned his head, hearing a twig snap, a bird fly up out of a thorn bush, and seeing what was moving in on them from the east along the Ridgeway, cried out to warn his comrades. As they tried to comprehend this thing that was outside nature, beyond any ordinary comprehension, Black Uigh's warriors wavered, hesitated—for no more than a blink of an eye, a single heartbeat, less than the time it takes to drive a spear through a man's ribs, an ax-blade through his skull—but it was enough, and it was to cost them the day.

As she loosed her first arrow, Naeri saw in her mind's eye what the enemy must have seen, bearing down on their left flank: a wall of luminous whiteness, milky-solid at the center, fringed and tattered where the wind tore at the edges, and glowing faintly gold where the sun lit it from above.

Men began to sway and drop, clutching the small deadly bolts that hissed like serpents' tongues out of the mist, catching them in the throat before they had time to bring their shields up. And with the arrow-storm came a shower of stones from unseen slings, toppling those in the near ranks that the arrows had spared.

The spear-throwers came last, a solid swift-moving wedge driving out from behind the fog-curtain. In shock and superstitious terror Uigh's ranks thinned, faltered, broke, the lines falling back the one upon the other like grass before the wind. Naeri could hear Rudra bellowing at his men above the arrow-hiss and thud of stones and clang of metal; turning and steadying his scattered forces, bracing them for a fresh assault hard on the heels of what had seemed a certain rout.

Rudra's war-band drove in mercilessly, now that the advantage was theirs again, herding Uigh's men westward along the Ridgeway until they pressed in panic and disorder against Rath's troops in the forward lines. The Old Tribes moved west along the high ground above the road, shooting down into the stragglers; the last tendrils of mist trailed into nothing as they ran. Naeri loped along with the others, somewhere near the head of the column, her quiver bouncing on her shoulder blades. It had not occurred to Cathra to send her back.

As they came around the shoulder of the hill, almost into the thick of the battle, the clangor and blood-reek burst upon them with staggering force. Clouds of chalk dust eddied up to thigh- and waist-level, so that those swaying, reeling figures had a curiously disembodied look. Naeri could see the glinting arc of an ax rising for an instant out of the swirl of battle, then crashing downward. Knots of men broke off from the mass and spun away like burning bark scraps whirled out of the fire. She caught glimpses of faces with a crazed, drugged look; eyes red-rimmed from dust or battle-madness, with little that was human in them.

Then suddenly they were into it themselves, swallowed up by it willy-nilly as the battle surged and boiled around them.

Naeri snatched up a dead man's spear. She could not manage it one-handed and tossed aside her bow. As she came upright she caught a flicker of movement, saw the dull gray gleam of a stone ax-head arcing down. With both hands on the spear shaft, she threw her full weight desperately into the thrust. The shaft jarred all the way up to her shoulder as the head struck bone, and she saw the ax slide harmlessly to the side. She set her foot against the man's ribs, frantically wrenching at the spear. It came loose with a sudden lurch as she twisted it, jetting blood across her tunic-breast.

She felt faintly sick, and there was cramping pain in her arms and shoulder muscles. An ax came at her, and dropping the spear, she dodged, sidestepping; somehow managing to skip out of the way long enough to draw the sky-stone dagger out of her belt. The thought flicked through her head that Cathra was right, the spear was no weapon for her; and then she came up under the axman's arm and slid the blade neatly between his ribs. She snatched up his fallen buckler and stood gasping for breath.

After that the thick of the fighting seemed to move off, like a great snake writhing over the ground, leaving her almost alone on a little rise of the chalk, circled by a single coil of the serpent's tail. From then on she did little damage to anyone as far as she could tell; but was herself more or less out of harm's way.

For a long time the lines of battle seemed hopelessly locked; swaying and heaving from side to side, but moving neither forward nor backward. Then, very slowly at first, but with gathering momentum, Ricca's forces began to lose ground.

It was at that moment that she heard above the roar of battle a high clear sound of chanting. She looked up, and saw Cathra standing alone on the high slope of a hill overlooking the fighting.

As the singing went on, Naeri felt her throat and chest tighten; her mouth was dust-dry, and her heart crashed against her ribs. Only a furious effort of will kept her from throwing down her shield and taking to her heels. As Iohnna had called up the Cloak of the Goddess, so now did Cathra unleash upon the northern host the curse or gift of the antlered god, the terror-wind.

She saw a kind of ripple run through the northern ranks, as a field of barley shivers and parts in a gust of wind. A gap opened suddenly between the front lines of north and south, where an instant before the dark feathers and the red and gold had been close-mingled. A long shrill wavering cry went up, a sound like the noise of wild beasts caught in a grassfire, fleeing in terror before the flames. The front lines fell suddenly into chaos, the shield-wall crumbling as the men turned in their blind fear and crashed into the ranks behind. In that frenzied retreat men fell to their knees and were knocked aside and trampled: the feet of their comrades pounded their faces into the dust.

The warriors of the south stood in disorder and confusion, feeling the clutch of a cold fist on their hearts, the dry taste of terror in their mouths. Though the full fury of Cathra's magic was turned upon the north, the weakening fringe of it caught them and lashed through their ranks like the gales on the hurricane's edge. They too might have broken and bolted, scattered like sheep down the hillside, had it not been for the bellow of Ricca's war-horn, and the sound of his great voice rising above that unearthly din— cursing, raging, exhorting; threatening worse deaths than anything the field of war might bring.

Rallying behind Ricca, the southern host steadied, closed ranks, and charged eastward over the bodies of the fallen. Cathra had raced down from her vantage point and with Iohnna was leading the Dark Folk. A storm of arrows and javelins followed Rath's warriors as they scattered eastward, spilling along the margins of the Ridgeway and down the slopes. Those in the rear that survived that rain of flint were picked off by Ricca's axmen, who chased them down like wolves in pursuit of hares.

Through the rest of that day the herb-women moved among the injured, cauterizing their wounds and packing them with moss; and the wagons came to gather up the dead. For two nights after, the sky was stained crimson by the death-fires. On the third night there was a great clan-gathering in Ricca's hall that served both as a funeral-feast and victory celebration.

At such times, Ricca was much given to expansive gestures; tonight he invited Cathra to join his own captains and clan-chiefs in the war-circle. The war-lords shifted nervously to make room for her, looking as if they feared she might suddenly cast a spell on them. Cathra herself sat stiff-necked and dour, toying with a pigeon leg and twisting her beaker nervously in her hands. Naeri caught her eye, from her place on the woman's side, and Cathra's dark face relaxed a little.

Daui had already made a song for the occasion: a hurried effort that would need to be polished later, but with a rousing beat and many loud chords building up to a heart-stirring crescendo. He made sure not to leave out the part that Cathra and her tribes-people played in the victory, making a very faint, silvery, shimmering music for the magic mist and an immense storm of sound for the final rout of the northern host.

Daui's battle-song crashed to its climax. In the brief hush that followed, before the feast din could build again, Ricca got to his feet and nodded to one of the household slaves, who scurried off with a look of self-importance. The apron of horsehide over the door was thrust aside, and the man came in, leading by one arm a ragged, skinny, red-haired girl. She looked bewildered, her large eyes blinking anxiously in the sudden glare of the firelight.

Naeri's heart leaped into her throat, and she saw that Cathra was already on her feet, her beaker clattering across the boards. Ricca's eye caught Naeri's over the heads of the other women. "Tell the Captain of the Dark Host," he said, "that I keep my bargains." He looked good-humored, jovial almost; and un-mistakeably pleased with himself. He must, Naeri realized, have dispatched a messenger to Rudra's camp almost before he had time to wash off the chalk dust and clean his weapons.

She watched Cathra leading her *fidais* back to the war-circle, stroking her and soothing her like some small frightened wood creature she hoped to tame. The girl shivered and hid her face in Cathra's neck. She was grimy and disheveled, her hair long and wildly tangled on her shoulders; and clearly, for all her joy in seeing Cathra, overcome with terror.

There was another matter too, that Coran had neglected to mention—or that his friend Kirith had not looked closely enough to notice. The ripped and tattered hand-me-down cloak that Fearnn clutched under her chin did little to conceal the fact that she was six months gone, at least, with child.

A stir had rippled through the hall when Fearnn appeared. Now, as Ricca began to speak, an abrupt and attentive silence fell. He said, "Listen well, my kinsmen. We have won a great victory, one that harpers will celebrate for a hundred years—but it was not won by us alone. I tell you this, that the Dark Folk, the Ancient People, who fought at our side and used their battle-magic against our enemies, will from this day live under Ricca's ax-peace. There will be no more raids on the forest camps and the houses under the hills; no more slaves shall be taken from among them, and the slaves who sleep at your hearthsides shall be set free."

The silence went on for another heartbeat, as they weighed the meaning of what Ricca had said; then there was a rustle of surprise and disbelief that built up quickly into an outraged clamoring.

"Lord Ricca, this is not the reward we were promised. Already you have taken our warriors, our farmers and herdsmen. Now you take the very slaves from our hearths."

"Be silent." The shouting died abruptly as Ricca bellowed out the command; though the clan-chiefs kept up a resentful muttering among themselves.

"This treaty have I sworn in blood with the Ancient People. I do not break such treaties. Remember this: we have chased away Uigh's men, and Rath Wolfslayer's men, like stray hounds who would steal bones from our table; they have broken my ax-peace and are no longer true men like ourselves. They have no right to call themselves warriors. If you need slaves, steal them from Black Uigh's and Rath Wolfslayer's lands."

The servants were run off their feet, keeping the beakers filled at the men's side of the hearth; the women's side was left to fend for itself. On her way to fetch a mead jug, Naeri passed near the war-circle. As she ducked her chin dutifully in Ricca's direction, he smacked his beaker down on the boards and caught her by the elbow, pulling her over to him.

"Woman," he said, glowering ferociously at her, "it comes to my ears that when you should have been in camp with the other women, you were seen in the thick of the fight on Sheep Hill, shaking a war-spear."

She looked at the floor; not sure whether his displeasure was real, or if he was feigning anger to amuse his war-lords.

She said in a small voice, "My kinswomen fought, and so I fought also."

Ricca grunted. "And how many men did you kill, witch-wife?"

"Only one that I know of. Maybe two," she added on reflection.

~ 26 ~

Temple-Raising

In the last hot days of summer, just before the leaves turned, Naeri made a journey into the hills. There she witnessed the birth-naming of a small, wizened, squalling girl-child with flame-red glints in the brown mouse-fuzz of her hair.

There was little about Fearnn, now, that was childlike. She had suffered much in Rudra's camp, and it had marked her. Where once her green eyes had shone with the dazzle and mystery of the Bright Land, now they held only a tired, sad, diffident look. Nor could the birth have been an easy one, narrow-loined as she was, and in a half-starved, exhausted state. But the child was strong and thriving; and Fearnn's eyes softened when she turned back the doeskin wrappings to show Naeri the small, angry red face. She and Cathra had chosen the name Mara for the babe. One of Cathra's ancestresses had borne that name, and she had been a great huntress and warrior-woman, renowned in song. So, too, should this girl-child one day have songs made about her, Cathra said. There was a kind of wonderment in her eyes as she held the babe, and stroked its petal-soft face with a gentle fingertip.

In her twilit place beneath the hill, the Old One's heart still went on beating faintly in its cage of bones; but it was plain to see that her spirit had gone to dwell in the Bright Land. And so Grania, who was the Old One's daughter and Cathra's great-aunt, became the one who sat in Council—the voice and living presence of the Mother.

"Stay with us a little longer, Naeri," Cathra said. "The deer in the upland runs are thick as woodticks. Who will notice if you bide here till hunter's moon?" But after harvest-rites, with the first gold upon the beech leaves, Daui came for her, and they traveled to the temple-ground.

An army of stonemasons, most of them flint folk and half-folk, swarmed over the site, laboriously coarse-dressing the stones by pounding them with sarsen boulders, then grinding them smooth with finely crushed flint. The ground underfoot was covered with sand and stone chips; the air was thick with dust. The work had been going on for months, and was still a long way from being finished. They had uprooted the old half-circle of blue stones and had moved them aside, filling up the holes with chalk rubble. The tower of crossed logs that would be used to raise the new stones stood waiting.

Now Daui was checking that the new holes had been dug according to his precisely calculated plans. Following him as he moved around the circle, Naeri peered curiously into the huge stone-sockets, steep on three sides and sloping on the fourth. As she watched, a work party began pounding wooden stakes into the back of a hole, opposite the ramp side, to shore it up when the stone slid into place. Presently they would drag the dressed stones on their heavy rollers into position over the holes, maneuver them into their sockets and haul them upright with ropes.

"After that," said Daui, "Ricca must be patient for a while. The stones will need time to settle into their foundations before they can begin work on the lintel-seatings."

Naeri observed that a curious shift of power had taken place. Now it was the Ancient Folk, the light-boned, narrow-limbed people of hill and forest and river marsh, who—under the watchful eyes of Ricca's warriors—oversaw the work and gave directions, while the stockier horsemen and half-folk swung the stone-mauls and worked the grinders.

The bones of the Great Ones, the Master-Builders, lay in the dark earth in their tombs of stone, or drifted with the gray tides of the Western Sea. Yet something of the old arts, the old knowledge, had survived. In these Dark Folk there persisted some deep blood-memory of a time when the circles of stone sprang up as thick as faerie-rings across the chalk.

Naeri glanced up and saw Nhiall approaching across the level plain; moving a little stiffly, but still with that long-limbed, unflagging and unhurried stride. They embraced with a quiet joy, and then Nhiall stepped back and gave her a long considering look. He said, "It is in my mind that you are happier than when I saw you last. It goes well with you?"

She nodded. "As well as may be."

"That was a great battle fought at Sheep Hill, they tell me. Even in my little village they are singing songs about it. I am glad I did not hear, till afterward, that you had a part in it."

She said, "I am not sorry I was there . . ."

"But you are in no great hurry to do it again?" She laughed as he finished the thought for her.

"Well," he said, "there should be peace for a while, and you have done your part to bring it about. It is enough to make me think that this wild scheme of Daui's will have a chance of succeeding."

He seemed to notice her silence, and glanced down; their eyes met and held.

"If," he said, "you still wish it to succeed. I am thinking, the world has turned a few times on its pivot since last we met.".

"I must keep my promises," Naeri said.

Gently, he laid his hand against her cheek, and she saw the depths of weariness in his eyes. "I know. I always believed that of myself, and I believe it of you. But sometimes we make too many promises, and in the end we must make a hard choice among them—or else keep none of them at all."

She could not think of any way to reply. They stood on the edge of the temple-ground, their voices almost drowned out by the interminable scrape and thud of the stone-dressing. The gusting wind blew sand and chalk dust into their faces.

"This was a moon-temple once," Nhiall said. "That old ring of marking-holes was used to chart the moon's pathway, long before the blue stones came from the west. In the village where I grew up there was another such circle. I remember, it was my task to move the marker-stones as the moon's phases changed." He held up an arm, sighting along a pair of stone-sockets. "In my day," he said, "there was not much science left in the world—even among the priests we called the Watchers. Then, we were taught that the marking-circles held the sun and moon in their power, so that they rose and set as the stones ordained."

Naeri smiled. "That is like saying, snow fell on this Winter's Eve, and was recorded; therefore snow must fall on every Winter's Eve."

"Just so. But that is what we believed." Nhiall added wryly, "It was a belief you could take a certain comfort in. In time I learned differently, and then the world seemed a much more dangerous place."

The stones of the Sun-Temple rose quickly in the mild open winter that followed. Black Uigh and Rath Wolfslayer raided no more cattle in the west and south. Fearnn's baby grew pink-cheeked and plump, and her mother's people prospered under the sheltering wing of Ricca's ax-truce. At Winter's Eve old Magha looked into the rowan-fire and saw that the Sun-God's face, which in the unfathomable way of gods had been turned aside in anger, once more smiled upon the horse-clans.

If another, darker shape appeared to Magha in the red roar of the flames, he did not speak of it. But within the month the old man was stricken with a lung fever that consumed his frail body like a brushfire. The horsemen built a cairn of stones on his barrow so that those dry brittle bones would not rise again to prowl upon the chalk.

On a morning in the middle of whitethorn month Naeri stood with Daui on the temple-ground, watching the first of the great stone lintels rising into place. The workers at the top of the raising-tower seemed puny as dolls as they maneuvered the huge unwieldy stone onto its uprights. She held her breath, almost afraid to watch, convinced that the immense slab would at any moment slip and come crashing to the ground. What she was seeing, surely, was the work of gods, not men and women like herself. Yet she could not deny the evidence of her eyes: men and women had built this place.

The morticed cross-stone slid out across its uprights; was shifted, pried, levered, adjusted. A great shout went up from the top of the raising-platform as it settled solidly onto its tenons.

"Now they have done it once," Daui said, "they have the trick of it, and the rest will go quickly."

She made no answer; she was lost in contemplation of this wonder she had helped to make: the monumental perfect geometry of this circle of thirty stones, with its half-circle of paired stones towering within.

No two of the stones were quite alike, she realized. Some were dull gray, the color of storm clouds, some rusty brown, or rose-tinged; others were pale and smooth-grained with a hard white glitter where the sun struck them. Together, they made a singing harmony.

Here was a pattern complete in itself, and completing a vaster pattern: the inmost circle of an immense and intricate web of circles radiating outward, over the downs, the fens and forests and moorlands, out and out to the world's rim, and farther; encompassing the moon, the sun; vanishing somewhere, beyond imagining, in the dark behind the stars. Where there had been an empty place, a gaping rent in the world's order, they had made this thing as complex and lovely as a harp-song, as stark as chalk cliffs falling sheer into the sea. She could feel the pulse, the surge and shudder of power, like a great heart beating deep inside the earth; no longer diffuse, but channeled, patterned—a dragon caged and slumbering within the loops and spirals of the earth-web.

She felt the hard grip of Daui's hand on her upper arm. She turned, met his eyes, saw the anguish in them as he struggled to grasp a thing he had neither art nor instinct to perceive.

"Cousin," he said softly, "tell me what it is you feel."

She shook her head. How could she put into words what was no more than a throbbing in the nerve-ends, a singing in the blood? So, she thought, does a blind man reach out in fear and desperation as he gropes his way in darkness along a high dangerous path. And she felt for him, suddenly, a great pity, and a sad affection.

At the moment that the last lintel-stone was juggled and shifted into place, a messenger was dispatched to Ricca's gates.

"It is finished," he shouted in a great voice as he clattered into the courtyard. "Today the House of the Sun is finished."

Presently the call went out to all the scattered clan-camps, and to the tribes of the alliance: summoning them to gather at midsummer on the Great Down, in the House of Many Doorways.

A slave-child, big-eyed with self-importance, came to Naeri in the women's bower. "Lady, the minstrel bids you meet him in an hour, at the spring outside the gates."

Naeri's stomach knotted with a cold foreboding. She nodded, waved the boy back to his master, and returned to her cloak-mending, delaying the moment as long as she could. She had known it must come, this summons. Since the first stone was hauled across the chalk and toppled into its place, she had seen it written in the Pattern.

Daui was pacing restlessly beside the hill-spring. He had left off his cloak in the summer's heat, and she saw that he wore a new black tunic of some finely woven southern stuff. At his throat was a necklace of incised gold plaques. A slender wristband of white-gold gleamed pale against the darkness of his sleeve. He looks like a prince in an old song, she thought, a sorcerer-prince out of the Drowned Lands.

Daui said, "I thought it would be better here, where there are no listening ears . . ."

She waited. He began to walk up and down again, striding in his soft boots over the summer-faded grass. She walked beside him.

He said, "The dragon is waiting, cousin. Waiting for the hand that will unleash him."

She thought of the Great Circle—no longer a tumbled, shattered thing, but a great heart beating at the center of the world. Ricca's dream, that somehow had become her own dream, made tangible in stone. Created, at what cost of years and lives, to crumble again to nothing at her touch.

"At midsummer," he said, "they will be gathered together in the temple-ground—all the clan-chiefs, the chiefs of the allied tribes, the war-captains. Destroy those, Naeri, and you destroy the horse-clans. Without their leaders, the war-bands will scatter in confusion. And the war-host of the Old Tribes will be waiting to sweep down on them."

"The Old Tribes . . ." She stared at him, feeling a small icy shock in the pit of her belly. "You did not say that before."

"Did I need to? I have great respect for your powers, cousin, but I do not think that even you, single-handed, can destroy all the armies of the horse-tribes."

At once she saw the flaw in his plan and seized upon it. She said, "There was a treaty. Cathra will not break a treaty that I have sworn in my own blood."

He turned to look at her. There was something in his eyes that was dark, and old as the stones themselves, and terrible: that had nothing to do with treaties or blood-truces; that was untouched by those small laws that rule the acts of ordinary men.

"Cathra is war-captain," he pointed out. "She is not the Old One. Nor does she speak for the Old One."

She saw it then as clearly as though he had written it in blood on the ground before her. "It was Grania," she said. "Grania has forsworn my treaty." Rage swelled in her throat, bitter-tasting as bile.

"She has that right," Daui reminded her. "And she has reason enough . . . she has lost many kinswomen to the horsemen—and two of her own daughters besides."

He reached out to take her by the shoulders. Furiously, she shook him off. "Naeri, what did you believe? How did you think to destroy the horsemen, without the breaking of vows and without bloodshed?"

From the beginning she had known this was the dark thing that lay at the Pattern's heart; and like a child that will not look into the shadows above the roof-tree, she had feared to gaze upon it. All the while she had been nurturing . . . what? A small, foolish, formless hope that this ax-truce, bound as it was by the Circle and by the mingling of blood, might somehow, against all logic, endure.

Stubbornly, hopelessly, she said, "But we are at peace now, the raids have stopped . . ." And groping her way uncertainly through the thought—"I have lived among the horse-people. Surely a treaty is not so unthinkable . . . "

Daui laughed—a dry harsh sound that grated along her nerve-ends. "Cousin, I see it is true what they say, that women think with their loins and not their heads. Because you have bedded with Ricca, now you would have the witchfolk lie down with the horsemen. Can the hare lie down in peace with the wolf, Naeri? Have you so quickly forgotten your mother and your sisters?"

She flinched, as he meant her to. Then, as she saw the deliberate cruelty and injustice of those words, her anger flared again. She held up her wrist, where a faint pink line was still visible across the blue cord of a vein. "I have not forgotten. Maybe you have forgotten this."

He did not look at the mark. "What does that mean, in the end? A matter of convenience, to be broken at Ricca's whim. Or maybe you are telling me to trust a horseman's oath?"

"His oath, yes." But she knew her words were falling on air. The wound that in her had begun to heal, a little, was for Daui still an open festering sore.

She said, "Who will rule this land, Daui, when we have driven out the horsemen? Now that our kings and queens are dead and our people are scattered through the hills? Will the Old One rule? Will Grania?"

He turned on her that bleak, hawk-fierce, implacable gaze. What she saw in his eyes was a long fever-dream of vengeance; and beneath it the desperate grief of a boy who had fashioned himself a kingdom of ice, and watched it perish. At that instant she knew that she feared Daui more than she had ever feared the horsemen.

"No," she said. Though the word was hardly more than a whisper, she saw him go suddenly tense, and his eyes flickered.

"If I must choose," she said, "I would sooner Ricca ruled this land than you, minstrel."

His face went the color of ashes. He reached out as though to shake her, or strike her. Then his hands dropped to his sides; and without warning there leaped out at her a wordless, shapeless fury that raked her mind and her spirit, searing them like flame.

He knew too well where her guard was weakest—knew how to use that raw-nerved sensitivity that exposed her to the grief and rage of others as though it were her own. Now she felt storm-battered, lacerated, as she recoiled before the terrible blind power of his need.

"Don't," she heard herself screaming. She clapped her hands to her ears, as though in that way she could block out this brutal assault on her inward self. And then she said, in a calm, quite ordinary voice, "If you go on, you will drive me mad, or kill me. But you cannot make me do the thing you ask."

She saw the glint of something behind his eyes that was not sane, not human. With a sudden sick certainty she thought, he means to kill me. She turned, then, and ran down the hillside toward the gates of the camp, without once daring to look back.

~ 27 ~

Midsummer

At the sight of her stricken face, Gwi caught her hands and pulled her down beside him on the smithy bench. She leaned against him, and he waited, holding her quietly, while she caught her breath and the thudding of her heart slowed.

Presently she said, "I have destroyed it all, Gwi—the plan, the Pattern, everything that Daui has worked for."

He said with a hint of irony in his voice, but no particular surprise, "Suppose you begin at the beginning."

She turned her head, met his calm, uncritical gaze. "All along I saw what was happening, Gwi—and I would not admit it. It was all for Daui, in the end. Not for our people, not for the Old Tribes. Only for Daui. He let me think it was order, pattern we were building; and all the while it was the Lords of Chaos he meant to serve."

"And now?"

"And now he can do nothing. Without me he *is* nothing. The power he needs . . ." She held up her hands, regarding them with a kind of horrified detachment. "With these I can call fire out of stone, power from the earth's roots. It may be these two hands can destroy the Westland. But afterward, they cannot put it back together again."

She was trembling, from sheer nervous reaction. "What would you do, if the thing you had schemed and plotted for all your life was snatched out of your hands, just as your fingers were closing on it?"

. "I am not Daui. The workings of his mind have ever been a mystery to me," Gwi said. "But I have seen him angry—and I think it is past time you left this place. There is a look in his eyes sometimes . . . I have seen that look in the eyes of madmen. Maybe I should have said that to you a long time ago." He hesitated. "Still, if I had, would you have believed me?"

"I might have believed you," she said, "but it would have made no difference. No difference at all." She paused, dismayed at the hard simple truth contained in those words. It was as though Gwi had held up a mirror in strong sunlight, and she had seen her true self revealed in all its self-deluding, headstrong stubbornness.

Gwi put up a hand to stroke back her hair. After a while the tension and anger began to drain out of her. She felt immensely weary. She said, "The wheel has come full circle, it seems. Once again I have no kinfolk, no place in the world. Daui will tell the witchfolk that I have betrayed them, and they will believe him."

"You have betrayed no one," Gwi said. "No one. Daui led you into a trap, and you have found your way out of it. That is all. He held you captive, and you have broken free."

"But," she said, "I am bound by other vows besides."

"To Ricca."

She nodded wretchedly.

"Listen to me," Gwi said. "Ricca has his Sun-Temple, and there is peace in the land, for a while. He had no more need of you. In the courts of the east, they know this Westland only as a damp gray isle in a gray sea, ruled by savages and wizards. A place of very small importance in the great scheme of things. A place it will not break my heart to leave. Naeri, you tell me you have power to draw fire from stone, to crack the earth's foundations. Since it is you who tells me this, I must believe it; though I cannot imagine such a thing. What I know is this: that these hands of yours were not fashioned to destroy the world. They belong to a craftswoman; there is art in them, the power to create beautiful things—and that is how they were meant to be used."

Presently he lifted her to her feet and led her to his bed-place; and for a while she forgot everything else in the pleasure his hands and his mouth and body gave her, the passion that each time came as a wonder and an astonishment.

Just as she fell asleep she thought she heard a faint sound, the ghost of a footfall, in the outer room; and imagined she saw the horsehide curtain stir as though a hand or a breath of wind had disturbed it. But there was only silence, afterward; and so she rolled over, fitting her body into the shape of Gwi's, and went back to sleep to the sound of his slow, regular breathing.

Much later she stirred a second time. It was the deepest hour of the night, that dangerous time when the heart beats slowly and the bond between flesh and spirit thins to a slender thread. She groped her way up out of the black depths—some deep instinct, some smell of danger, making her heart race as she jolted abruptly into consciousness.

Why in this black hour was the room filled with red flickering light, why were there voices shouting? She sat bolt upright, heart pounding. Beside her, Gwi was fumbling for his knife.

The torches filled the room with a smoky, blood-colored light, and sent strange shadows leaping against the wall. There seemed to be at least half a dozen men shouldering their way into the narrow chamber. Among them was Gruah, the war-captain, and Ket the horsemaster's son. Ket looked embarrassed, apologetic almost. As Suais's lover he must have seen all too clearly the irony of the situation.

These, Naeri realized, were the men that Ricca trusted most in the world. These men—and Gwi. With that thought came a sick horror at what was happening.

Gwi was on his feet, backed against the edge of the bed-place, clutching a knife. Naeri sent up a wild plea to the Goddess, that he should not try to fight his way out. Maybe this time the Goddess was listening—or maybe Gwi saw the hopelessness of struggling—for he gave a kind of tired sigh, and his knife-hand dropped to his side.

The warriors fell back then, crowding against the walls to make way for the big blond man who had pushed aside the curtain and was thrusting his bulk through the low doorway.

"Get up," said Ricca, speaking to Naeri but not looking at her. His voice, though low-pitched, was cold and harsh as the wind that comes down in winter off the northern chalk.

She swung her feet to the floor, pulling the top rug with her and trying without much success to wrap it around herself.

"In the name of the Mother," Gwi said—forgetting how little power the Mother had in this place— "Ricca, she is your wife, let her cover herself before your men."

Ricca's face was like stone, but he jerked his chin sharply, signaling his warriors to turn away. She groped for her kirtle and tunic and put them on, thinking, since she would be dead soon enough, it mattered little whether she was naked or clothed. Gwi, with some presence of mind, had already pulled his tunic over his head.

Ricca said, "It is not me who must be reminded that she is my wife, smith." He was high-colored, as though he had been drinking earlier, but he was clearly dead sober now. "You had your chance once, and refused it. Now you would make mockery of me before the camp."

Gwi said nothing. There seemed nothing to say. But in the midst of her shame and fear, a cold clear part of Naeri's mind went on working. As she fastened up her tunic laces with stiff, fumbling fingers, she thought, it is Daui who has done this. He knew, and this is his revenge."

She felt a curious sympathy for this loud-voiced, fierce-visaged bear of a man who was her husband. There was a somberness in him tonight, a bleak, defeated calm; the look of a man who has taken a grievous wound, and knows that the certainty of his death is on him.

To Gwi, Ricca said, "Maybe it would not have mattered, this . . . I could have turned my head away, for the sake of friendship. But I had to see for myself—to be sure the other was true, also."

"What other?" Naeri had suddenly found her voice.

"This woman," Ricca said, "this woman who was my wife, would have betrayed me to the Old Tribes. There was no ax-truce on their side, only on mine. At midsummer they meant to come down upon us with their witches' weapons, slay my war-lords and seize power for themselves."

Anger rose bitter and scalding in Naeri's throat. "Ricca, go to the one who has told you these things. Ask whose plan that was—for it was never mine."

"He was loyal to me," said Ricca, "when those I called friend betrayed me. He has warned me of the she-wolf in my camp who wears a woman's face. Now I have seen with my own eyes that he speaks truth."

Naeri thought, I have woven this net with my own two hands, and now it will strangle me.

"Put them in the stables," Ricca said. There was an edge of contempt in his voice that was like a knife turned in a wound. Gwi had gone chalk-pale, and there was a sick, shamed look in his eyes.

Gruah came forward with two lengths of braided sinew in his hands. He twisted Gwi's hands behind his back and tied them; as he started to bind Naeri's hands he noticed the dagger-sheath on her belt. Reaching down, he drew out the sky-stone dagger and tossed it onto the bed.

As they led her out of the smithy, Naeri glimpsed a tall, cloaked figure lurking by the doorway. Daui's features were shadowed by his close-drawn hood; still she could feel his eyes, afire with hatred, burning like coals in his gaunt face. He could not stay away, she thought bitterly. He has come to rejoice in what he has done.

They took her to an empty stable, and fastened her bound hands to a stanchion with a length of rope, high up so that there was no way she could reach the knot.

Ket said, "It is cruel to leave her with her hands tied behind her. I would not treat a beast of the fields in such a fashion."

Gruah shrugged. "Bind them in front, then—but have a care how you do it. Remember she is a witch, and who knows with what spells she may try to loosen the ropes." He looked down at her, his eyes narrowing. "And hobble her ankles," he said.

And so, when she was trussed like a bird for the cooking pot, they left her sprawled in the straw by the stable door. Toward dawn, worn out by grief, she dozed, only to be woken by the sounds of the camp stirring.

After a while the door opened, admitting a shaft of dusty sunlight. A hearth-slave sidled in with a beaker of water and some barley-bread. Her eyes were wide and wary in the half-light.

Naeri gulped the water gratefully, but could not bring herself to eat. Then the door slammed to, and the woman was gone.

The day passed somehow, and another, and then another. Trying to work free of the ropes, she chafed her wrists until they began to ooze, and finally had to give it up. There was always food, sometimes hot from the hearth, and milk or water. After the first day she ate everything she was given, as much to pass the time as from hunger, for the food tasted like chalk in her mouth. Once or twice someone came to change the stinking straw where she had relieved herself.

Much of the time she thought about Gwi, wondering where he was, and if indeed he was alive at all. Thinking of him made her weep, until after a while there were no tears left, and she fell into a kind of stupor, a dull apathy of mind and spirit that left no room for fear, or remorse, or rage—that was like a quiet death of the soul.

She knew that among the hill-folk those who were sick beyond hope of healing, or who were overcome by grief, simply lay down and willed themselves to die. Perhaps if she did not eat, her spirit would find its way into the Bright World. But once she imagined that Gwi's voice was calling out to her, and she thought, if I live, then surely he lives also. So at sundown she ate the gruel they brought her, and lay down to endure another night.

At first she had kept track of the days with bits of straw, but soon gave it up, not caring enough to make the effort. Each night, though, the gray light through the roof-chinks seemed to fade a little later; and in the daytime she could hear a great bustle and commotion in the courtyard and sometimes the creak of wagons rolling through the gate. From time to time the fragrance of roast meat found its way from the cooking pits into her prison, and it occurred to her that the camp must be preparing for the Midsummer Feast.

Then one morning the door was flung open and Gruah stood there, a dark ominous shape against the flooding light.

He put his fingers to his nose and made a sound of disgust as he bent to untie the thongs that held her. She realized that she had grown almost used to the foul smell of this place.

"Get up," Gruah said, and put out a hand to help her to her feet. Ragged, dirty and bad-smelling as she was, she was still the Fourth Wife, and must be treated, if not with kindness, at least with no overt disrespect.

She blinked in the sudden dazzle of the morning sun as they led her out; her eyes began to water, and she felt light-headed. Just then Clia came into the courtyard, carrying an armload of clothing. Catching sight of Naeri, her eyes widened and she looked ready to weep. She thrust a clean tunic and kirtle into Naeri's arms and slipped into her hand a little deer-bone comb that Naeri knew was a treasured possession. Clia hovered there a moment, with tears glazing her great scared doe-eyes, while Naeri smiled her thanks and wrapped the comb carefully into the bundle of garments. Then the Third Wife turned and vanished without a word around the corner of the appleshed.

Naeri's own eyes were stinging. She wiped the moisture from them with the back of a grimy hand.

Gruah was standing close beside her, watching her nervously, as though he was afraid she would bolt without warning. There was a clattering of hooves and wooden wheels, and Ket drew up beside them in a pony cart.

"Get in, lady," said Gruah, almost gently. "You are to go with Ket."

Numbly she climbed into the cart, clutching her bundle against her.

"What day is this?" she asked Ket. Her voice sounded hoarse, disused—a frog's croak.

"The Eve of Midsummer," he told her. He was concentrating on the ponies as he steered them through the gate and over the causeway. There was a long silence as they went down the slow slope of the hill and onto the southern track.

Finally she could bear the quiet no longer, and she said, "Ket, you must tell me where we are going."

He gave her a look of mild surprise. "Why, to Ricca's temple. To the House of the Sun."

She had known that, of course, from the beginning. Still, hearing it spoken, she felt a small hard shock in the pit of her stomach and a dryness in her throat.

"Have you seen it, Ket?"

He shook his head, his eyes on the road in front of them. "Not since the lintels went up. But they say it is truly a dwelling-place for gods."

She thought, there is a kind of order here, the working out of a pattern. Among the horsemen, as among her own people, a new dwelling-place must be sanctified with blood. Surely the death of a lamb, a kid, a stallion even, was too small a sacrifice for the Sun-Lord's house.

It was almost noon, a day of clear skies and gusting winds. Half in a dream, she watched the slow surge and plunge of the clover-dusted hills, the shadows of clouds racing across the turf.

"Ket," she said, and stopped, as though the question had stuck in her throat.

He turned his head for an instant. "Lady?"

"Ket, tell me what has happened to the smith."

"Gwi?" He did not answer at first, and she read in his hesitation a slow searching for words that would seem to answer her, without in fact revealing anything.

"He is alive, lady. He is unharmed. Soon you will see him."

And why should he have been harmed, she asked herself, with a sense of relief that was like a sudden inrushing of air and light. Gwi was Ricca's friend, and she had led him into this by her own weakness and wrongheadedness; the fault, and the betrayal, was hers entirely.

The Great Circle seemed to rear up suddenly before them, out of the wide sunlit plain. On this summer midday, with no mist to shroud it, it was more immense than she had remembered, and somehow more intricate-seeming: an infinite series of gateways dissolving into other gateways.

A city of tents had sprung up on the bare plain outside the earth-bank, as the clans swarmed in from all the wind's directions. Ket led Naeri to a small tent set apart from the others. He did not attempt to bind her hands or tie her to the tent-pole, but instead left one of Ricca's household warriors on guard just outside the door flap.

Even with the flap up it was stifling hot inside the cowhide tent. She called out for water, and presently heard footsteps approaching. Silently her guard handed in a goatskin.

She could hear pony carts and wagons rolling up the roads, children shrieking, a snorting and stamping of horses. Later on there was a hum of voices as the women gathered at the cook-fires to prepare the evening meal.

Someone brought food for her, but her stomach was clenched into a small hard knot and she could not bear the thought of eating. Eventually, as the light faded, a breath of night air found its way through the door hole to stir the heavy, clinging heat. She dozed for a while until something—a faint movement, a whisper— brought her abruptly awake. As she rolled over and sat up she felt the light touch of a hand on her forearm. She could see, crouched beside her, a dark indefinite shape.

"Lady," a voice said. Then, "Be still, or you will give me away." She breathed his name in disbelief. "Coran?"

"Aye, lady. I told your guard I would relieve him for a bit. We must be quick though—he has only gone to stretch his legs."

"Coran, how did you come here?"

"Why, we are all here—all the youth's house, the new spears, everyone. But listen, Naeri, when I heard they had brought you here, what was to become of you . . . Here," he finished awkwardly, and she felt something thrust into her hand. She closed her fingers on it. It was the doeskin pouch that she had left in Gwi's bed-place. She could feel through the thin leather the outlines of a few small hard objects—bits of copperwork and beads that she had put there for safekeeping.

"And this also." His fingers touched hers in the darkness, and hen, with a quick irrational leaping of her heart, she recognized he haft of the gray sky-stone dagger.

"I found it in the smithy," he whispered, "and I knew it was yours, for I have seen it in your belt in the feast-hall." He hesitated, then said all in a rush, "You are not just a woman, you are a warrior, and you should not go unarmed into the Country of the Sun."

"Coran," she said. There was a great swelling pressure in her throat.

"Lady?"

"You are my true friend, Coran—in this world, and when we meet in the Bright Country. But go quickly now, before the guard comes back."

"Aye," he said. She saw his hand lift in the darkness—a warrior's salute. Then he slipped out, dropping the door flap behind him. In a moment she heard him exchange a casual goodnight with the guard.

She sat in that dark, airless place, stroking the blade of the gray dagger. It could not save her life now—though she wondered if that thought had lurked unspoken in Coran's head. The time was long past when she could fight her way out, but still there was an odd comfort in the feel of the knife, the perfect weight and balance of it in her hand. She hung the pouch around her neck under her clothing, and put the knife in her belt with her tunic hanging loose over top to hide it.

In the dead of the night, while the world slept, her mind turned and turned like a wheel spinning aimlessly in darkness. It had seemed to her, before, that her life had been a journey along a tangle of paths, like deer tracks in a dark wood that crossed and recrossed, trailed off aimlessly and doubled back upon themselves. Now she saw that from the instant of her birth her feet had been set upon a straight track, leading arrow-true and unswerving from one landmark to the next until it brought her inescapably to this high, lonely place.

Her hand strayed to the sky-stone knife. She drew it out, stroked it, pressed it against her forehead. It was no longer cold, but warm with her body's heat. Gwi had held this knife, burnished it, carried it. It was a link between them. Her thoughts drew in upon themselves, shrank down to the aching place where the knife-blade touched her flesh. But this time there were no visions, no sense of contact or communion. All that came to her were blurred, feverish images; and under those, an anguish, a yearning, a wordless dread. He is asleep, she thought, and in his sleep he grieves, and is afraid, like me.

Much later she heard whispering outside the tent, and presently two women crept in, carrying a cauldron of water between them. They set down the copper, and one of them handed Naeri a handful of clean rags.

When she had scrubbed off as much grime as she could and had dragged the worst of the tangles from her hair with Clia's comb, she shook out her bundle of clean garments. They smelled fresh and sweet, as though they had been sprinkled with herbs. Pulling the tunic over her head, she thought with bleak irony of her bride-rites. Then she had thought that she would prefer death to a horseman's bed. Now—as though the Goddess had overheard, and laughed—it was that dark bridegroom, death, who was waiting to embrace her. Once a hill-warrior, recovering from a grievous wound, had told her that he scarcely felt the knife's thrust; it was the pain that came after, with the slow healing of the flesh, that he remembered. She could bear pain. But it frightened her, not knowing what came after that last swift thrusting of the knife.

The witchfolk believed that as the soul gained wisdom and self-knowledge it rose like a bubble of light through the bright worlds that lay like the rainbow's circles beyond our own. She had gained little enough wisdom in her short life; and less self-knowledge. And so, she thought with a sense of utter desolation, her spirit must be condemned to dwell until time's end in the Gray Lands.

It was Gruah, glittering and splendid in his ceremonial dress, and the new priest Wydda, who came to fetch her. She thought it odd at first to see this full-fleshed, pink-cheeked youth in Magha's wizard-garb; but Wydda's robes were clean and new, not long from the loom, the madder-red dye unfaded, with a glint of river-gold at wrist and throat.

The air felt damp and cool on her face. The fires on the hills had faded, grown almost colorless, now that the first gray glow of morning was brightening in the east.

They led her between the two sentry-stones that guarded the entrance, into the inner half-circle of ten paired stones. She stood with her back against one of the pillars of the great southwest trilith, with her hands bound behind her and her face turned into the dawn-light.

The stones of the outer circle, rising out of a sea of shadow, made black brooding doorways against the silvery pallor of the sky. There was perhaps an hour remaining until sunrise. She drew in a great breath of the chill gray air, with its fragrance of wet grass and smoke and chalk dust. She could hear a lark singing; and the thin sad music of the dawn wind whistling among the stones. She shivered as a cold tendril of ground mist curled around her ankles.

She made herself stand straight, her chin held high, though she was almost too weary to stand at all. Her vision was starting to blur a little from hunger or lack of sleep; there was a dull prickling all through her body, and a faint hum in her ears like a distant swarm of bees.

She closed her eyes for a moment, shook her head to clear it. Then as she looked again she caught her breath, feeling as though she had been plunged into icy water. Gruah and the priest were leading another prisoner into the circle—a man, cloakless and barelegged, with his hands bound behind him, shivering slightly in the chill predawn air. He was a young man, strongly built, but with a gaunt, tired, defeated face.

Gwi's head lifted, and his eyes met Naeri's. His mouth twisted in the wry semblance of a smile.

They made Gwi stand against the other pillar of the trilith. He and Naeri were close enough to speak, though not to touch: two insignificant figures flanking that enormous gateway that lay in the chariot path of the Sun-God. A pair of nervous young warriors just out of the youth's house guarded them at spear-point.

Naeri turned toward Gwi, saw the angry bruise across his cheekbone and the ragged cut that had made his lower lip swell, giving his mouth a lopsided look. There were deep shadows under his eyes, like charcoal smudges. Bound as he was, and under close guard, still he leaned toward her—would have crossed the space that separated them had not Gruah warned him back. Neither of them spoke; it was not necessary. There was a tenderness in Gwi's face that wrenched at Naeri's heart—and a queer kind of apology, as though somehow he were at fault, not she, and he was asking her forgiveness. She took no comfort in his presence, feeling only a black rage at the pointlessness of his death, and the injustice of it.

There was a gathering brightness in the air. The light in the east grew; thin streamers of rose and gold appeared. In minutes now there would be a flash of fire over the Sun-Stone; and then the bright flash of Wydda's knife.

She could hear the distant ebb and flow of the crowd noise carried up on the wind. Somewhere an ox-horn blew, and with that signal the people of the horse-clans surged up the slopes and across the ditch and bank. For such a vast throng they made surprisingly little sound.

She did not look at Gwi, but was achingly aware of him. Her bones hurt with cold and weariness, and with the slow throb of power in the stones.

Then her eyes widened. The young men of the clans were winding their way in a ragged procession up the avenue, past the tall flame-shape of the Sun-Stone and through the entranceway. They were carrying armloads of furze and thorn and juniper brush, tinder-dry from the sun; bundles of faggots, and logs which must have been cut from the timbers they had used to raise the lintel-stones. One by one they entered and set down their burdens in front of Gwi and Naeri, like holy offerings; and a great tower of brush and wood took shape at the Circle's center.

As Wydda stepped forward, carrying the sacred fire-drill, a scream ripped its way out of Naeri's throat. It was not blood, after all, that would be offered up to the Sun-Lord; but the living and devouring flame.

The light in the northeast was a fierce yellow furnace glow. Naeri sent up a swift, silent prayer to the Goddess: let them kill us first.

The fire-drill squeaked and spun in Wydda's hands. Soon the flames would leap up, and the guards would reach out to seize her and throw her upon the pyre.

Rigid with terror, she set her shoulders hard against the pillar-rock, pressing her bound hands flat upon the sarsen's face.

Something leaped from her, or leaped from the stone through her. She felt her hair crackle; her body arched, bow-taut, until she thought her spine would snap. The breath rushed out of her lungs as though some immense unseen force were pressing down upon her. Brain, bone, blood, sinew, she was fused with the stone's huge, intractable, patient strength. She could feel the steady sea-surge of caged power as it twisted and spiraled through the nerve-tangle of forcelines. Her roots reached down and down through turf and soil and living rock, to touch the raw fire at the world's heart.

As light flashed on the Sun-Stone, and the spark leaped from the fire-drill, and the tinder caught, she sent a blast of naked, shattering, sundering power into stone and earth. One by one the delicate links of her binding magic snapped; the dragon-lords who dwelt in the deep rocks stirred in their age-long sleep.

The ground shuddered; blue flames leaped in a circle, dancing along the lintels, sheeting down the sides of the stones; huge tongues of flame sprang out of the earth where the stones pierced the chalk, and raced over the surface of the plain through the tinder-dry grass, along the outward-radiating web of forcelines.

As the dragon-fire leaped up, fracture-lines tore through the deep substructure of the earth. Naeri could see one of the great upright stones in the outer circle begin to rock and sway in its socket, threatening to unseat its lintel. There were ripples of movement along the surface of the chalk, like still water ruffled by the wind. And now a smoky pall was creeping over the northeastern hills, blotting out the horizon and the new-risen sun.

All this happened in a breath, a heart's beat. A spear-length from where she stood, the faggots and logs of the sacrificial fire had just caught hold, and the flames rushed up. She could feel the fierce heat of them on her face.

Their guards had bolted. The ranks of the clans were breaking, scattering; surging in a great wave up over the banks, across the plain and into the chalk hills beyond. She could hear, over the roar of the flames and the rising wind, and the terrified wails of the womenfolk, Gwi shouting to her to follow him.

She wrenched at her bound hands, and all at once the leather thongs, charred through by the fierce heat of the sarsen-stone, broke and fell away. A gust of wind caught her and she staggered sideways. Something struck her on the side of the head, and she threw up her arms to protect her face. Huge hailstones, the size of hen's eggs, were plummeting out of the storm-dark sky.

Dizzy and disoriented, she followed the sound of Gwi's voice. As she caught up with him she saw how badly he was hampered, thrown off balance, by his bound arms, but there was no opportunity to cut him free. That brief terrifying storm of hail was over, but now the wind had risen to a driving gale, flattening the grasses against the earth, tearing off branches and uprooting trees. The ground beneath their feet was vibrating, humming like a plucked harp-string.

Fanned by the wind, the tongues of blue fire that had rushed out along the serpentine patterns of the forcelines now were spreading and joining; before long the whole of the plain and the surrounding slopes would be engulfed in flame.

"This way," she heard Gwi shouting, and she followed him blindly on a weaving, twisting path among the flames.

As she ran her light-headedness increased. Her temples throbbed and there was a sour taste of nausea in her mouth. Her bones ached, as with the onset of fever. She remembered stopping in the lee of a westward-facing scarp long enough to saw through Gwi's bonds with the sky-stone knife.

Then it seemed that the shouting and the crackle of flames had grown faint and distant behind the dip and swell of hills; and Gwi was half-carrying, half-dragging her along a grassy track, where the only sound was the shrieking of the hot, fierce wind. Once they took shelter in a deep hollow of the hills, and Gwi held her while she retched on an empty belly until her throat burned with bile and she was too weak and ill to raise her head.

After a while Gwi lifted her in his arms and they went on, following pack trails and cattle paths through country that was strewn with ancient barrows and earthworks, keeping always to the folds of the hills and avoiding the high exposed ridge tracks.

They came to the edge of the chalk, where the high country ended in a maze of streams and tumbled hills and waterlogged forest of alder and willow scrub, which men of those parts called Sallow-Wood.

By late afternoon Naeri was steadier on her feet, but looking at her wan, exhausted face as she stumbled along the reedy pathway, Gwi said, "Enough. This is as safe a place as any to spend the night." And he searched out a dry cavelike shelter under the root-tangle of a fallen oak.

Curled up on leaves and moss, she drifted into a leaden, feverish sleep. In that halfway place between dreams and waking she saw the stones of the Great Circle swaying and rocking like saplings in the wind. She murmured, "Gwi, did you look back? Was the Circle standing?"

He drew his cloak over them both, and his arms tightened around her. "It was standing," he said. "Some of the stones are loosened in their sockets and leaning—but even your magic was not strong enough to topple them."

She gave a small sigh, and did not stir again until the morning sun slanted down through the alder branches.

~ 28 ~

The Summer-Road

That day they moved westward again, and coming to the edge of the woodland, saw spreading away before them a wide level country of lakes and marsh and water meadows. To the west and north the plain was encircled by low hills; nearer at hand, a huge cone-shaped tor rose abruptly and inexplicably out of the marsh.

"It puts me in mind of the Mother-Hill," Naeri said, and because she was dizzy and out of breath in any case, she paused to stare at it.

"I climbed it once," Gwi told her. "There are spiral pathways winding to the top, and the ruins of a temple. They say it was the Great Ones who built the temple, in the days before Flood-Time."

"And who built the tor?"

Gwi shrugged. "Maybe it has always been there. Or maybe it is the work of the same geomancers who built the Mother-Hill. This much I can tell you—if you look down from the summit in high summer when the water is low, you can see how the whole countryside has been shaped and molded, given pattern."

She gave him a startled look. He said, "Did you think you were the only one in the world had discovered that secret? I come from the Old Tribes, as you do. And anyway, a good craftsman must know something of pattern and harmony. I can guess—a little—the meaning of the pattern you made, when you built the Great Circle. And I can guess what it must have cost you to destroy it." And then he said in his usual matter-of-fact tone, "Well, all that is in the past, and should remain so. What we must think of now is finding a safe place to hide and rest."

Once out of the forest, the pathway vanished in a morass of sallows and reeds and alderbrake. Gwi caught hold of Naeri's arm. "Stay close behind me," he said. "There is a summer road through these marshes that runs from the chalk hills to the coast. I have traveled it often enough that I should be able to find it in my sleep."

He led her along the marsh edge until they came to a solid roadway of planks and turf, fringed with tall, plumed swamp grasses. Some ancient road-builder had driven posts into the marsh at regular intervals to mark the course of the track. On either side stretched the fenlands, a wilderness of reed banks, shallow sour pools and winding, interlacing channels.

Here and there, on islets of high ground, or set on posts at the marsh edge, were the wattle-and-daub huts of the swamp-folk. They passed a fisherman carrying elvings in a basket; a solitary hunter with a brace of moorhens on his belt. A coracle bobbed idly on a distant lake. The air was thick with the sweet-sour smell of the marsh and the sharper tang of bog myrtle. It was always hazy here; even in midmorning the sunlight had a veiled, uncertain quality.

There was a sadness and a strangeness about this fen country that in the midst of the summer morning touched her like a small chill breath. Everywhere in the landscape she could feel the lingering presence of old magic, ancient ghosts.

"Maybe," said Gwi when she remarked on it, "it is because it is summer country, that vanishes under the mere in winter, when the tides and the streams rise. I have seen it in the cold months—a gray waste of water lapping around a few desolate islands of high ground. Any place seems melancholy, that is beautiful for so short a time."

"It is not only that." She could not put into words this sense of loss and age-long grieving that lay like a shadow over the quiet land. Finally, "It is a place of mourning," she said.

Presently Gwi spotted what appeared to be the ruins of a hut standing on a grassy knoll far out in the midst of a lagoon. They set out across the narrow causeway of brushwood and packed earth that linked the islet with the summer track. The door of the hut was half-hidden by rank grass and loosestrife; the roof had long since fallen in, but the four walls offered at least a semblance of shelter. They gathered thorn and alder scrub for a fire to take away the damp moldering smell of the place; and to cook the two perch they had bought from a fisherman, in exchange for one of the beads in Naeri's pouch.

The sun slid down behind the western hills, staining the clouds with rose and amethyst and madder-red. The glassy surface of the mere threw back the shifting hues of the sunset so that sky and water glowed with the same vivid jewel-colored light.

Twilight came, and darkness, and the marsh lay glittering in moonlight. Small flickering lights danced over the water—the spirits of the drowned, some said. The night was loud with the voices of frogs and a myriad of small nameless sounds. From the doorway of the hut they could see the strange smooth thrusting shape of the tor outlined against the stars: a black mysterious presence, ominous and unexplained.

Gwi said, "On top of that hill, according to the swamp-folk, there is a gateway to the Dead Kingdom."

Naeri shivered and moved closer to him. The hair stirred on her nape as something—some vague unsettling premonition—touched her. It was fleeting as a cloud shadow on the water, cold as the icy breath of winter.

"Gwi," she said, "there are too many ghosts in this place, the walls are too thin between our world and the spirit-land." There was a pleading note in her voice as she asked him, "Is there nowhere else that we can hide?"

"It is only for tonight," Gwi reminded her, "and the night after. Then we will move on, to the coast. There will be a ship from the Western Isle in Hefryn-Mouth on the first full moon after midsummer—it is bringing me a shipment of river-gold. The master knows me, and will trust me for our passage."

Naeri said, "Why then wait three days? Why not push on to the coast at once?"

"In the first place, because you are still in no fit shape to travel. And in the second place, because Ricca knows I was born of coast-dwelling folk, and the coast is the first place he will think to look—especially if he gets wind there is a ship due in port. My guess is, by now Ricca will have all the war-bands of the west out searching for us; but he won't risk bringing horses into this morass, for fear of foundering them. If he should blunder in here on foot, I know these marsh paths well enough to outrun him."

"But why," she asked, "should Ricca trouble to follow us at all? He has his temple. The earth-web is broken, but the stones remain. What am I to him now, but a weak foolish woman who has betrayed him?"

"He will follow us," Gwi said quietly, "because we have stolen from him the thing that makes him Great Chief, the thing that lets him call himself a horse-warrior. Until he takes back from us his power, and his honor, he is nothing. He is not even a man."

In the morning the marshland steamed with mist, a drifting veil of luminous white that shrouded trees and huts and islands, with only that single haunted mountain-summit floating mysteriously above it. One saw the landscape then as it must have appeared in the days of Legend, when summer and winter there was only the mist-swathed tor rising out of a gray rolling waste of sea.

When they had finished the second perch and a handful of rush shoots gathered from the water's edge, they pondered what they would eat for the rest of that day and the day after. Ghosts or no, Naeri had slept soundly; today her head was clear, and she was ravenously hungry. Rummaging in the corners of the hut, she found a length of fishnet and a broken basket. While they waited for the mist to rise, she mended the basket with wattle rushes, and then set to work to fashion a sling with a strip of leather cut from Gwi's tunic hem.

Some time after midday Gwi set out along the marsh track to try his luck with the basket and net. Naeri spent the rest of the afternoon practising with her makeshift sling; and finally, toward sunset, brought down a pair of mallards. As she waited in the gathering dusk for Gwi's return, she built up a fire on a patch of firm ground above the waterline and sat down to pluck the birds for the evening meal.

Somewhere across the lagoon she heard a rush of wings and the harsh cry of a waterbird, and then the slow slap and splash of a paddle. She looked back idly, thinking it was a fisherman returning in his coracle. Suddenly her breath caught in her throat, and her belly knotted. It was not a basket-boat, but a dugout, like the ones that plied the Great River and the western coast. Its two passengers were, at this distance, no more than huddled shapes, unrecognizable in the dim vague light.

The craft drew nearer, slipping wraith-silent through the dark still water, like a ghost ship out of the Gray Land. For one wild instant Naeri imagined that it bore the shades of men who had died at her hand and had returned to haunt her.

But these were not ghosts; she knew that, long before the

narrow craft nosed into the soft ooze of the shoreline. She leaped up, dropping the mallard in a flurry of feathers, and stood with her back braced against the wattle of the hut; staring into her husband's cold and unforgiving eyes.

Ricca's face had a closed, heavy look. In his right hand was his great drooping-bladed ax, the Skull-Splitter.

In a bid for time, for a chance to think, she whispered, "How did you find me?"

It was Daui who answered, with a kind of mocking triumph. "We rode to the coast, and though you were not there, we found men who had crossed from Sallow-Wood over the marsh track, who had seen fires burning in deserted places. They were ready enough to part with what secrets they knew for a horseman's gold—and lend us a boat into the bargain."

"Witchwoman," Ricca said. That one word only, through his teeth. In his rage he was moving his head slowly, deliberately, from side to side, his heavy plaits swinging against his shoulders. So does the great boar of the wood swing its savage head before it charges.

Naeri's eyes flicked sideways as a pelican launched itself from the lagoon with a startled splash. She saw Gwi walking along the causeway in the twilight, carrying the eel basket in one hand, and in the other hand the piece of net twisted up like a sack. She cried out a warning; glimpsed a silvery squirming as the basket dropped on the track; heard Gwi's feet pounding along the causeway. She saw the flat of the ax-blade glimmer red as it caught the light of her cooking fire. Then somehow, suddenly, Gwi had thrust his broad back between Naeri and the ax.

For the first time in her life she saw a hesitation, a flicker of uncertainty, in Ricca's eyes.

He said, "Stand aside, smith. Time and time you have come between this woman and me. Now I mean to finish the thing."

As calmly as though he were remarking upon the weather, Gwi said, "If you would kill her, you must kill me first."

"Go on your way, smith," said Ricca. "I would have seen you die in the fire, gladly. But now I am tired, and my anger has cooled, and it will give me no pleasure to kill you."

For answer, Gwi's feet sought a firmer footing on the muddy slope. Ricca's eyes narrowed. For an instant Naeri thought that he would simply thrust Gwi aside like a stray hound that had come nosing between him and his kill. Then the ax came up, slowly, steadily, in a deadly arc.

Naeri's hand flicked under her tunic, the gray dagger slid like silk from its sheath. She drew a quick breath and, tensing, took a step to the side and came forward; her left shoulder jarring against Gwi's and knocking him off-balance as her right hand brought the blade up hard under Ricca's ax-arm. She felt the shock of the knife as it glanced against a rib; then it slid smoothly home. Ricca staggered, and the ax fell sideways from the top of its swing to half-bury itself harmlessly in the mud.

Ricca was on his knees, his face abruptly drained of color, his breath rasping and rattling in his throat. She saw the froth of blood on his lips, heard the faint hiss of air around the dagger handle; and she guessed that although she had missed his heart, the wound was mortal.

He looked down with a kind of surprise, then put his two hands on the haft and wrenched the blade out. A gout of blood foamed after it. He said, in that straining, breathless voice, with a slow bewilderment in his eyes, "You heard the augury, woman. You saw the rowan-flames. You were there when Magha said that death had sworn ax-truce with me."

The bright blood gushed out of his side, and she saw the clear ice-blue of his eyes glazing with shock and pain. She knew—as he knew, all too clearly—that the wound was beyond any power to heal.

There was a strange look of pleading in his gaze. She knew it was no ordinary fear of death she saw there, but the shadow of a greater horror. For an instant his lids dropped, and she thought his spirit had left him. Then he looked full at her, his eyes clearing, and he said in a low and quite steady voice, "Woman, do not leave me to rot here in this foul place. Give my body to the clean flames, so my spirit is set free." With the last of his strength he reached out and gripped her hand. "Witchwoman, say you will do this thing for me."

She bent her head over his neck, and hot tears ran down her face as she gave him her promise.

Ricca's final words were for Daui, who was standing at his feet with a queer, shocked look. "Minstrel, I know you make your own truth, as a smith molds copper—and so you must make a better death for me than this." And then his life boiled away in a hissing and frothing of crimson.

Naeri looked round, for fear of what Daui might do to finish his dead chief's work for him. But he was already gone; she could

ear the faint splash of paddles lifting as the long dark shape of the
oat slid away into the reeds.

After a while Naeri got up and went to the water's edge to clean
the gray knife that was made of no substance of this world, but the
cold dark metal of the stars: the cruel narrow blade that in this
place that was neither land nor water, at the gray hour that falls
between light and dark, had betrayed into death's hands the Lord
of All the Horse-Tribes. And she thought how Magha's omen-fire
mocked those who would seek truth in its riddles.

At first light, when the mist had risen, they bore Ricca's body
between them, along the treacherous marshways to the little
wooded isle that lay beneath the tor. They wrapped him in his
cloak, with all his gold and bronze upon him, and his ax beside
him; and they gathered brushwood and branches to make a funeral
pyre: with limbs from the alder, the tree of doom, and ash for the
promise of rebirth. The flames leaped up, copper and gold and
crimson, out of the shadows at the mountain's foot. Thick white
smoke, from wood that even in summer had dampness at its heart,
billowed up and up to the heights of the tor, until it vanished at last
in a shimmer of mist.

A small wind had risen, shivering through the reeds. It made a
plaintive music—a lamentation, Naeri thought, for all those who
must journey through that high gateway. At last the fire burned
down to embers, and shadows crept back into the wood. She
turned and followed Gwi along the Summer-Road and through the
western hills, to where the clean cold winds blew along the coast.

AUTHOR'S NOTE

As I finish this book, archaeologists are moving toward a new prehistory, one in which the old notions of invasion and conquest give way to movements, influences and cultural process. Still, as Christopher Chippindale notes in *Stonehenge Complete*, ". . . culture process models may have a weakness when it comes to accounting for single, unique events in prehistory, of which the building of Stonehenge appears to be one."

In a novel of prehistory one can only attempt not to violate what is known to be true. This story borrows something from the old prehistory, something from the new; the rest is pure invention.

For those who wish to read more about megaliths and about earth-magic, I recommend the following:

Atkinson, R.J.C. *Stonehenge*. Harmondsworth, Middlesex: Penguin, 1979 (rev.)

Burl, Aubrey. *Prehistoric Avebury*. New Haven and London: Yale University Press, 1979.

Chippindale, Christopher. *Stonehenge Complete*. Ithaca: Cornell University Press, 1983.

Dames, Michael. *The Avebury Cycle*. London: Thames and Hudson, 1977.

Hitching, Francis. *Earth Magic*. London: Cassell & Co., 1976.

Michell, John. *The Earth Spirit*. London: Thames and Hudson, 1975.

Pennick, Nigel. *The Ancient Science of Geomancy*. London: Thames and Hudson, 1979.

Underwood, Guy. *The Pattern of the Past*. London: Abacus, 1972. (Reprint.)